BREAKING TIME

Books by Sasha Alsberg
available from Inkyard Press

Breaking Time

The Androma Saga by Sasha Alsberg and Lindsay Cummings

Zenith
Nexus

BREAKING TIME

SASHA ALSBERG

inkyard
PRESS

ISBN-13: 978-1-335-28489-1

Breaking Time

Inkyard Press
22 Adelaide St. West, 41st Floor
Toronto, Ontario M5H 4E3, Canada
www.InkyardPress.com

Printed in U.S.A.

To Joanna Volpe,
who lit the torch that helped guide me
to the light at the end of the tunnel.
For you, I am forever grateful.

SCOTLAND

ISLE OF LEWIS

Fairy Glen

ISLE OF SKYE

INVERNESS

Fairy Pools

FORT WILLIAM

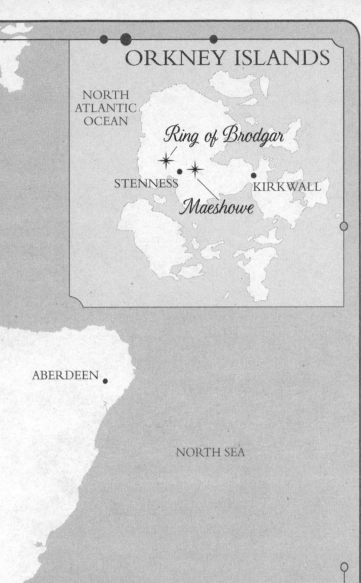

ORKNEY ISLANDS

NORTH
ATLANTIC
OCEAN

Ring of Brodgar

STENNESS

KIRKWALL

Maeshowe

ABERDEEN

NORTH SEA

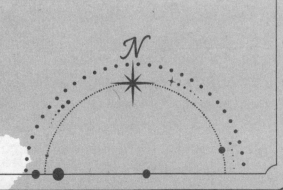

N

Rosemere

EDINBURGH

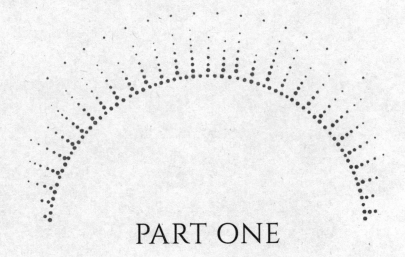

PART ONE

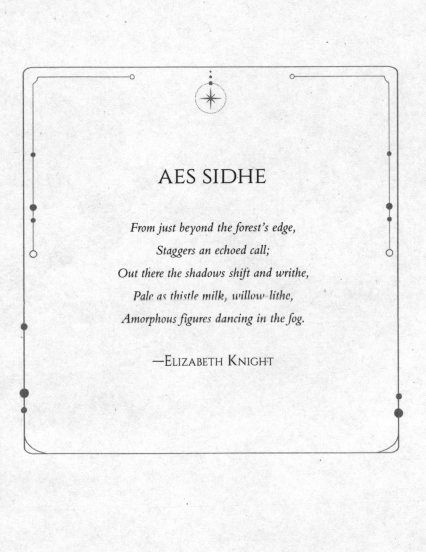

AES SIDHE

From just beyond the forest's edge,
Staggers an echoed call;
Out there the shadows shift and writhe,
Pale as thistle milk, willow-lithe,
Amorphous figures dancing in the fog.

—Elizabeth Knight

CHAPTER ONE

CALLUM
1568

"Thomas!" Callum yelled as he left the pub. The wall of crisp night air dizzied him, causing him to stumble over cobblestones that seemed to shift beneath his feet. Drunken laughter muffled as the door slammed shut behind him.

"Where the hell are ye?" he shouted. His voice echoed through the deserted streets.

No answer came.

Lanterns flickered along the main road, setting the heavy fog aglow. In a wee town like Rosemere, the slightest whispers could be heard a mile away. They carried farther than that, Callum knew; the windows around him were shuttered, but candles burned low just inside. How many prying eyes watched from behind the slats? How many would speak of his friend, the disgraced fighter, in hushed voices at tomorrow's market, over bread bought with the coin they'd won betting on him mere weeks earlier?

Callum clenched his fists. The whole pub had shouted and jeered while Thomas got pummeled that night. Sounds still rang in Callum's ears: the thud of fist and flesh, the sickening crunch of bone. It was the third time this month that Thomas had lost—only the third time, in two years of fighting.

Brice would be angry.

Master, keeper, devil, father. Brice MacDonald was all of these things to Callum and Thomas. Whatever Brice's wrath tonight, Callum could not let Thomas face it alone. Not when Thomas had looked after Callum for so long, raised him up from a nipper as well as a real older brother would.

But he would not abandon Thomas like his mother had abandoned him.

The thought sobered Callum. He called again, lowering his voice to a taunt.

"Thomas! You owe me three shillings!" Thomas could usually be drawn out with a jab.

Callum paused, straining his ears for a response but was met with unease instead. An owl watched from its perch atop the baker's roof, golden eyes unblinking against the dark night sky. The shining orbs fixed on him.

He tore his gaze from the bird and walked on, moving away from the firelight and into shadow.

Even more worrisome than Brice was the fact that Thomas had given Callum his most treasured item earlier that night: his notebook, small sheaths of vellum bound in leather. When he first began carrying it around, Thomas claimed to have stolen it from the apothecary when he went in for a poultice.

He had kept it on him, always, and had never let Callum lay eyes on what was inside. Yet he had pressed it into Callum's hand, just before the match tonight. He said something to Callum when he did, but his words were inaudible within the roar of the pub. Then after, he disappeared from the pub without even a goodbye.

Now Callum was wandering the streets, alone.

It was unlike Thomas to behave so strangely, to lose so badly. The Thomas he knew—boyish and rowdy, tough as leather but never mean—had fallen away with the autumn leaves these past months. Instead of spending evenings at The Black Hart Inn, weaving stories he'd learned as a child of selkies and sailors for red-cheeked barmaids until the sun rose, Thomas began to disappear for days, weeks at a time— stretches too long for Callum to explain to Brice. He took a beating or two for it, too. When Thomas returned, he was sullen, sometimes violent, and consumed by a strangeness Callum had no words to describe. His eyes stared but did not see, as distant as stars burning in his skull. If he spoke at all, he told tales of the demons that terrified them as children: like the Sluagh, spirits of the dead who wandered in flocks, flying around the sky like soaring reapers and stealing souls, flesh hanging off them like blackened rags. Or the *bean-nighe*, banshees, messengers from the Otherworld and omens of death, who lingered in lonely streams, washing the clothes of doomed men. Normally Callum heard of such dark crea- tures within the stories of heroes, but Thomas's stories didn't end in life...but death. He fixated on that fact, as if it were coming for him.

I saw her, he'd said of the bean-nighe. *I refuse to die.*

It worried Callum, but just as his worry morphed into confrontation, Thomas would come back to himself. This was enough to comfort Callum as he watched Thomas return to tales of ancient heroes and kings. Maybe he accepted his relief too soon since the nights of those stories were fewer these days, and more often Thomas's speech would turn dark again. He would speak of strange visions, of men who leaped from one world to the next.

They're coming, Cal, you'll see. It's as simple as stepping through a veil.

Who's coming, Thomas? What veil? Callum asked, and Thomas would laugh.

It was no tale that Callum knew. He'd warned Thomas not to tell it. He didn't like the wary looks it earned him. It was one thing to be a bard who told these stories for a living, but it was another thing to speak like a madman of evil spirits and fairies as if they were tangible things away from the lyrics of a song or the pages of a book.

Callum reached the end of the main road—the turn for Kelpie's Close. If you wanted trouble, you found it in Kelpie's. The narrow backstreet edged Rosemere like a blade pressed against the town's throat.

A chill clung to his skin. Here, there were no lanterns to light the way, his only guide sparse slivers of moonlight. The wind picked up suddenly, lifting his hair and reaching under his woolen cloak. He tried to shake off visions of the Sluagh hovering above him, raking their cold fingers down his neck.

"It's as dark as the Earl of Hell's waistcoat," he mumbled.

Callum reached for the dirk tucked under his arm and found the carved handle concealed under layers of wool, feeling a sting of guilt. It was Thomas's knife. Callum had slipped it away from him before the match, worried about what his friend might do in the crowded pub if he got enough drink in him. He tapped it, drawing enough strength to plunge into the darkness.

"Scunner!" he cursed, meaning it. "Where are you?"

A cry pierced the quiet.

Callum's heart pounded as he followed the sound farther down the alley. He pulled the dirk from under his arm, certain now that he'd need to use it.

"Thomas?"

Unease, cold and metallic, crept up his spine. The alley appeared empty—strange, for this time of night—but the silence was thick, alive with a feeling Callum couldn't name. He pushed on, deeper into the gloom. "Thomas?"

Another strangled cry, ahead.

Callum broke into a run.

A single lantern flickered a short distance away, casting a wan glow over a lone figure slumped against the wall. A sweep of red hair, bright even in the dim alley.

"Thomas, ye bastard, do ye ken what—"

The insult lodged in his throat. Thomas lay on the ground, his legs splayed at sickening angles. Blood seeped through his shirt, blooming like ink on paper. Callum rushed to his friend and knelt beside him. He dropped the dirk and pressed his hands against the deep slice that marred his friend's torso. A knife wound.

"Dinnae fash, Thomas, dinnae fash," Callum repeated, voice tight and panicked. He glanced up, searching for friend or foe, and found no one. "We'll be back to the pub before Anderson kens we havna paid our tab."

Thomas stared up at him with glassy blue eyes. With each shuddering breath, more blood spilled through Callum's fingers. He ripped the cloth stock from his neck and pressed the fabric onto the wound. It did little to stem the flow of blood. Within a few heartbeats, the cloth was soaked through, red and dripping.

If he pressed any harder, would it be doing more harm than good? Should he call for help, though it might draw the attacker? Callum hadn't a clue. He wished suddenly, ferociously, that he'd had a proper mother, one whose wisdom he could call upon to calmly guide his hands. However, Thomas was the only family he had.

His only family was dying.

Thomas opened his mouth, but instead of words, a wet cough came out, splattering red across his pale face.

"Dinnae move, Thomas," Callum shushed him. His uncertainty gave way to desperation, burst from his throat. "Help! Help us!"

His words dissolved into the night air, leaving behind only a tightness at the center of his chest. If he hadn't taken Thomas's dirk, he would have been able to defend himself, he wouldn't be dying in Callum's arms—

Thomas gasped, but it seemed as if no air reached his lungs.

Lowering his head, Callum gripped Thomas's hands, though his own were shaking. "I will find the man who did this, I swear—"

Then the world flipped sideways. A blow had hit Callum like a runaway carriage, throwing him against the alley wall opposite Thomas.

Pain exploded along his ribs. Grasping the mossy wall for

purchase, he struggled to his feet and wiped blood from his eyes, scouring the darkness for his attacker—and found no one.

"Show your face," he growled.

A cruel whisper cut through the quiet. "Are you certain?"

The man emerged from the shadows as if he had been one with them. He wore a dark black cloak, in stark contrast to his unkempt, pale hair. Deep set in his face, a pair of amber eyes seemed to emit their own light. Callum's gaze was drawn to a glinting shape in the man's hand.

A dagger, dripping with blood.

Thomas's blood.

Callum's heart pounded like a war drum in his ears.

The man sighed. "Move along. Unless you'd like to meet the same fate as your compani—"

Callum lunged forward, cutting off the man's speech with a guttural cry, striking with the speed of a viper.

The man ducked. He whirled around as Callum charged again. He overreached with the arc of his knife, and Callum used the moment to surge upward with a punch. His fist took the assailant in the chin—

And the force knocked Callum back.

He stared. A blow like that would have laid out the toughest fighter, yet the man stood and smiled, rubbing his chin with a gloved hand.

"I'm going to have fun with you," the stranger whispered. "I like a man with a bit of fight in him. It's more fun to play with your prey, don't you think?"

Callum didn't see the blow coming, only felt the pain searing across his temple as he was thrown to the ground again.

He lifted his head, vision blurring. He blinked it clear, took in his friend's ashen face. The sight flooded Callum with rage.

Whoever said to never fight with anger fueling your fists was a fool. Thomas's best fights had been powered by emotion. Callum wasn't fighting for money now. Or for Brice. He was fighting for Thomas. Because Thomas was—

"Stay down, little man," the attacker's voice hissed.

Callum dragged himself to his feet. His body, corded with muscle from a lifetime of training, screamed for him to stop. Instead he stood, swaying.

"I dinnae believe I'm going to Heaven," Callum said, raising his fists once more, drawing strength from the familiar ache that radiated through his arms. "But I cannae wait to bring you to Hell with me."

Lunging forward again, Callum poured everything he had into a single strike. He swung, landing the punch more out of luck than skill, half blinded by blood and dirt.

The man merely flinched, then caught Callum easily by the throat. A grin curled over his face.

How could that be possible?

"My, my, you are a feisty one," he hissed.

The man lashed out, and pain flared along Callum's torso. He released Callum and stepped back, red-tinged silver shining in his fist.

Callum touched his side, and his fingers came away wet with blood. He watched as crimson spread across his shirt. He tried to take a step, only to crumple to the ground beside Thomas, whose head rested limp against his chest.

Callum had never feared death, but now as he looked into its eyes, terror seized him.

"Many thanks for the entertainment," the man said.

To Callum's horror, he bent low, holding a vial to the spreading pool of Thomas's blood. He was gathering it.

"If you'll excuse me, there's one last Pillar I must find."

Pillar?

The unearthly amber eyes melted into darkness as his opponent backed away and turned, disappearing into the shadows once more. Softly hissed words echoed in the alley. *Àiteachan dìomhair, fosgailte dhomh, Àiteachan dìomhair, fosgailte dhomh...*

The words the man spoke were Gaelic, but Callum's fading mind couldn't make out their meaning. A dark, mist-like substance rose from the ground and curled around the man's feet, nearly indistinguishable from the dim of night. Like a sudden fog had rolled in.

Callum sputtered a curse, lacking the strength to spit. He tried to lift himself, but with each breath, pain flared in his side like a web of fire.

"I'm sorry, Thomas," he croaked. Tears fell freely down his face, mingling with blood and sweat. He pressed his forehead against his friend's. Grief washed over him at the still-warm press of his skin.

Thomas was gone, and Callum would soon follow.

A shiver raked his body. His eyes drifted shut.

Take me already, he pleaded to the darkness.

And the darkness answered.

No, not the darkness—Thomas's voice, a memory now, though it was solid as stone.

"Get up, scunner."

The warmth of the words turned electric, spreading through Callum's body like wildfire. His eyes shot open and he gasped, breathing in a shock of cold air still sharp with the smell of blood. His fingers found the dirk he'd dropped earlier.

Grief and agony and pain and rage lifted Callum onto his feet, thrumming in him as he charged after Thomas's murderer, knife raised and eager for flesh. He grabbed blindly, finally grasping a handful of fabric—the man's cloak. Turning, the man's eyes widened, making two white rings of surprise in the dark. Callum's hand grabbed the man's neck and aimed his dirk at the pale slash of his throat.

Suddenly, they froze. Callum could not move. His hand remained around the man's neck, the tip of the dirk pressed against his vein. Light flowed around them. *It's not time for sunrise*, he thought. Dimly, he noticed markings along the man's collarbone. Knots carved into his skin.

The man cried out—not in pain, but in anger—but then, the cry was stifled by a rush of silence, so thick Callum thought he might drown in it. His stomach turned violently as the ground seemed to drop out from under him, forcing him to squeeze his eyes shut. He was falling, flying, falling.

I must be dead in the alley. The man must have killed me. This must be death.

A bright glow burned against his lids. He closed his eyes tighter and welcomed whatever might follow, only hoping he'd find Thomas there. A wall of light had formed above, descending as if the sun were pulling him through the sky. His body rose into its searing embrace.

He waited for the long drop to the ground, but it never came.

Callum kept soaring.

Not just through the street.

Not to death's embrace.

But somewhere else.

Leaping to another world, like the man in Thomas's story, Callum thought.

So he leaped.

CHAPTER TWO

KLARA
PRESENT DAY

Klara usually thought of rain as Scotland's natural lullaby, but right now it felt more like the bars of a prison cell.

It had been three days since Klara had been outside, thanks to the seemingly endless torrential downpour. Three long, uneventful days cooped up with a gradually dwindling number of entertainment options. Not that she went outside much when it *wasn't* raining.

Having read every one of the dozen sappy romance novels that guests had left behind and having watched an embarrassing amount of reality TV over the last six months, she was out of options.

Maybe it was a good think that Klara's Aunt Sorcha, who usually manned the reception desk, had gone to visit a friend in Cowdenbeath this afternoon. Since Klara's dad had asked her to cover for Sorcha, at least she'd have something to do.

Klara opened Kingshill Manor's check-in portal on her phone. An American couple was due to arrive at 3 p.m.

She hoped this couple would prove to be better guests than the one who'd checked out yesterday after knocking over the vintage Morrison & Crawford ceramic sugar barrel. Jockie Boyle, who'd been the manor's caretaker since Gram was a girl, had spent most of the afternoon trying to glue it back together.

At least her mom had been spared the sight of one of her favorite antique pieces lying on the floor in shards.

Brooches. Coins. Antique dirks. High crosses forged in mist-covered monasteries. At least three bagpipes. Her mother spent much of their annual summer visits scouring antique shops and flea markets for treasures, collecting enough to fill one of the old storage barns on the manor property by the time Klara was in high school.

The plan had been for her mom and dad to retire once she was finished with college and move to Scotland permanently. They'd looked forward to moving into the manor and transforming the manor from the lackluster, dusty bed-and-breakfast it had been for many years into a truly special inn.

Klara's dad used to call the jumble in the barn "Loreena's buried treasure." But when, a year after she died, he'd decided to move to Scotland and fulfill her dream, he'd lovingly restored each piece and put them on display in the inn's common rooms.

The giant oak doors in the manor entryway were her mom's favorite salvage. Celtic knots wove their way down the door's edges, simple yet beautiful. The knob, now burnished with age, was a rearing horse's head. Klara's throat tightened at the memory of her mother, Loreena Spalding, hauling them back to the manor in the bed of Jockie's rusty pickup truck.

Barking erupted in the other room. Klara hauled herself up. "Finley!"

Her collie-shepherd mix was a terrible watchdog for intruders, thieves, and murderers, but all hell broke loose when the mailman came around.

Pulling her hair into a hopefully decent bun (okay, the mailman was cute and looked her age), Klara jogged to the kitchen, passing several rooms. Placards bearing Scottish clan names blurred by: Campbell, Brodie, Cameron, Fraser. A little cheesy, sure, but it allowed them to distinguish the rooms, which also meant charging different prices for each. Her dad might be a mild-mannered innkeeper now, but he'd been the CFO of a boutique hotel chain back in the states, and he knew a few things about the business.

Steps sounded outside the door, which set off another series of barks. "FINLEY!" Klara picked up speed through the dining room and slid into the gilded grand foyer—the manor's pride and joy—where her dog pressed his nose against the mail slot, snarling. A clutch of white envelopes fanned out on the floor.

She glared at Finley. "You chased him away. Thanks to you, I'll be single forever."

Finley gazed up at her and wagged his tail.

Sighing, Klara patted Finley's head, then scooped up the mail—and froze when she spied a familiar academic seal. Her stomach dropped.

When Klara applied to the University of Edinburgh during the spring of her junior year at Vandam Academy in New York City, she had no idea her world was about to fall apart. That June, her mother was diagnosed with Stage IV cancer and in less than two months she was gone.

For a while, Klara and her father seemed to be drowning in the numbness of their grief. Klara withdrew from her friends, her extracurricular activities, even her riding lessons at the Central Park stables, and graduated a semester early. When her acceptance letter arrived and Klara learned she'd been accepted into the astronomical sciences program, her dad seemed happy for the first time since her mom got sick. Klara couldn't bear to tell him she wasn't sure she still wanted to go.

Her parents had met while in grad school at the University of Edinburgh. Loreena had grown up in New York City with Grams, but had fallen in love with Scotland when the two went back for a visit. Klara's dad might have grown up in Ohio and was only half Scottish, but he liked to joke that he'd been born "tearin' the tartan." Since he had little family left of his own, Grams and Aunt Sorcha and their many cousins welcomed him into theirs.

So when he decided they should move right away so Klara could help him refurbish the inn before she started college, she couldn't think of a reason to say no. And most of the time she was happy they'd come.

Only now, as she opened the letter with trembling fingers, Klara knew that studying at her parents' alma mater had been her mother's dream, not hers.

Klara wanted more than to study the stars—she longed to discover new ones. New worlds.

Dear Ms. Spalding, We received your notice of withdrawal and have removed you from the matriculating Fall 2022 undergraduate class. We wish you all the best in your future endeavors.

It was done, then. No going back.

Klara waited for second thoughts to hit her, but all she felt was a massive wave of relief. She swore to herself that she'd tell her dad as soon as she could explain it. She just needed to find the right explanation, the right combination of words that wouldn't break his heart.

"Klara!"

She jumped at her father's deep voice. "Crap," she hissed.

Quickly, she jammed the envelope into her hoodie pocket and whipped around just in time to see him emerge from the east corridor.

"Mail's here!" she practically shouted, brandishing the other envelopes like one of the many swords that hung on the walls.

"You seem really excited for the mail." Her dad took the envelopes from her and paused, consulting Finley with an arched eyebrow. "Or is it the mailman?"

"*No,*" she lied.

"Just passionate for bill paying?" He nodded approvingly. "Good for you."

The thing about her dad—the thing that made it so hard to just *tell* him—was that he never *ever* suspected Klara of doing the wrong thing. When she was a kid, he had even walked in on her when she was stealing *actual* cookies from the *actual* cookie jar and believed her when she said she was just picking up the cookies after their cat, Jasper, had knocked the jar over. He was weird like that.

Sure, her dad teased her—a *lot*—but he was a total softy, a man who was moved to tears by movie trailers and the occasional insurance commercial. That's why Klara tried to avoid any talk of her mom. Eighteen months had come and gone, but it almost always made her dad cry.

She had to be strong for him. Just like her mother always had been.

She cleared her throat of its tightness and forced a smile. "What's on the agenda today, Dad?"

He brightened. "I just got us a deal with a band to come and play music here on weekends," he said, pumping his fist in triumph.

"Yaaaaay," Klara said weakly, trying to sound encouraging. Her ears were still recovering from the last Scottish folk group her father had "discovered," who turned out to be four American study abroad students with an affinity for the bagpipe but no actual skill. "Are they...local this time?"

"Yes," he chuckled. "Your mom had the eye for all things Scottish, not me. But I'm trying, kiddo."

She shrugged. "The tourists can't tell the difference anyway."

If anyone were to look at the two of them, they'd never imagine she and her father were related. Ethan Spalding was tanned and stocky, a stark contrast to Klara's tall, pale frame. Her red hair was identical to her mother's, though Klara kept hers long and her mother had worn it in a short, professional bob. Her dad's hair was an ashy brown before it went gray.

"What about you? Maybe...going out for a walk?" he asked hopefully.

Klara crossed her arms in affront. For dignity's sake, she felt she should at least pretend to be offended at her dad judging her for choosing an indoors lifestyle. "A walk? In all this rain?"

"It's been, what—" he furrowed his forehead, making a show of doing math in his head "—three days since you've been outside?"

Okay, now she *was* offended. He was keeping count! Rude. She smiled sweetly. "It's been, what? Zero days since you minded your own business?" she asked, giving him a cheeky wink. "Plus, it's pouring. Just like it was yesterday, and the day before, and the day before that..."

Her dad raised his eyebrows in disapproval but said nothing. Until—

"I was thinking..." The words came out slowly, as if he was reluctant to speak. He tucked the envelopes under his arm. "How about we invite your grandmother over to hear this band play? I bet she would love to talk about what classes you're taking—"

Her stomach clenched with guilt. She wanted to see her grandmother but talking about nonexistent classes probably wasn't a good idea.

Klara had dreamed of living near her grandmother ever since she could remember. Grams had fallen in love and moved to Edinburgh when Loreena was in college, but ever since Klara was a baby she and her parents visited Grams and her wife, Granny

Laura, every summer. They stayed in the manor, which Grams had inherited but had no interest in running, because there was no room in the tiny, ancient Edinburgh apartment, but Klara slept over almost every night and spent hours listening to Grams' stories and made-up tales. Someday, she thought, she'd pop over to Grams' apartment when she wasn't studying, bring her college friends over to get their tea leaves and palms read late into the night. Klara had grown up on her grandma's free-spirited wisdom about everything from finding her path in life to what to do if you crossed a witch in the wood.

"Yeah, I'll send her a text." Maybe she could get her news about college off her chest. Grams had always been a problem solver, but this wasn't your run-of-mill white lie.

She pulled out her phone.

Hey Grams, can I come around this weekend?

Her response was instant. Y
Klara scrunched her brows. Because I want to see you lol.

Y as in yes.

Grams may be a fast texter but she also had the tendency to create her own lingo. Great, I'll give you a call later to sort out a time.

She looked at her dad. "All set!"

"Great!" He leaned in and kissed her forehead.

She saw the car keys dangling from his pocket. "You know what, maybe I *will* get out. I'll take this," Klara said, snatching the keys. She turned and strode to the oak doors.

"Okay," he said. "Be safe."

She turned back again, smiling, leaving one hand on the doorknob. The horse's cool brass nose pressed into her palm. She met his eyes. Dark green, like hers. It was the only feature she'd inherited from him.

"What's going to happen, are the fairies going to get me?"

"Don't say that in front of your Grams! All right, have fun, kiddo. Craig is picking me up for dinner, his wife made a roast if you want to come, but if not, you are more than welcome to come see the band with us at The Black Hart."

Klara shrugged on her red raincoat and smiled up at him. Craig and his wife were like family, but she could do without listening to them reminisce about their grad school days tonight.

"Thanks, Dad, sounds delicious but I am still stuffed from breakfast, but I'll try to swing by to see the band. Though no promises."

At eighteen, she could legally drink in Scotland. It should have been every normal American teenager's dream, but Klara had never felt normal—not even before they uprooted their lives to a country across the ocean. Going to a pub to socialize with strangers was the last thing on her mind. Cute mailman aside, she preferred the leading men of romance novels, who were hot and charming and broody and didn't try to pull her into any awkward conversations.

Maybe she was just easily annoyed but on-the-page boys didn't bother her with silly questions about things she didn't want to talk about. Like watching too much TV. Or college. Or her mom.

Klara pulled the great oak doors open and was greeted by

a gust of cold wind and a slap of Scottish rain. The breeze swirled around her, filling her nose with the scent of earth and kicking up locks of her hair. A memory flashed into Klara's mind: leaning out their third-floor window, spying on the saucers of milk her mom had left out on the fire escape for the fairies.

She would go for a drive, dispose of the letter from the University of Edinburgh, and return to an empty house, at which point she would figure out how to 1) finally tell her dad, or 2) wipe his memory so he never remembered she'd been accepted in the first place.

She pulled her hood over her whipping hair with a determined tug. Her reality TV and romance novels would be waiting for her when she got back.

Driving on the left side of the road would never feel truly natural to Klara, even though she hardly drove when living in New York, where the A train was her go-to mode of transportation. Then again, she couldn't cruise in her dad's beat-up Mini Cooper in New York. At least not after that third speeding ticket.

She drummed her fingers against the steering wheel, keeping time with the windshield wipers. The rain was pouring down harder now—the squeaking wipers could hardly keep up with the torrents of water. She loved Scotland, she really did, but this weather and gloom made her miss the sunny, cluttered skies of New York.

She eased her foot off the gas pedal. The winding roads were too slippery and narrow to risk more than a snail's pace.

Then, to make matters worse, the music abruptly cut out, replaced with a steady stream of static.

"Really?" Klara groaned.

She fumbled for the radio, glancing down to change the channel. When she looked up, something was in the road in front of her.

No—someone.

A figure stared back at her, dark eyes locked onto hers with a gaze that seemed to burn through the sheet of rain.

Too late, Klara jerked the wheel to the right with a strangled scream, the car juddering and banging as she swerved, just barely avoiding the ditch. Her body pressed against the seat belt with incredible force, only slamming back when the car finally screeched to a halt.

Panting, Klara forced her eyes open. She hadn't remembered closing them in the first place. Her whole body shook.

"Owww," she groaned.

So much for airbags.

She willed her thundering heart to slow and looked into her rearview mirror, ready to give the man the kind of road-rage-fueled dressing-down that only a New Yorker could deliver.

But he was nowhere to be seen.

Or so she thought, until she saw the body crumpled in the middle of the road.

CHAPTER THREE

KLARA

Holy crap. She had hit something.

Someone.

She had hit *someone.*

Snapping back to reality, Klara scrambled for her phone. Her stomach dropped when she realized it was back at the manor, collecting lint between the couch cushions.

Klara yanked off her seat belt and vaulted out of the car, boots smacking across the wet pavement. Splayed on his back, the stranger's arms were wrapped around his torso, hands balled into loose fists. As she got closer, she saw that his knuckles were bruised and bloodied, like he had just tried to fight her car and lost.

Up close, he didn't look much older than her. Long, dark

curls clung to his beardless jaw. His cheeks were rosy. A good sign, she thought dizzily.

"Hey? Can you hear me?" Klara gently poked his cheek. Nothing. She gathered her nerve and jostled his shoulder "Hello?" Still no response.

This guy had to have a phone. She looked for a pocket, but his weird clingy pants had none. Gingerly, she brought her hand to his heavy coat. "If you can hear me, I'm sorry, I'm not being a creep I just need—"

She pulled the coat open, revealing a huge red stain across his torn white shirt.

Blood.

"Shit. *Shit*." Klara half cried, half yelled. She lurched back onto her heels and shouted, "Help! Help us!"

Her voice was lost in the sound of the rain. The road remained empty.

Klara had a vague memory of someone telling her that you shouldn't move an injured person. But out here, it might be hours until another car passed by.

Klara's throat burned. She had to do something.

"You are *not* dying on me. Not today." She tried to hoist the guy into a sitting position. After a few hard tugs, he groaned and picked himself up slightly, making it easier for her to do the rest. She slung his heavy arm around her shoulder and together, they stood up shakily.

"Great! You're doing great!" She screamed to hear herself above the rain.

He was hobbling with her now, thank god. Her oncoming heart attack subsided into a run-of-the-mill panic attack.

After easing his body into the passenger seat and buckling

him in, Klara slid behind the wheel, soaked and shivering. How far was the nearest hospital? Rural Scotland wasn't like Manhattan, where emergency care was no more than a few blocks away.

Kingshill Manor was much closer than the nearest town. She would take him there. Then call an ambulance.

Her hands turned the key in the ignition, and before she knew it, she was speeding in the direction of home.

Her conscious mind lost all sense of where it was until she heard the familiar crunch of gravel beneath the wheels. Klara slammed the car into Park, jumped out, and opened the passenger door.

"Dad!" she screamed, though the manor was silent. Craig must have picked him up already for The Black Hart and they weren't expecting guests for another hour or two.

The guy muttered something under his breath. Talking. Talking was good. "Thomas," he said, voice hardly above a whisper.

Thomas? Was that his name? Klara eased his arm around her shoulders. "Thomas, don't die on me, okay?"

She hauled him into the open air, and the boy stumbled against her chest, his chin falling on top of her head. Finally, he managed to find his feet, if a little unsteadily. Klara winced as he pressed his weight on her. "Come on, help me out here."

She used her butt and upper thigh to lower the door handle of the grand oak doors, and eased them into the dim hallway. Finley, who was resting by the fireplace in the study, lazily turned his black-and-white head to Klara as she and the boy stumbled into the room.

"Fin, stay," she ordered unnecessarily.

After successfully circling Finley without incident, Klara led them to a brass claw-foot rotary phone sat on a writing desk alongside pamphlets for Highlands tours and Edinburgh nightlife. It was the manor's only landline. Strength failing her, she eased her unwitting captive down into a chair beside the desk. Keeping a hand braced against his shoulder, she grabbed the receiver with her other. The dial tone buzzed in her ear. Shakily, she dialed 9-1-1. Then, cursing, she hung up and punched 9-9-9.

"Hello? I have—er—someone's been hit by a car. Thomas? We're at the Kingshill Manor—"

Something gripped her wrist fiercely. She jerked her head up to see the guy staring at her, his eyes wild. One was a piercing blue and the other, a muted hazel.

The next thing she knew, Klara was tumbling down in a shower of glossy pamphlets as the guy's knees buckled and he crashed to the ground, pulling her down with him. Her fall was cushioned when she landed on top of his muscled chest, but his head hit the floor with a sickening thud. His eyes fluttered closed again.

Klara hoisted herself up. The desk had tipped over and the rotary phone lay on the floor, cracked down the middle. Just like the guy's skull probably was.

Panting, she jumped up and frantically scoured the manor, trying to remember where her dad stuffed their extremely well-equipped first aid kit. When she returned a few minutes later with a roll of paper towels from the kitchen, her captive was still sprawled on the floor, muddy coat and all, his bloodied shirt riding up his chest.

She knelt next to him again—and stopped.

There was nothing under his shirt—no wound or injury or even a fresh scrape—only muscle, and smooth, tanned skin. A faint scar.

Was the blood…someone else's?

Klara went cold, snatching her hands to her chest. Who *was* this guy? Why *was* he in the road? Nobody in their right mind would be out in this rain, unless they were a lost hiker or water nymph. His uncomfortable-looking wool coat, snug fabric pants, and billowing linen undershirt were not exactly suitable rainwear. Maybe he was a Scottish-obsessed cosplayer or battle reenactor who got lost in the woods?

Maybe he was an escaped murderer from the local asylum, using an elaborate ruse to find his next victim.

Or maybe she was paranoid from watching too much *Criminal Minds*.

"Get it together, Klara," she mumbled to herself.

For the first time since she hit him—or maybe *didn't* hit him, she realized with a jolt—Klara stopped to study him. Though he was slim, there was muscle on him. She took in his dark, curly hair and sun-bronzed face. Even in his rain-soaked, filthy state, she couldn't help but notice how attractive he was. He kind of resembled the guy on the cover of *A Loch Ness Lass in Love*.

Cautiously, she leaned forward again, and began to gently tug free the cloak that was wrapped around his shoulders and neck to look for a cell phone or ID. Something heavy fell out and stuck into the floor.

"What the—"

She froze. It was a knife.

Well. That would confirm her murderer-on-the-loose theory.

Keeping one eye on him, Klara picked up the weapon. To her surprise, she recognized it. It wasn't a knife. Not exactly.

It was a dirk, a Scottish weapon dating back hundreds of years, which she knew because several of her mother's collection were displayed in the library. The one she held looked old—antique, medieval in the style of her mother's—but perfectly new at the same time. The blade was covered in dirt, but Klara could tell it was well taken care of, regularly sharpened and polished, free of rust. The studded handle was wound in leather, which was soft and worn. Cold crept up her spine. Like the dirk was used often.

Taking a mental inventory of where their Scottish weaponry was displayed around the manor in case she needed to defend herself, Klara began to slink backward on her hands and knees, yelping when she butted against something. She whipped around to see Finley's furry face. He barked once.

"A little late for that, don't you think, Fin?"

But Fin had never been a good guard dog. It only took a few more seconds for the ambulance's sirens to reach Klara's ears before she saw its red flashing lights coming up the driveway.

CHAPTER FOUR

CALLUM

Callum's legs were aching from exertion.

At first, they had burned, but now, they scarcely felt a part of him. He just wished Thomas would slow down. The mountainside was becoming increasingly steep. Lush grass had turned to rocky soil and the debris slid underfoot, leaving Callum as clumsy as a newborn calf.

"Come on, Callum, keep up!" Thomas yelled. Callum could see the muscles straining in his friend's back, yet Thomas's voice sounded impossibly far away. He glared at the back of Thomas's red mop of hair as it disappeared over the crest of the peak.

Put Callum in a boxing ring, and he could end the fight in one swift punch, but hiking up a mountain was altogether different. He was only here because it was a special day—though Callum, head swimming with heat and exhaustion, could not remember why—and if his friend wanted him to climb a mountain, he'd climb the damn mountain.

It was Thomas's birthday, after all. Oh. That's why.

Callum's head pounded. The sun flashed in his eyes. Forcing himself to take the last grueling steps, he reached the top and let out a low whistle.

Now he understood why Thomas insisted.

The Cairngorms mountain range.

The view took what little breath he had away, but Callum was more than willing to part with it. Greens, blues, and browns rolled out before him like an oil painting. The sapphire waters of Loch Avon pooled between two mountains, still as glass. Beyond the loch, rolling hills spilled out in all directions, the wilds of Scotland endless and untamed. Dimly, Callum wondered how they had traveled so far from home.

Thomas hooted, his voice echoing into the valley below.

A breeze gusted past, chilling Callum's damp skin. The wind seemed to carry voices on it. He tugged his shirt higher on his neck. "Do you hear that?" he called.

Thomas cast a glance back at him. "No. Maybe the altitude is gettin' to ye."

Callum scoffed, though his head ached fiercely. "Maybe, but who would willingly climb up a Munro such as this."

Thomas flashed him a wicked grin in response. "Well, who in their right mind would follow?"

"A man daft enough to follow a bampot like you."

Callum's heart twisted. Why? This was a happy occasion. His friend's birthday.

Thomas's blue eyes shone in the afternoon sun, a perfect likeness of the loch below. His expression turned grim, darkened by the rapidly shifting shadows.

"Ye're lost, Callum," he said. "It's time to wake up."

The sun flashed in Callum's eyes—back and forth, back and forth, like it was swinging at the end of a rope. Callum groaned. His stomach roiled. His master, Brice, had once hoisted one of the younger boys by their feet into the rafters, as a punishment. Now, with his head throbbing, Callum couldn't remember what the boy had done to deserve it. Likely nothing. A pair of hands grabbed at his face.

All at once, the memories flooded back to him.

Thomas. Blood. The man made of shadow.

Gasping, Callum sat up. His hands flew to his chin, prepared to strike.

A man hovered over him. A red-haired woman—no, young lady—stood a few paces behind him. With a lurch of his stomach, Callum recalled Thomas's account of the bean-nighe who foretold his death. The creature could pose as a maiden when it suited them.

Seeing the concern in their eyes—at least in the man's, as the lady's eyes squinted—Callum lowered his hands. Dimly, he realized he no longer held the dirk, though it didn't matter: the man in front of him seemed to pose little threat. The lady—well, he couldn't be sure.

"All right, son?" the man asked kindly.

Callum nodded, even though it wasn't true.

The man—light brown eyes, hair to match, and brown spots on his face—shone a torch in his eyes unlike any Callum had seen. It was made of black metal, not wood. Light burned at one end, but there was no fire and little heat. Child-like and dazed, Callum reached out, tapping the torch softly with one finger to assure himself it was real.

The man turned to address the girl. "Has he been drinking?"

Her mouth opened and closed a few times, like she was coming up with an answer. "I—I don't know. All I know is he was hit by a car." The man looked critically at Callum.

Swaying with nausea, Callum blinked. His eyes adjusted to his lavish surroundings. He was sitting on the floor in an unfamiliar hallway. His white-knuckled fingers sunk into a rich red carpet far softer than the straw he was used to. Fine paintings hung on the wall. In the adjoining room, he glimpsed wood-carved furniture and a grand, yawning fireplace.

Had he been brought to the local laird's manor? His heart stilled in fear, like a bird caught in a closed fist. Did they think him Thomas's killer?

"Have you been drinking, son?" the man asked. Staring at him now.

"Aye," Callum answered. It felt like ages since he had watched Thomas lose his fight—but by his count, Callum had stepped out of the warm, hazy safety of the pub mere hours ago, if that. He could still taste the whiskey on his tongue. Confusion churned in him, but awareness of the red-haired maiden sharpened his mind. Bean-nighe or not, he didn't want her to think him a fool. "At The Black Hart."

The man sighed, sitting back on his heels. Behind him, the lady quirked her brow, it was nearly the same copper color as her hair. Shame welled in Callum. "I havna paid yet, but I will. Anderson knows I am a man of honor."

"Right, then, I'll be going," mumbled the man angrily to himself like the drunks at the pub, and he began to toss several metal instruments into a dark leather bag. A healer? "A man of honor. Just like the rest o'em…"

Callum clutched his side. The memory of his wound seized hold of him. He yanked the fabric up to reveal a clean scar.

The wound was gone.

Callum raised his eyes again to see the young woman staring intently at the place where the wound had been. Then, the man spoke to her. "Aspirin."

The copper-haired girl started. She took her eyes off Callum and addressed the man. "Aspirin?"

"Yes. This young man needs aspirin, water, and perhaps to reconsider his life choices, if he's already this drunk so early in the morning." He stood and began to retreat down the hallway. The harshness of his voice as he addressed the lady made Callum's fingers twitch.

Darting a wary glance over her shoulder at Callum, the young woman followed the man out the door, voice fading as she walked farther away.

"He's lucky to not be dead." The sound of her voice was strange, an accent unlike anything Callum had ever heard. Not Scottish—nor English, nor French—but spirited. Perhaps she was Scottish, after all.

Her words lingered in the air. She had tried to save his life. Done something, perhaps, to heal the fatal wound on his torso. The miracle kindled suspicion in him, at the same time his cheeks warmed with shame that he had needed saving at all.

Callum slumped against the wall, letting his muscles relax. He breathed in deeply. Though the manor smelled of cinnamon and a recently put-out fire, the scent of blood still lingered in his nostrils. His senses sharpened as his ear became attuned to the pattering rain outside.

When he closed his eyes, the image of Thomas's empty, dying eyes burned in his thoughts. It was no fevered dream, as much as he might wish it so. The shadowed man had escaped his grasp. Despair filled Callum again as he remembered his own helplessness.

But where was he now?

Preparing to stand, Callum shifted his weight to his hands and knees and noticed several shining slips on the ground. He picked one up. There was no printing press in Rosemere, but Callum had seen religious pamphlets before. None had color like the pamphlet he held in his hand, which depicted a grand manor in brilliant greens, browns, and blues.

A painting? He had never seen one so small. But then, Callum was not accustomed to the habits of the rich—though he was familiar with their whims. He thought grimly of a few of the doughy, sweating faces that bet on his bouts regularly, trying to pass as common folk for a thrill.

Callum began to collect the other pamphlets that had fallen, vaguely knowing that he had somehow caused the mess. Suspicions aside, he did not want to cause any more trouble than he already had.

"Hello, sweetheart, can you help us?"

Callum whirled. A lanky man and plump woman stood in a grand hall. Both wore strange clothing, but then, the rich surely had strange fashions as well as tastes—though the garments did seem awfully strange nonetheless, made from a transparent, shiny material and not wet though they were speckled with rain. Strange dress aside, both man and woman were well-groomed and had finer teeth than anyone he knew.

They must have been the manor's owners. Maybe they had knowledge of the man he sought. Callum bowed his head in respect. "My lord, have you heard news of a man—a strange man seeking shelter, perhaps bearing the marks of a struggle?"

The woman giggled. "Pardon?"

The man looked at Callum's clothes with a bemused smile. "We're looking to check into our rooms."

All Callum could do was blink. Brice never taught his boys to read, but he did make certain that they spoke passable Scots, Gaelic, and English, and had enough manners to conduct themselves for the rich—they were more valuable that way, able to understand their opponents as well as the men betting on them. Callum knew the lairds of the lands lived different lives, but he could hardly understand *this* man.

"We have our reservations, if that helps," the woman said.

The woman held out a small box. Strange lettering had been engraved against a glowing light. As he watched, her fingers skimmed its surface, and the letters moved with it. His eyes widened.

"What in the devil…" he breathed.

"Oh, he's in *character*!" the lady said, clasping a hand to her chest.

The man chuckled. "No wonder he's wearing a costume. What a charming touch!"

The woman turned to her partner. "Sometimes they

method act at these places, I read all about it on the Yelp reviews."

The redheaded girl ducked in through the main door and hurried toward them. "I'm so sorry, ma'am, can I help you? I'm Klara. My family owns the manor."

Only minutes had passed since Callum had seen her, but his memories did her little justice. She was absolutely stunning. Her hair flowed loose around her shoulders, each strand shining with rain. Surely a bean-nighe would not be speaking so freely, acting so human, or be named Klara. Her beauty reminded Callum of the stories sailors told as they passed through Rosemere on the way to the coast—of the beautiful mermaids that ensnared men's hearts and dragged them to the depths of the sea. He had never understood why, if the men knew what fate lay before them, they didn't turn away from the sea-devils before it was too late.

Now, looking at the lady before him, Callum understood.

He glanced away, fearful of the feeling that now ensnared him. His head was filled with the tales of the maidens who appeared to guide kings and heroes on a journey—or to tempt them away from their fates, like the Morrígan attempted to trick the demigod, Cú Chulainn.

The girl—Klara—was entirely focused on the couple. She extended her hand and the man and woman took it in turn.

"This...*lad* was just helping us," the woman giggled. "Ain't he just *darling*! Y'all really pay attention to detail." She turned to the man. "He's even put some fake blood on it."

Callum understood that much. "'Tis not false, my lady," he replied, offended.

The woman clapped delightedly, but Klara fixed him with

a glare that would strike a lesser man dead. "Please give me a moment while I check these folks in, Thomas."

The name struck him like a blow. His chest tightened. "My name is Callum," he added quickly.

Klara watched him, eyes softening. "*Please*, Callum." She pointed further down the hall, where there was a row of doors. "You can wait for me in the Cameron suite."

Callum went in the direction she pointed, not wanting to incur her ire further. How had she known Thomas's name? And what had she meant by Cameron? True, he was familiar with the Cameron clan—was she one of them? He stopped at the first threshold he found and stepped inside, closing the door behind him.

Inside the room was just as fine as the hall. A four-poster bed stood in the center, its blanket as blue and wide as the sea. The walls were lined with shelves made of dark, glistening wood, each bearing gold instruments and fine dirks that glinted between towers of leather-bound books. The only book Callum had seen was Thomas's notebook, yet here there were hundreds. Resentment stung him, quick as a snake's bite—why was he in this fine house while Thomas was lying on the ground in Kelpie's Close, cut open and cold?

Trembling at the thought, Callum sat on the large bed. His weight pulled back the coverlet to reveal a crisp white bedsheet underneath. Yesterday, he would have given anything to sleep in comfort, but now Callum saw white winding cloth instead of welcoming sheets. He imagined the women of Rosemere wrapping Thomas's body in the fabric, preparing him for the grave. The deid bell would have tolled by now, to ring out the news of his friend's passing.

Head heavy, Callum's chin fell to his chest. Seeing Thomas's blood splashed across his shirt made him ill. He tore the fabric down the middle and cast it to the ground. Only then did he realize that he had lost Thomas's prized possessions— his notebook and his dirk.

He passed his hand over his closed eyes, and a sob erupted from his lips. Instinctively, he clamped his mouth shut and braced his body. A harsh, scarred face cut into the darkness behind his lids.

A quiet child is a good child. Brice's voice in the darkness, menacing eyes aglow.

Callum's entire body tensed—but Brice was not here, or even close. Callum could feel the distance in his bones.

Slowly, Callum let his grief flow, though quieter this time. Hot tears streamed down his cheeks, dampening the soft pillow clenched in his fist. A chilling wash of numbness swept his body, penetrating so deep it was as if he were no longer tethered to his own soul.

He had seen plenty of death in his short years. Every day, the deid bells rang out in Rosemere, their sad, steady song echoing in the streets. Callum had even buried boys and men he'd fought in the ring, some of them younger than he was now. Some thought him brutal, to be sure, but Callum had no taste for killing. Yet had he not fought fiercely he would be dead many times over.

To survive required hard choices. Callum's own mother had abandoned him as an infant, leaving him in the cold care of a devil, so that she herself would have enough to eat. Callum could not blame her for that, even if sometimes he wondered if he was dead inside, unable to feel more than pity for her.

Yet sitting in this strange house thinking of Thomas, Callum experienced a rush of grief so powerful he felt as though it might drown him.

He had watched his best friend die horribly at the hands of a stranger—and he'd failed to stop it. The one time killing could have saved a man, he'd been too late, too weak.

Thomas had been his only family. But maybe Callum no longer deserved such comfort. He was meant to be a fighter, but he had failed. And now he would be alone.

Callum closed his eyes. It should've been him who died.

He knelt, pushing his pain down deep with a shuddering breath. Even with so much uncertainty, one thing was certain.

On one knee, he vowed to find the man made of shadows and take his life, no matter how strong the man was, no matter what unearthly blessings had been bestowed upon him. Callum fought the chill that moved over his body and finished his vow to kill this man, no matter what world he came from.

Callum would get revenge.

Only then would he allow himself to mourn.

CHAPTER FIVE

KLARA

After getting the Texan tourists settled in their room—an "upgrade suite" that put them as far away from Mystery Man as possible—Klara headed to Cameron and raised her fist to knock on Callum's door, then stopped. If he was some killer, she wasn't about to give him an advantage. Briefly, she thought of retrieving the literal dagger she'd found on him from her bag where she'd hidden it, but who was she kidding? She'd probably accidentally kill the guy if she tried any self-defense moves on him. After narrowly avoiding murder once today, Klara didn't want to press her luck.

"Hey, sorry about—"

When Klara entered and locked eyes with a naked Callum, she stepped backward out of the room and snapped the door shut again.

Okay, he was only mostly naked. But *very* shirtless. Had he been kneeling? Praying? Doing squats? Ugh, was he a Cross-Fit bro? Klara was too flustered to remember. What she did remember was the image of his bare chest and toned muscles. Other than on TV, which didn't really count, she hadn't seen many men's bodies in her eighteen years of life—except for Steven, her ex-boyfriend. She would've felt guilty for almost forgetting about him but then again, he was forgettable. And Steven seemed to have forgotten about her when he cheated on prom night…

Callum's body was…not forgettable.

Muscled. Ripped. Svelte. Bonnie. Tan and lean, with a dusting of dark hair on his upper chest which also sprouted below his belly button and went lower than she cared to admit she had noticed. Definitely not forgettable.

Clothes. Maybe she should get Callum some new clothes.

Kingshill Manor had an unofficial lost and found, a dusty kitchen pantry where Klara stashed the assortment of random items guests left behind.

Klara began to sort through the pantry's musty contents, turning her thoughts to how snugly various articles of clothing might fit over Callum's body. Tossing aside a few XL tank tops, galoshes, a pair of sunglasses, and one rubber snake, she hit the jackpot: a men's T-shirt and a crumpled pair of jeans that looked to be roughly Callum's size. Sure, the T-shirt said Kiss Me, I'm Scottish and the jeans dated back to when acid wash was in style the first time, but anything was better than the mud-and-blood-stained outfit that Callum was sporting.

A voice rang out from above. "Hello?"

"Coming!" Following Callum's call, she retraced her steps

to see him poking his head out of the open doorway. From what she could glimpse of his toned and tanned shoulder muscles, he was still shirtless.

In Klara's opinion, the best thing to do in awkward circumstances was to completely avoid whatever was causing the awkwardness. So as she handed him the jeans and T-shirt, she averted her eyes upward, taking a sudden interest in the crown molding that lined the hallway.

He chuckled softly and took the bundle from her hands. "Dinnae fash, it's just skin."

She allowed her gaze to drift downward. He looked back at her, eyes sparkling.

He held her gaze. Time seemed to slow and stretch, like freshly made taffy.

God, what love potion did she accidentally take? She wasn't the insta-love crush type, and she didn't need to become one all of a sudden.

"Are you sure you're not hurt? I did *not* trust that EMT," she said.

"Aye, I'll survive. Thank you for—" He stopped short, his expression suddenly twisted in confusion.

"Saving your life? All in a day's work."

His mouth twitched, like he was about to smile but thought better of it. In fact, his whole face was tense and drawn. The dark curls hanging over his forehead only added to the broody vibe. "Did you find a dirk among my things? Or bound vellum pages?"

Klara flushed and swallowed, trying to give her best poker face. No way was she handing a weapon to this guy. "No." At least she was only half lying.

His jaw tensed and lips pressed together, giving Klara the distinct impression that he was holding back a curse. Then, he spoke again, lowering his voice. "Did you heal me?"

"Heal you?" Klara laughed. "No, definitely not. Actually..." She trailed off, not sure how much she should divulge. But he seemed nervous, and it made her want to trust him. "I thought I'd killed you."

He paused before finally answering, "I see."

"I'm Klara," she said, offering her hand gently, like she would to a scared puppy. "We haven't really been introduced."

Hesitating slightly, he squeezed her hand. "Callum."

"I know. Definitely better than Guy-I-Hit-With-My-Car," she said.

Klara waited, hoping he would elaborate or laugh or— *something*. But he only nodded, retreating into the room with the bundle of clothes. Through the partially closed door, Klara glimpsed the flash of a heel. She watched his odd pants fly in an arc and land on top of his dirty, blood-stained shirt, adding to the heap at the foot of the bed. The sight of blood reminded her that no matter how much of this guy's skin she'd seen, he was a stranger. An attractive stranger, but a stranger, and a blood-drenched one at that.

"I didn't find a phone on you, either, but you can use mine if you want," she shouted. Callum said nothing. "Or I can call a car for you." Still nothing. "Or my dad can give you a ride when he gets back from The Black Hart," she tried. Utter silence.

Her competitive streak, long dormant now that she wasn't in school anymore, flared. She *would* get this guy to talk. "Are you hungry?"

The rustling on the other side of the door stopped. "Quite," he replied huskily.

Klara was pretty sure that meant "yes."

"Meet me in the kitchen in ten minutes. It's downstairs."

Mysterious strangers had to eat, too.

"Sorry the jeans are a bit eighties."

Roughly fifteen minutes after the accidental peep show, just as the microwave beeped, Callum appeared in the doorway of Kingshill Manor's kitchen, looking surprisingly fresh in his not-so-fresh clothes. He tugged at the T-shirt warily, like he half suspected it was going to bite him. Klara tried not to stare too long at the shape of his chest underneath the fabric.

"Eighties?" he repeated.

"Yeah. Come on, they scream vintage."

She put the nuked breakfast burrito onto a plate and turned to see a bewildered Callum sitting at the other end of the table, staring at his hands.

"Acid wash? Scrunchies? Lots of hair spray?" Nothing. "Taylor Swift's *1989*?" He looked even more confused.

Poor Callum, she thought. Dirk aside, every moment, he seemed less "serial killer" and more "out-of-touch farm boy." Her father had told her about some communities, deep in the Highlands, that kept their kids isolated from the rest of the world. Maybe Callum was from there. It would explain a lot. He must have been *really* backwoods if he didn't know T. Swift.

A darker possibility occurred to her. Maybe he suffered a brain injury or amnesia before she found him in the road.

Or who knew, maybe he was one of those insurance scammers that jumped in front of cars to get a payout and this was all part of an act. Then again, those guys tend to act injured. It was the opposite with Callum. Klara couldn't say exactly why, but she sensed Callum was hiding pain—at the very least, he definitely wasn't shouting it from the rooftops.

"These clothes," he said, plucking at his shirt. "They're strange." The seriousness of his observation made a laugh bubble in Klara's throat. "Yours are strange, too," he added, looking her up and down.

Okay, not so funny anymore. Today, she wore her favorite outfit: worn red jeans and an old, soft Metallica T-shirt.

"Well, I could say the same thing about yours," she said, thinking of his dirty, old-fashioned woolen clothes. Callum stared at her blankly in response.

Oh so witty, Klara.

"Well, if you don't like Metallica, you're definitely not an eighties buff. I'll try to avoid any *Back to the Future* references." She removed the wrapper from the steaming burrito.

Klara slid the plate of food across the table. "I hope you're not a vegetarian."

He gave her a questioning look. "I'm no Lutheran, if that's what you're asking."

"Uh…" Was that the famous dry Scottish humor she still didn't get? "Do you like meat?"

He nodded, shaggy hair flopping with the movement. "Very much."

Klara gave him a tight-lipped smile. His deep Scottish brogue was probably the thickest accent she had ever heard, which was saying a lot because a Glaswegian school group had once visited the manor. Callum was a strange one, no doubt about that—though he felt less like a stranger every second they spent together. Klara quickly dismissed the thought.

Callum looked at the burrito curiously before taking a bite. To her surprise, his face lit up with pleasure, eyes half closing as he chewed slowly. "This is heavenly," he moaned through a mouthful of egg and bacon. "Give your cook my gratitude."

She laughed. "Tell her yourself. You're looking at her."

Callum stared at her in that confused way she was starting to get used to, then took another bite. "*You* prepared this?"

If you can't beat 'em, join 'em, she thought wryly. "Are you shocked at my culinary prowess, my lord?" She gestured with a flourish to the microwave and added a sarcastic half curtsy.

Callum tilted his head and stared at her like she was an animal at the zoo.

"I thought the rich always employed a kitchen staff. You're a…different sort of lady."

"A different sort?" Was that a compliment or an insult? Klara laughed, mostly to hide a wince. Her family wasn't rich—far from it—she couldn't blame Callum for assuming. She *did* live in a massive, cool manor house brimming with antiques and oddities.

A few more moments passed in awkward silence—awkward for Klara, not Callum, who was quite occupied wolfing down his burrito. While he ate with abandon, Klara gathered herself to ask the question she should have asked outright, or at least before she started internally comparing his eyes to a pool she'd like to swim in. "I'm glad to see you're feeling better, but—what the hell were you doing in the middle of the road?"

Smooth, Klara! Put his feet to the fire!

Callum's chewing slowed. He put down the crescent moon of his remaining burrito. "I canna say."

"You...don't know?"

"I was at The Black Hart. Drinking, aye, but not drunk," he said quickly. "I left in search of my friend..."

Callum trailed off. His expression twisted.

"Thomas?" she guessed.

His eyes widened in surprise.

"I'm not a mind reader or anything. You said his name while you were unconscious," she clarified. "Listen, I'm not like that judgy EMT. If you want to get wasted with your friends after breakfast, it's a free country, right? If Thomas is wandering around the woods somewhere near where I found you, we can go look for him. The Black Hart's not that far—"

Callum's head dipped low between his shoulders, as if a weight had been slung around his neck. A kicking, panicked feeling shot through Klara's body. All at once, she recognized the look twisting his face—she saw it in her father's eyes every day, and in the mirror every morning.

Grief.

Callum spoke. "It was Thomas I was referring to. But he's gone now."

A story clicked into place: Callum was mourning someone, so drowned himself in grief, lost time. In the days after losing her mom, Klara half remembered stumbling around in a haze, without any sense of time, direction, purpose.

"Losing someone you care for is painful."

Callum considered her, then nodded sadly. "An untimely loss pains the soul, especially when the one who is responsible still breathes." He continued softly, more to himself than her. "There is a man who needs to pay the price, and I plan on finding him."

Well, she didn't exactly like the sound of that. "How are you going to do that?" she asked. It was clear there was more to say on the subject of Thomas. And as for this other man—Nope, Klara decided not to push it. They weren't friends, she reminded herself. He didn't have to tell her anything. So why did *she* almost spill her guts to him?

"If I'm to be honest, I dinnae ken yet." He scrunched his thick brows, as if trying to pull his forgotten memories forward. "All I know is that I think I have traveled far from home, and I have to get back. That is where I must start."

"Where is home? I could drive you there," she offered, to her own surprise. "Or call you a taxi."

He raised a hopeful eyebrow. "Rosemere."

"Rosemere," Klara repeated. "I'm sorry, I've never heard of it." Her mom's passion for local knowledge and history would've come in handy right now. Luckily, Klara had the internet. She pulled out her phone and searched maps, but came up with nothing. A tingle moved its way up her spine. She looked up to see Callum staring at her, an intense, blazing look in his eyes. Color returned to his face.

"If I'm to avenge Thomas, I must find my way home."

He looked determined. "I can take you to The Black Hart?"

Callum stood up. "I'd be obliged to ye. I can find my way from there, and not impose on ye any longer."

He bowed his head low, and Klara smiled at the odd mannerism. She tried not to think about how this stranger had made her smile more times in an hour than she had in months. The upward pull of her cheeks felt foreign.

"As long as you address me as Lady Klara. It suits me, don't you think?" she said airily. Of course she was kidding... maybe.

"I think it does," Callum said, a smirk pulling at his lips. "Lady Klara."

The rain had stopped and the sun was actually visible and utterly gorgeous, a fact Klara tried not to read into. She had already exceeded her daily quota of smiles, laughter, and butterflies. Plus, Grams would be way too smug if she started interpreting signs from the universe.

Rays of light broke through the lingering clouds, striking the Kingshill Manor lawn in wide beams. The air was thick with the scent of damp soil and pine. Klara could taste autumn in the air, creeping in with the changing leaves.

"What kind of carriage is that?" Callum said in awe, examining the little blue car.

"A Mini Cooper. You have the weirdest sense of humor," she said, trying not to laugh, and opened the creaky door for him. "Get in. You missed out on my great driving while you were unconscious, so you're in for a treat."

Klara rounded the car and slid behind the wheel, comforted by the pepper spray on her key chain that her dad insisted she carry. The car rocked as Callum climbed inside. His eyes roved all over, taking in the steering wheel and the dashboard in front of him. Trying to ignore his general weirdness, she turned the key in the ignition. The engine sputtered to life like a chain-smoker's cough.

"Where are the horses?"

Klara laughed. "Getting fat on hay in the stables. Shall I fetch them?"

She eased the car down the driveway, Callum turned a deathly shade of pale. She really hoped he wasn't the type to get carsick. Cleaning up vomit was not on her agenda for today. Or any day really.

Klara cracked the window, allowing the breeze to rush into the car. It smelled of burnt leaves, still smoking from the kiss of a fire. She wound the car around a twisting bend, across the same sturdy stone bridge she'd crossed not long ago. In the river below, a fly-fisher stood waist deep in the current. Callum watched as his figure whipped the pole forward, shooting the line impossibly far. They were silent, but it was a comfortable silence—like the kind Klara would always interrupt when her mom and dad were doing separate crossword puzzles on the couch.

Soon, the Elder Forest enveloped them under its thick, multicolored canopy. She slowed the car as they passed the crash site, recognizable from the churned-up earth that marked where the car not-so-gracefully swerved to avoid Callum.

"That's where I found you," she said.

Less than a minute later, The Black Hart came into view. It stood at the edge of the forest, standing out from all that green with its walls the color of wool. Red neon signs glowed faintly inside the dim pub, behind the many-plated windows. A sign boasting Oldest Public House in Scotland swung in the breeze. She pulled in behind her dad's friend Craig's car and shifted into Park.

"Are you sure this is where you want me to leave you?" she asked.

"Yes, I am sure."

Callum began to leave the car, then turned back, embarrassment plain on his face. It was nice to see him blushing for once.

"Thank you, Lady Klara." He spoke her name slowly, and she couldn't help but love how it rolled like a rumble from his tongue. It sent flutters through her stomach. Callum looked at her for a long moment. His body went still.

Oh my god. Was he going to kiss her? Her heart pounded harder the longer his gaze lingered on her face. He was definitely going to kiss her. She closed her eyes.

"Lady Klara?"

Klara's eyelids flew open. Heart-pounding turned to mortification when she realized that he wasn't trying to kiss her. He just couldn't open the car door.

She reached across him to pull the door handle and practically shoved him out of the car. A knot formed in her chest as he walked away, but she ignored the feeling. Through the still-raindrop-speckled windshield, she watched him approach the bar entrance, wrench open the door—and freeze like a deer in headlights.

Callum backed away slowly. The heavy door slammed closed with a bang. Then, he walked toward the edge of the forest, hesitating only slightly before he plunged into the thick, dark woods.

"What the hell," Klara muttered.

She moved to open the car door and follow him, then stopped. Callum wasn't a bird with a broken wing that she nursed back to health. She wasn't responsible for him. All she'd done was give him a change of clothes and a meal. She should be grateful he *wasn't* a killer.

And yet, though she had only known him a few hours, she felt a tinge of sadness.

Well, less of a tinge…more like a pull.

Klara pulled the car back onto the road, muttering to herself to get a grip. Deep in her chest, a knot formed. It was the strangest thing. Like nothing she had felt before. It wasn't love, or empathy. It was a physical feeling, like a rope was tightening around her ribs. Swallowing hard, she punched the radio on and cranked the volume until the slashing guitars and beating drums were louder than her thoughts.

Plenty of charming strangers had come through Kingshill in the last six months. Hot ones. Like, an entire rugby team full of hot strangers. Why was she feeling this way *now*, about some rando who had never been in a car before?

But the farther she drove from The Black Hart, the more the feeling intensified. It felt as if something was pulling her back. The longer she resisted, the tighter it became, until it was so tight, she felt like something would break inside her.

"What *is* this," she choked, turning the wheel around. Her body moved of its own accord, but her brain was still trying to catch up.

To her relief, the feeling lessened as she got closer to the pub. Klara pulled onto the side of the road—far enough away where she hoped her dad wouldn't notice her car—and sat there, listening to the engine hum.

Trust yourself.

Her mother's words came to her, so loud and real in Klara's

mind that she actually looked to see if her mother was standing just outside the car, calling to her.

But of course she wasn't. Klara was alone.

She looked behind her, in the direction of where Callum disappeared, then reached for her bag in the cramped back seat, top flap slightly open. The heel of the dagger poked out—the one she hadn't given back to Callum.

She grabbed the bag. Callum's muddied footprints led into the woods, and so, Klara did, too.

CHAPTER SIX

CALLUM

Ducking low-hanging branches and navigating thick tangles of rock and root, Callum pushed on, driven forward by the pulsing beat in his chest.

Klara had left him at The Black Hart. It was the tavern he knew—the familiar shape and visage, the same sweet smell of ale and frying meats inside—at the same time it was not. Not at all. It was more akin to a painting of The Black Hart, with its lines and colors slightly askew.

Confusion, frustration, and anger urged his legs forward as he let his muscle memory find the path that he had walked earlier. *It was only hours ago*, he thought dizzily, insistently. But trees grew in place of the familiar homes and merchant shops, their chimneys puffing with thick smoke. Instead of the cobblestones that held Brice's prized horses aloft and soaked up Callum's blood when he scrapped, earth lay under his feet.

The weather was turning. Newly shed leaves left slick patches along his path, causing him to slip and curse as he pushed onward. A copper leaf lazily spiraled to the ground in front of him, the same color as Klara's hair.

Callum stopped, catching the leaf in his palm. The sight of it grounded him. It was the same as any that littered Rosemere.

Callum turned the leaf over, feeling a dull twinge of recognition. It was the leaf of a yew tree. He knew of only one yew tree, and he knew it well. He looked up.

The Hanging Tree. Its black, skeletal branches were far thicker and more twisted than he remembered—its bark had grown bulbous knots, and its roots jutted upward from the earth, too—but Callum was certain it was the same tree. He had watched too many men die there to mistake it for another.

Everything had changed except The Black Hart, which was still standing, and the Hanging Tree. Which meant that Rosemere *had* once stood here, even if it did no longer.

Callum sunk down, coming to rest on a fallen trunk. Was it possible that Thomas had come down with an illness that had somehow afflicted Callum? But that would not explain the man—the *demon*—who had killed Thomas and attacked Callum. The scene in Kelpie's Close, Thomas's murder, Klara's strange house and clothes and carriage, all converged in his head with sickening force.

He reached under the shirt Klara had given him and traced his fingers over the faint scar, remembering the bloody slash that had been there before. He clung to the memory. The mark was proof that he *had* followed Thomas out of the pub, *had* fought for his life in Kelpie's against a man who had the strength of ten.

When Thomas had spoken of leaping to different worlds, he had spoken of the old gods, of fiery skies, of creatures that gave children nightmares. But since Callum had woken up in Klara's home, he felt like he'd arrived in a world he knew, though distantly—like he was looking at his world through a strange glass, or in a dream.

The wind whistled through the trees. The Hanging Tree groaned, its branches shuddering. A chill ran along his spine.

His head ached again, like it would burst into flames. He crushed the leaf in his fist.

Something snapped to his left.

Instinctively, Callum jumped up and crouched, bracing himself for another attack. "Show yourself!" he shouted.

But no murderer or evil spirit stood in front of him. He stared back at a wide-eyed Klara, a mere few steps away.

Surprised at his sudden movement, she lost her footing and stumbled. Callum darted forward and caught her by the upper arms. Her loose hair spilled over his wrist. Quickly, he righted her and let go when he was sure she was steady.

"Easy, weirdo. Just me," she said breathlessly.

His beating heart slowed. "You followed me," he said, impressed that she had done it so quietly.

"Well, it doesn't sound great when you say it out loud like that." She let out a short nervous laugh. She plucked a twig from her hair and tossed it aside. "But yep, I followed you, a total stranger into the woods, miles away from any other human or cell service."

Cell service? Would she throw him in prison? "Why did you follow me?"

Klara watched him, brow furrowed in confusion. Then— "Oh my god…are *you* suspicious of *me*?" She let out a laugh. The sound rang out, making several birds take flight. "You've got to be kidding."

The thoughts he had been considering swirled in Callum's chest, like a storm threatening to pour out of him all at once.

"You look terrified. No offense," she added.

Callum's heart raced. Would she believe him if he told her the truth—at least what he knew of it? "I was attacked," he said finally.

Klara's mouth fell open. "Someone attacked you? Here? Why didn't you call the police?"

"Police?" he repeated.

Klara waved her hand dismissively. "Or whatever they call them in Scotland! Why didn't you say this earlier?"

Callum grimaced. Telling the truth, if only in part, had been a mistake. It would only lead to more questions, ones he could not answer. He needed to be rid of her. He needed to find his way home. "Lady, ye dinnae understand, I must—"

"Okay, okay," she said. "I change my mind. Enough of the 'lady' stuff."

His blood flared. Suspicion and fear got the best of him. Perhaps she was Fair Folk, or a selkie, or one of the many otherworldly creatures who took on the guise of a beautiful woman. "Are ye not a lady?"

She groaned. "I'm a lady. I just don't want you to call me that when my name is Klara."

Klara shrugged off the leather bag fastened to her back. Callum had never seen such a bag before, but it no longer shocked him. What did shock him was what she pulled out of the bag.

Carefully, she opened the top flap, reached inside, and drew out Thomas's dirk.

Sadness swept through him and he reached for it eagerly. The weight of the weapon in his hand brought the memory of the attack swooping back again, the truth and certainty of it.

"I found it on you. It fell out of your clothes when I was helping you." Her cheeks flushed rose.

He looked at Klara. "Did you find the folio?"

"A folio?" she asked. Her brow furrowed.

"It's leather-bound with parchment inside."

"A notebook?"

"You've seen it?" he said hopefully.

"No. Just that *lethal weapon*."

Callum felt his cheeks burn. He had no reason to feel shame for carrying a dirk, but her words were a sore reminder of why he had possession of Thomas's. He had taken it from Thomas without his knowledge, and if he had not—

Tucking the dirk under his cloak, Callum turned away from her and continued on his path, navigating the best he could with the Hanging Tree as a reference.

"Wait!" She grabbed his arm. "Can we go back to the part where you were attacked?"

"No." He pulled gently out of her grasp and walked on. "I need to get home." *To find the man who killed my friend*, he wanted to finish, but stopped himself, unsure whether he could trust her.

"Fine," she said, and followed him anyway. "I guess it's none of my business. But honestly, it seems like you could use some company, considering you nearly got hit by a car earlier. If you insist on finding your way home, I'm going to tag along," she said firmly.

"Lady—"

Callum turned. Klara crossed her arms.

"*Klara.*"

"Well, what are you waiting for? Go on," she said. "What if you need your life saved again?"

Turning back, Callum clenched his jaw and continued on the narrow path ahead. He still did not know for certain where he was or how he had arrived there, but after only a short time in this strange world, he felt sure that Klara was going to have her way.

"I did tell ye there was a dangerous man out here."

"No, you said you were *attacked*. Now I know you were attacked by a man," she said smugly.

He glanced back at her. "Who else would attack me?"

"A woman?"

Callum laughed, and the joyful noise sounded so strange coming from him that he almost did not recognize the sound of his voice.

"What's funny?" Klara asked. "Or is that a secret, too?"

Callum glanced back at her again, uncertain if she was joking. "I wouldn't need a *dirk* to defend myself from a woman."

He faced forward again, contemplating whether he should tell her more—that his attacker wasn't a man, but possibly more than a man—when his ankle was swept out from under him from behind. He plummeted forward and hit the ground with a hard thud. Still struggling for the wind that was knocked out of him, Callum flipped over to see the mud-stained sole of Klara's slipper as she stepped over him.

"I don't know what passes for feminism wherever you're from, but that was a fail in my book," she said lightly.

A smile tugged at the corners of his mouth—the first in a long while. He let it fall. The unfamiliar feeling was a betrayal of Thomas. "That was not exactly a fair fight."

"Life's not fair," Klara said breezily.

"Aye," he agreed darkly. "It is not."

"Here." Klara extended a hand: an offer to help him up. Hesitating slightly, Callum moved to grasp it when Klara darted forward, past him, leaving his proffered hand to hang in the air.

"Hey—"

Callum lifted himself up, brushing loose dirt and leaves from his clothes. She had picked up an object. His breath caught.

Thomas's notebook.

Relief washed over him, along with a new wave of grief. If this was not all a devilish trick, Thomas's notebook was more proof that Callum was not imagining things—that he had indeed traveled through this forest—but it also meant that Thomas was dead, and this was not all a terrible dream.

Klara turned the book over in her hand and ran her fingers along the frayed edges. "Is this what you were looking for? This is beautiful. And old." She opened it. "Are they draw—"

"'Tis not old," Callum said, snatching the notebook from her swiftly. The pages were private. Even he did not know what it contained. But he knew that the notebook was precious to Thomas. Callum slipped the small folio into his pocket.

Klara looked at him, lips slightly parted in affront.

He blushed. He had been rude, he realized. Having spent the majority of his time with men, Callum felt awkward and brutish in front of Klara—whether he trusted her or not. "Thank you for finding it," he said, softening his voice.

"No problem," she responded slowly.

Avoiding her gaze, he trained his eyes forward again.

Treading close behind, Klara followed Callum deeper into the forest as he searched for any clues as to how he arrived here, any sign that might lead him back to his Rosemere. Soon, the dense trees around them opened slightly into a small clearing. Klara stopped abruptly, her mouth parting again, though this time in surprise. "Look."

Callum followed her gaze. The clearing wasn't a natural clearing. It looked as though a great storm had passed through. A few slim trees lay felled on the ground, broken decisively at the base. Those that stood, their branches were snapped cleanly in half, though the damage stopped abruptly six feet up the trunks, where the branches were untouched. Stranger still, the ground was marred: the green grass gave way to slices of black earth, but the boundaries between the black and green were crisp. The image of a giant stamping the earth with its foot entered Callum's mind.

Klara cast a wary glance at Callum, then turned away again. "What happened here?" she said, but it was as if she was talking to herself. She stepped closer and gently touched one of the dangling branches. "It's like a really strong wind passed through, but just on this spot. Or a burst of energy…"

"Energy?" Confusion racked his brain for what felt like the hundredth time that day.

"Yeah." Klara narrowed her brow at him, nearing an expression of concern the longer he remained silent. Again, he felt suddenly foolish in her presence. "As in, kinetic, potential, can never be created nor destroyed?" She paused, her mouth flickering between mirth and confusion. "'The fundamental entity of nature'?" she recited.

"Like God?"

"Um, I've never thought of it like that. But some people think about God—or their gods—like that. I'm more of a by-the-textbook science girl."

Approaching the area with caution, Callum noticed a line of small brown mushrooms rising up from the earth, like soldiers standing in formation. Fear gripped him.

"A fairy ring," he breathed.

Though Brice, through the teachings of the church, had taught Callum to turn away from silly childish stories that floated around the village, the tales whispered to him now, low and urgent. Fairy circles were to be avoided—humans could be ensnared in them, tricked into dancing to their own deaths. Why was there one here, in the strange wood that was both Rosemere and not Rosemere? The wee folk were known to whisk humans away to their realm, where time passed in unnatural ways. Could he have been taken? Had he offended a member of the fairy court? Had Thomas? His blood chilled.

"Klara, dinnae go closer," he said.

"They're just mushrooms." Klara approached the fungi. She seemed unaware of the fear prickling his skin, unaware of the danger. "My Grams used to tell me that fairy circles are where the barrier between the spirit world and ours is weakest," she said, walking carefully around the perimeter of the circle. She ducked a broken branch. "Which is kinda creepy, when you think about it."

Suspicion rose in him once more. Was that why she was not afraid? "Your grandmother," Callum said, eyeing her for a reaction, "is she a *cailleach*?"

"A *calli*-who?"

"Is she a witch?" he tried again.

"So she says," she replied, lilting.

Wary of the fairy circle, he stood an arm's length away from the mushrooms, examining the charred earth at a distance. Though the dark streaks radiated outward, the grass at the center of the circle appeared pristine. A perfectly untouched circle of green within the larger circle.

"If you dropped that book, you must have been here." Klara bent over the edge of the circle, lowering her head until her hair nearly swept the blackened ground. "The ground looks burned. Was there a fire? A freak weather incident? Do you remember anything like that?"

"I dinnae remember a fire. Only a very bright light," he said.

Gingerly, she prodded a patch of grass with one finger. Unsatisfied, she grasped a handful, uprooting it with a strong tug, and ran her thumb over the limp blades. She brought it to her nose and smelled it. "Weird. The grass isn't actually burnt. It's just...dead."

"Dead?" He shuddered at the word.

Opening her fingers, she let the dead greens fall from her grasp, then froze. "Do you feel that?"

Callum stiffened. "Feel what?"

No sooner had he said the words than something swept across his skin. It felt like a sickly shiver, it rippled over his arms and neck, rolling along his body until it penetrated his torso, where it soured and squeezed his stomach into a terrible knot.

A few paces away from him, Klara stood and drifted her hands through the air,

"It's like there's something *there*. I can feel it, I swear."

As soon as she stopped speaking, the air in front of her began to shimmer as if it was the height of summer—but the air turned suddenly cold. Still, sweat broke out on Callum's brow. The breath pulled out of his lungs like a receding tide from shore.

Klara inhaled sharply. "What the…"

Callum willed his limbs to move, but they refused. He was forced to watch as the shimmering air convulsed and thickened into a mist. It expanded in size until it was so close to Klara that it whipped her hair into tendrils around her face. She did not back away. The mist grew thicker still with every passing second, until it was a curtain of light and shadow, but still she did not back away.

Callum watched in horror as a hand emerged from the mist and reached for her.

CHAPTER SEVEN

KLARA

Something in Klara's chest pulled, snapped, *broke*—

Then a man stepped out of thin air and grabbed her throat.

Not thin air—not quite. The mist had appeared like something from a horror movie. But Klara couldn't think about that now. She couldn't think at all. Couldn't breathe. Her eyes moved up the man's arm to his chest, landing on a sallow face set with a sneering mouth and pale, blazing eyes.

He fully emerged. The wall of mist started to shrink and rapidly fade. Soon, only a few wispy threads remained, hanging in the air like smoke.

"Do not move a finger to help her, you insolent dog," the man snarled at Callum. He tightened his grip on Klara and she couldn't help but let out a squeak of fear. Callum stopped in his tracks. The pain and fear twisting his face made her heart race even faster.

Satisfied, the man turned back to her and grinned, revealing pearly white teeth. "*Finally*, we meet."

The voice was deadly, a venom that worked its way into her ears and seeped into her blood. Her pulse pounded wildly against the palm of his hand.

"And who the hell are you?" she rasped, trying to sound braver than she felt.

Annoyance deepened the lines of the man's forehead, but the look was replaced quickly by pride. His lip twitched. "A god among men."

She loosened a breath.

He squeezed tighter, making her sputter. Her lungs worked fruitlessly, burning and straining like her ribs had been welded shut. He was trying to kill her. *Was* killing her.

Klara reached for his face—to claw, scratch, anything that would remove the pressure from her neck—but her fingers only scraped uselessly against his exposed neck. Her nails caught on something: the grooves of interlacing marks carved into his skin.

The man titled his head. "To think that the final Pillar is only a little girl."

Pillar? She tried to suck in a breath but the man squeezed her neck again, cutting off her windpipe. The edges of her vision blackened and closed in.

Still gripping Klara with one hand, he reached under his cloak. To Klara's horror, he withdrew a sword with an elaborate hilt and pressed the cool metal of the blade against her neck. "Truthfully, I was hoping for more of a challenge," he said, smiling.

He's enjoying this, Klara thought dizzily, hopelessly. *I'm going to die*. Her stomach bucked with fear. Was this what her mom had felt when the cancer took over?

Through the deepening darkness, she caught a flash of movement. *Callum*. He lunged forward and sunk his dagger into the man's thigh.

Crying out in pain, the man released his grip slightly, allowing Klara to pull out of his grasp. She fell to her knees and scrambled backward on her shaking legs, gasping as cool air flooded her lungs.

In front of her, Callum lunged again. This time, the man was ready for him. He knocked Callum to the ground with a single swipe of his hand, sending his body through air as if Callum weighed nothing at all. Then the man rounded on his crumpled form, sword raised—

"No!" she cried out, her trapped breath erupting into a scream.

Springing forward, Klara collided with the man. She wrapped her fingers around his wrists. He turned his fiery gaze on her. Her grip weakened.

A god among men. Klara believed it now.

I'm going to die, she thought again. The image of her mom flashed into her mind, a flicker of longing and a wish—hope—that Klara might see her soon.

Behind him, the faint strands of mist grew thicker, doubling in size with every beat of her heart until they were surrounded by it.

The hope she felt moments before twisted into another emotion—fear. She didn't want to go, not like this.

Something inside her snapped.

A powerful burst of energy exploded inside her, moving in electric waves outward from her chest into her limbs.

Her fingertips felt like live wires, but instead of the power electrifying her as she thought it might...it targeted the wall of grayish fog. It suddenly sparked into a bright, white light that wiped away everything else.

"Perhaps I spoke too soon," the man said, strangely calm. "But nothing can keep me from finding you by Samhain."

Klara felt her feet lift from the ground—*flying*, she thought in disbelief—at the same time a voice called her name. "Klara!"

Callum. The sound snapped her into motion. She uncurled her fingers from the man's wrists and pushed away from him, hard, kicking with her feet. Her weightless body began to spin, slow at first, then impossibly fast. The weight returned all at once. She was no longer flying. She was falling. The white around her drained to blues, greens, browns, blacks. Shielding her face with her arm, Klara squeezed her eyes shut as she plummeted downward.

A thud echoed in her ears. A strangled moan. Dimly, she realized the sound was coming from her. The strange flying feeling was replaced by pain all over her body. She collapsed.

"Klara!"

Strong arms hoisted her up. She wrenched her eyes open. Callum was staring down at her. Behind his head, a graying sky shifted into focus, punctuated by broken tree limbs swinging perilously in the breeze.

Klara sat up and quickly regretted it. The movement caused

a wave of pain to crash through her body. But relief followed quickly. The man was gone. The mist was gone. They were surrounded by the Elder Forest, birdsong in the air. It was like nothing had happened at all.

Callum still held her in his arms. The warmth—his closeness—slowed her thundering heart by a fraction. "Where is he?" she asked.

"Gone. Are you hurt?" His voice was urgent.

"Gone? But—where?"

Callum had no answer for her. He just shook his head, looking as confused as she felt. Dizzy, she blinked again, clearing her vision as feeling continued to return to her limbs. Her once yellow flats were soaked through and caked in mud. Her Metallica T-shirt was covered in foliage and dirt. There was a new hole in her jeans. She stuck her finger through the tear and winced when she found an angry red scrape underneath.

"I'm okay. Not dead." She paused, unsure. "*Am* I dead?"

"Not dead." Though he offered a weak smile, Callum's face was filled with concern. But there was something else there, too. Tension in his forehead. Fury. Fear. Knowing. All etched on this stranger's face.

A complete stranger.

As Klara thought it, she spotted the dirk gripped tightly in his hand, its polished blade glinting in the sun.

The sight made fear explode in her chest. She pushed herself out of Callum's grasp and scrambled backward. "Get that thing away from me," she said, speaking through big gulping breaths.

Callum quickly tossed his weapon to the side. "Klara, I mean you no harm."

He reached for her again, but Klara pushed his hand away. "Don't come near me." She was shouting now. She backed away farther. Callum stared at her like a lost puppy. She relaxed—slightly.

"Sorry, it's just that you appeared out of nowhere, led me into this forest to this…" she waved her arms"…fairy circle, and then—then—that man tried to kill me."

"To be fair, lass, you insisted on following me, and I stabbed the man in his leg," Callum said quietly.

Annoyance stung her. But something about his earnest face slowed her heartbeat again. "It's still sketchy."

He stepped forward. "May I?"

"May you what?"

"See if you are hurt. Trust me, I've felt enough broken bones that I would know."

Klara shot him a questioning look. "Say what now?"

"I fight for my supper." He didn't clarify further, like she was just supposed to understand what that meant.

Sighing, she let him instruct her how to flex her fingers and wiggled them obediently. Then, he took each of her hands in his, gently pressing into her palms. It was the first time she really noticed his hands—his knuckles were scarred and his skin was rough, but his touch was shockingly soft. Strong, but soft. Warm, too, despite the chill in the air. He lifted her arms, then—with only the slightest hesitation that made her blush— he felt gingerly along the sides of her torso down to her legs, applying pressure as he worked his way to her thigh and calf.

"Ye'll live. Nothing broken," he said. Gingerly, he moved to touch her throat but she drew back. She could still feel the man's hand there, squeezing and gripping.

"What the hell just happened?"

"That was the man who killed Thomas." Callum growled the words, his accent thick in his throat.

"What?" Her head spun with confusion. "Thomas was—murdered?"

"Aye."

"By that man? Who is he?"

"The devil," Callum spat.

The color drained from her face as she glanced to the spot where the man had been and back again. "It's not possible."

Callum pulled her close, with his arms around her, so close that he felt the heat of breath on his skin, the pulse of her heart under his fingers. "I saw that man standing over Thomas's lifeless body with my own eyes. I saw the streets go slick with his blood. I saw his magic and felt his strength, his determination, his *ruthlessness*—"

Klara backed away. "Callum, are you okay?"

By now, Klara could see that Callum had a flair for the dramatic—or she would have thought, if she hadn't seen a mist appear out of nowhere with her own eyes, followed by a man. Fear trickled through her. With a lurch of her gut, she tried to reconcile the fact that he wasn't being dramatic at all.

"'A god among men.' That's what he said to me," she said, remembering the words with a chill. Then she remembered something else: the feeling that had overtaken her body when she was being attacked. It had opened in her chest with the force of an exploding star. She stared at her palms like the answer would be written there. They were slicked with dirt. The feeling must have been adrenaline—but it was nothing like she'd ever felt before.

Then again, no one had ever tried to *kill* her before.

Callum's eyes flashed as he looked somewhere over her shoulder in deep concentration, lost in thought. He spoke softly, almost as if to himself. "Before Thomas died, he told me, 'he's coming, Callum.' I didnae know this is the man he meant. I didnae know he would die." Callum still averted his gaze, but Klara could see that his eyes shone with ferocity and pain.

"Thomas knew someone was coming for him?"

He looked at her again. "Aye, and now the devil's tried to kill you."

Sense began to penetrate Klara's brain fog. "Let's be reasonable. He's not the devil. That makes no sense."

Something Callum said at the manor came back to her. *If I'm to avenge Thomas…*

"Was that the man you talked about taking revenge on?" she asked.

Callum nodded. Red pinched his cheeks.

"Oh my god." Klara's head sunk in between her knees. The thought of more death sent a new wave of fear washing over her, making her head light. She hugged her knees to her chest. "It's just…hard for me to wrap my head around." *Murder.*

Callum didn't respond right away. The birdsong grew louder in her ears the longer he was quiet, providing a strangely cheerful soundtrack to the heaviness that seemed to be rolling off him in waves.

Klara gave Callum a beat to gather himself before she pressed him further. "Tell me exactly what happened with Thomas."

"We were at The Black Hart, after a fight, and Thomas

left without saying a word. I went looking for him down Kelpie's Close—it's an alley in Rosemere, where I live—" he clarified, seeing her confusion "—and I found him. He had been attacked, stabbed. I encountered that man and—" He stopped, voice full.

Klara cleared her throat and stood up, making a futile attempt to brush the dirt from her T-shirt. Her eyes grazed the mushroom circle and the discarded dirk lying close by. The memory of the man's pale hand, his tight grip, sent another convulsion of cold down her body. Steeling herself against the chill, she refocused on Callum.

"The man—that devil—who attacked him, attacked me," Callum spit. "He had such strength as I've never known, Klara. He was not of this world, and he nearly killed ye. Just like he killed Thomas."

Fear prickled the back of her neck. "But you escaped?"

"I didnae mean to escape. I charged at him with my dying breath and then—" Callum faltered. "I was falling, though it felt nothing like falling—"

"It felt more like flying, but you couldn't tell what was up or down?" she finished eagerly.

"Exactly that. And then I woke up in your home."

"He attacked you here?"

"No. The murder happened in Rosemere. There are traces of my home here—" He gestured around. "The Black Hart, the Hanging Tree—"

"*What hanging tree?*" she said, alarmed.

Callum continued, ignoring her. "It is like I traveled far away, but nowhere at all."

Klara sighed. "If you told me you fell out of the sky, it would seem believable at this point."

A blush spread over Callum's face. The red warmth deepened the colors of his eyes. "Do you think I am lying?" he eventually asked.

Klara shook her head. "No, I don't."

He paused, considering her. "Have you heard of the wee folk kidnapping people into their realm? They say it can be like the human realm, but changed. That is how this place appears to me. Like a changeling child—familiar and different at once."

She nodded. Her grandmother used to tell her stories like that—that if she strayed too far or took a wrong turn, she would wind up in the fairy realm, whisked away by the Fair Folk—but it was only something her Grams said to keep her from running off when she was a kid.

"Is that what you think happened? You think you traveled to the fairy realm?" Klara asked. "This isn't the fairy realm, Callum. I know this world, this *time*. And if this is somehow the fairy realm, and if I spent the majority of my teen years doing homework, I am going to be *pissed*. Trust me, I am not a fairy."

Callum appraised her. Despite the circumstances, the idea of him mistaking her for an otherworldly being made her stomach dip in flurries. She crossed her arms and looked away, hoping he didn't notice the color that was definitely rising in her cheeks.

Something that he said earlier popped into her head. She hadn't given it much thought at the time, but...

"That notebook you found—Thomas's notebook—if he

knew the attacker was coming for him, maybe he wrote something down in there that will give us a clue?"

"Thomas cannae write or read, my lady."

"At all?" The words were out of Klara's mouth before she had a chance to think, and the shift in Callum's expression suggested she should have kept quiet.

"We didnae have schooling, Klara."

"I'm sorry," she said quickly. "I didn't mean—"

"But I can read some." He lifted his chin. "Brice didnae know. No one knew...even Thomas."

"Oh," Klara said, even more confused. She thought about what it meant not to read or write; she knew the difficulty of reading well. Her dyslexia made reading challenging, but at least not impossible.

"He only drew," Callum continued, as he pulled the notebook out of his pocket and held it gingerly, like it was an egg he didn't want to break.

Klara took in the worn leather, the thin leather pages. "But that looks—" It looked like it ought to be in a museum. "Callum, how old is it?"

He shrugged. "I think Thomas had it since he was a boy. He came to Master Brice in the year of our Lord, 1550, when he was but 5 years old, so—well, I suppose it's about as old as me."

Klara stared at him, waiting for him to tell her that he was kidding, that this was a classic Scottish joke she just didn't get. But he said nothing. Either he had the world's best poker face or...

"Callum," she said slowly. "It's 2022."

Understanding dawned in his eyes. He sucked in his breath

and let it go all at once, blowing locks of dark hair away from his face. "I was born in 1549."

"1549?" It took a few seconds for the meaning of his words to sink in, and when they did, she laughed again. "So you're telling me that you're, what…like five hundred years old?"

"Do I appear five hundred years old to you?" He puffed out his chest a little as he said it.

Klara blinked. Was he serious? "So the logical conclusion is that you traveled. In time."

He nodded, eyes blazing with an almost religious fervor. "Aye. Aye, that must be it."

Klara laughed. "Come on, Callum. That's ridiculous."

"That may be. But that doesna mean 'tis not true."

"Actually, that's exactly what it means." Her frustration rose as she watched him run his hands through his hair with renewed energy. She felt it, too—a restless, nervous feeling inside her—but it was nudging *her* closer to a breaking point. "Am I on a prank show, like some Scottish one I don't know about?"

Callum's eyes filled with hurt. "I knew ye'd think I wasn't truthful."

Anger bubbled under her skin. His strange humor had lost its charm. In fact, it was starting to feel downright cruel.

"Tell me the truth," she insisted.

Callum crossed his arms and stood, immovable as the trees that surrounded him. "I told the truth. And what happened just now," he said, pointing to the fairy circle, "was not of this world."

"I'm sorry, Callum, it's just—none of this is possible." She snorted. "Which is like the understatement of the century."

"Of several centuries," he said seriously.

"There has to be a rational explanation for whatever it was that happened."

"I thought that was a rational explanation. Do ye have another, Klara?"

She looked at him: the boy who had appeared from nowhere, the boy she had nearly killed with her car, the boy who now claimed he was born in another century. Another century? Seriously? But earnestness radiated off him in waves. She thought of the damage around the fairy circle, the mist that had appeared from nowhere. *Like a burst of energy...*

Her heart thrummed.

Had he traveled through time? Had the man? Was that where Klara felt like she was flying to, only a few minutes ago—through time itself?

Impossible.

"I can't believe this. What you're saying is—it just can't happen." Klara backed away from him, disbelief and panic rising in her the longer she let the reality of what he was suggesting tumble around in her head. "I felt sorry for you. I don't know what's going on with you, Callum, but you can't just...mess with me and make up stories," she said, letting emotion fill her voice as her chest tightened. "Some of us have lost people, *really* lost people, and it hurts."

Callum's expression hardened into stone. "I lost someone. I watched Thomas die. And I'll do right by him, whether or not it agrees w' you. I won't deny the truth."

Klara couldn't wrap her mind around everything else, but the grief in his eyes was definitely real. She was sure of it. But after what she had just been through, she was also sure as hell that she didn't want to have anything to do with it. Her hand flew to her neck again, remembering how the blade had been pressed against it.

Callum surveyed her with his mismatched eyes, every muscle in his face taut. "But of course you cannot understand. Ye are privileged. Go back to your fancy estate—"

"You don't know the first thing about me." Her chest hitched. "I *do* understand. Losing someone, I mean. I don't understand you."

"I'm not surprised, lass. No one understands me, save Thomas. That is just fine with me."

Hot, angry tears stung Klara's eyes. What had she gotten herself into? She had decided to follow this stranger into the woods based on a feeling in her gut—and she had almost paid for it with her life. "You know what's true? My life has been relatively normal until *you* showed up."

Determined not to let any more emotion show, Klara clenched her jaw until the tears shrank back. "I saved your life, you saved mine. Let's call it even."

His mouth flattened into a thin, determined line, then took a deep breath. "I will not leave ye. I was wrong for insinuating ye should go. That devil may return at any time—"

By Samhain. The words swirled in her head. She pushed them out.

"No. I'm done with this," she said firmly, not wanting to be a part of his internal back-and-forth. She shifted from foot to foot. Doubt fluttered throughout her body. But she shut the feeling out, tucking it away in a little box in the farthest corner of her mind. What she needed now was familiarity. Logic. Food. A nap. She needed to go home, where she could forget Callum existed and forget this ever happened. "I don't need any protection. Especially yours."

"But, Klara—"

"Goodbye, Callum."

Klara didn't wait for a response. She turned her back to him and plunged back into the trees again, toward the car— toward home.

CHAPTER EIGHT

KLARA

"Dad?"

The manor was eerily silent. Klara was alone. The American tourists seemed to be out. There was only Finley, who barely lifted his head up from his bed by the fireplace to greet her.

"Thanks for the warm welcome." She wrapped her dog in a hug, burying her face in his fur. "I've never been so happy to see you, you mangy mutt."

After inhaling a pound of Finley's fur, Klara collapsed onto the sofa without changing her clothes. She knew she should shower—she was still filthy, and her dad would not be happy that she was tracking dirt inside even though the manor was already a dust magnet, no matter how often they cleaned—but she was hollowed out. Plus, she didn't like the idea of going upstairs alone. Instead of relief at being home, she only felt a vague, pulsing uneasiness.

Shuddering, Klara remembered the words the man had spoken to her. *Nothing can keep me from finding you by Samhain.*

Her phone buzzed. The sudden noise made her jump. Incoming FaceTime popped up on the screen next to a photo of her best friend Brittany.

At least…Brittany had been Klara's best friend, until her mom died and she spent the next year hiding in her apartment, in too much pain to get out of the house most days. To say they'd fallen out of touch would be an understatement.

Klara started to tap the green phone icon, then slowly drew her hand back

Even if she was in the mood to talk, she could not find words, which was a rare occurrence. She always had something to say.

Until now.

What was there to say?

That she had saved a man from certain death, and he turned out to be just your average time-traveling scamp whose best friend was murdered in cold blood by what appeared to be a supernatural entity, and also that same supernatural entity had almost murdered her inside a fairy circle for reasons unknown? No biggie.

She silenced the phone and pressed it facedown into the couch.

"Time travel," she snapped at Finley. "Can you believe it?"

Klara just didn't believe in inexplicable things. Unlike her dad, she had never considered herself a religious person, either. Her eyes were rooted to the stars most of her life. The beauty and mystery of the universe had always been more than enough magic for her.

But she was a future astronomer—or at least she would've been if she went to college. This was why she also had a duty to unbiased, empirical observation and the scientific method. Observation led to hypotheses, and hypotheses were testable. But how could she test this—*time travel*?

Circumstantially, if Callum was from another time—big if—it explained some things.

The way he acted toward a car was not exactly normal. He called it a carriage, for Pete's sake. There were theories of parallel universes and timelines, not to mention Einstein's theory of relativity...

At the very least, Klara concluded that she had never met a guy like him before, and that was saying a lot. She lived in New York, and there were all sorts of unusual people there with larger-than-life stories and unbelievable pasts. Off the top of her head, she could name at least three people who had grown up in a traveling circus or show.

But time travel? Whatever happened in the Elder Forest was something she couldn't chalk up to fact or faith.

She needed to calm her racing thoughts, so she sprang up to start a fire.

As she tossed firewood into the hearth, she remembered the energy that had flowed through her. It was like adrenaline on steroids.

Finley barked. She got up and peeked through the heavy curtains. Willows bordered either side of the driveway, their hanging tendrils dancing in the breeze. Golden rays of evening light filtered through their canopy. It was nearly dusk. To her relief, Craig's car pulled into the driveway a few seconds later. Klara practically bowled her dad over with a hug as soon as he opened the door.

"Hey." He squeezed her back. "You okay?"

Klara pulled away. *Other than almost getting murdered? Peachy!* Instead, she said, "Just a weird day, that's all."

Her dad shrugged off his coat and plopped down on the modern cream love seat—the only artifact from their apartment in New York, his prized possession—and patted the cushion for her to join him. She sat next to him, sending his body jolting upward with her weight. The chair creaked as she tucked her legs underneath her.

"Remember how much your mom hated this thing?" he said.

She leaned her head on his shoulder. "It doesn't exactly fit with the decor in an old Scottish manor."

Her dad chuckled. "You're sure you're okay, honey? You seem…spooked."

Klara hesitated. "This really intense thing happened and…" She trailed off. How much of the truth could she tell him without totally freaking him out? Probably none, she decided. "I just feel like nothing makes sense anymore. Like everything's spinning out of control."

Her dad pulled his shoulder out from under her, forcing her to lift her head up. "That's okay, honey. That's life. And sometimes figuring out the meaning of life *is* life." He paused. "Do I sound like your Grams?"

Klara laughed. "A little."

Her dad squeezed her shoulders and let loose some "I'm looking into your soul" eye contact. It brought her comfort… familiarity.

Now that she wasn't facing down a murderer, the secret was gnawing away at her again. Nothing like a near-death experience to get you in the confessing mood. She pushed herself to say the words. *I'm not going to college anymore. I dropped out.*

Instead, Klara thunked her head back onto his shoulder and sighed. "I think I'll just be the Kingshill innkeeper forever. I'll go prematurely gray and wear frumpy sweaters and watch my shows and yell at squirrels in the yard. And I'll change my name to Franny."

"A life well lived."

"I'm glad you approve."

"Speaking of living life to its fullest, your Gram called. She said to be *sure* to give you the message."

Her skin prickled. Was it a coincidence that her grandma was calling after what had happened today in the Elder Forest? "What was the message?"

"Hold on, I wrote it down." He consulted his phone. "She said, 'My door is always open.'" He looked back at her. "Mean anything to you?"

Disappointment swept over her. She sighed. "Nope."

Her dad shrugged and dropped his phone into his shirt pocket. "By the way, why do you look like you just got into a fight with a tree?"

Whoops. Her hair was a tangled mess and she was streaked with mud. She panicked and searched her mind for the least scary version of what had happened, some grain of truth. "I, um...hung out with a guy."

Her dad's eyebrows shot up. "Do I need to have a word with him?"

"It's not like that, just—a friend, I need more of them here anyway."

Her dad lifted a brow. "Well, invite him to dinner sometime."

"For sure, Dad." Klara laughed. "I should change." She jumped up and practically sprinted to her room, leaving him bemused with a wave.

★ ★ ★

Exhausted, Klara forced herself to shower. It felt good to stand beneath the steaming water, and even better when she was dry and clean. Back in her room, she opened the window, letting the cool autumn air drift through her pajamas. She tried not to think about Callum, which only made her think about him more.

Now that she was safe in her room…it couldn't hurt to google Rosemere.

She pulled out her phone. Her friends always made fun of her for using it instead of her laptop. It was just easier for her dyslexic mind to absorb information on a smaller screen.

It didn't take her long to confirm that Rosemere—whatever Callum's relationship to it—was definitely real. It'd been centuries since Rosemere had burned, but throughout all the wars and border disputes, it didn't mean it was ancient history. If Callum was from the past—well that meant it was the future for him.

Soon she found herself deep down the rabbit hole. Time melted as her phone warmed with effort, and her eyes burned as images and information flooded into her head.

She went to The Black Hart's website and clicked through until she found a History tab. Her eyes skimmed until a line jumped out at her.

It is thought that pub fights were once all the rage at The Black Hart. Young men with no future prospects fought for their livelihoods—and enjoyed a pint after. Times may have changed, but our beer is worth fighting for ☺

Klara froze. Was that what Callum meant when he fought

for his supper? He said that Thomas had left The Black Hart after a fight...

Shutting her laptop, she gazed out the window. It was the first clear night they'd had in weeks. Hundreds of twinkling stars and passing satellites winked at her from the sky. The perfect night to stargaze. She hadn't used her telescope since returning to Scotland six months ago. There would be a rare total lunar eclipse in the northern part of Scotland next week—and for the first time in hundreds of years, it coincided with Samhain, a Gaelic holiday, similar to Halloween, celebrating the barriers of the human and spirit world thinning on October 31 through November 1, allowing crossover from both realms.

Klara felt the urge to look to the stars now, pulling in her chest. Hardly thinking, only moving, she went to her telescope at the window, heart fluttering with anticipation. Gently, she brought her eye against the eyepiece and held it there—perfectly still—until her limbs went slightly numb. Body forgotten, she became her own satellite in the night sky, floating weightless among the stars. For a moment, she became the old Klara again.

Countless stars twinkled before her, as if they were saying hello. Her gaze roamed across the sky, marking constellations and planets that she knew all too well.

But then her eye caught something: a shift in a milky cluster of stars a few hand lengths above the horizon. She stilled. Watched. The colors seemed to thicken, while the blackness between the stars deepened. The shape of a mouth. Two eyes. *A face.*

A woman's face, staring back at her.

Klara lurched back, accidentally jostling the telescope with her knee. It fell over and clattered against her bookshelf.

"Kiddo? You okay?" her dad called up.

"Fine!" she shouted. *Was she?*

Klara reset the telescope, heart pounding. When she looked again, the face was gone.

"Great," she chastised herself. Now she was seeing things. Maybe she could invite the woman in the sky over for tea next.

A cool breeze lifted the hair on her neck, sweeping a chill down her arms. That was enough stargazing for the night, she decided. Klara moved the telescope back to its perch next to the window before washing her face and climbing into her bed.

The wind howled outside, making the glass rattle against the windowpane. She thought about Callum then. A pang of guilt ricocheted around her insides like a pinball. She closed her eyes. He wasn't her problem, she reminded herself. He looked all kinds of hardened and rough around the edges.

He could take care of himself, she told herself, as she fell into a fitful sleep.

Her dreams transformed into nightmares made of swooping shadows and glinting knives. The low cackle of Thomas's killer broke into her mind over and over again. *I'll find you by Samhain.* The haunting words echoed as she fell into a fitful dream and stayed there, caught between asleep and awake.

CHAPTER NINE
CALLUM

When the man returned, Callum would kill him.

He paced around the perimeter of the fairy circle like a rabid animal, dirk clutched in his hand. His fingers curled with heat despite the growing cold. His other fist worked open and closed, desperate to feel the searing pain of bone hitting bone. The sun sunk lower in the sky. Broken branches threw shadows across the ground.

Callum stood watch for hours, but no one came—neither Klara nor the man.

Blood still singing in his ears, he stopped and loosened his grip on the dirk. A dull ache had reached his chest. Part of him, he realized, thought that Klara might return. He cursed himself for being so foolish. Still, he could not fight back the feeling that their fates were intertwined.

He had fought plenty of men and bore the scars to prove it, but the idea of Klara gave rise to a strange, unfamiliar emotion in him. It felt like the shadow of fear, a crackling under his skin when he thought of her. Trying to understand it completely was like trying to see the bottom of a creek after a rain—it was blurry and indistinct, just out of reach.

Callum looked the way she had gone. Uncertainty surged in him. Should he have followed her? Should he go to her now? He could easily navigate his way back to the manor. But Klara had told him not to, and she did not seem like a person to be crossed.

And doing so would mean returning to the manor, where there might be armed guards, waiting to strike intruders down. In Callum's mind, the manor rose toward the sky, its lit windows partially shuttered in disapproval, as if it stood in judgment of his private thoughts. Callum knew in his bones that he did not belong there. He would be unwelcome.

Was Klara safer there than with him? Shame brushed the inside of his chest, burning where it touched. He could not protect his best friend from death, so why did he think he could protect her?

A stillness settled on him along with the chill of twilight. He gathered the driest wood he could find and stacked it like Thomas had taught him, stuffing the kindling to feed the upright sticks.

When the flames were high enough, Callum sat to rest. He was no stranger to sleeping outside. He did not belong in soft beds, like those in the manor. The crisp white fabric was too much like the winding sheets used to wrap the dead; their clean blankness spoke to him of death. Soon enough, though, loneliness sunk into him, cold and damp as the leaves that littered the forest floor.

Callum looked to the sky. What would Thomas do if he were stuck here, in a strange land five hundred years in the future?

Realizing with a jolt that he had a piece of his friend with him, Callum pulled the notebook out of his pocket. After wiping his hands clean, he opened the lightly worn animal hide.

The vellum pages bore drawings. With a fresh pang of grief, Callum recalled how Thomas would pull embers from the fire to use as an artist's tool. They left bright pink burns on his fingertips when he was too impatient to wait for them to cool—which was often.

Callum thumbed through the pages. The illustrations were landscapes—some crossed out violently, and other pages filled to the brim with smaller sketches in the margins. All strange and magical landscapes—all except the last.

The last was a portrait of Klara.

Callum froze. He angled it closer to the fire to see the portrait more clearly, expecting to see that he was mistaken. His friend had not known Klara. His friend was dead. But here she was, rendered in curving black strokes and furtive lines. The portrait, though crude, was undeniably her.

Beneath it was a knot. The design matched the mark on the murderer's neck.

Certainty seized him. Thomas must have known the man was coming for him. The night he died, he had pressed his only worldly possession into Callum's hands—Klara was right; it must have been a clue. A *mission*. Even in death, Thomas was still the only person Callum could trust.

"What are ye trying to tell me?" he whispered. He flipped back to the drawings, skimming through with a careful eye. Had Thomas been to these locations or were they conjured from his imagination? And why were some crossed out, as if in anger?

Out of ten landscapes, only four weren't crossed out. The first, was a sparkling pool next to soaring peaks. The second, a mound with a small door in the middle of a clearing. He turned the page but paused as his eyes landed on what looked eerily like this very clearing in which he stood. It even had the fairy circle. And smaller, in the corner: a tiny illustration of the alley in Kelpie's Close.

"Mhac na galla," he swore aloud.

Only the wind responded, howling through the trees. The eerie whistle turned into a thin melody that raked over his skin. He imagined the bean-nighe singing in the darkness, calling him to his grave, just like it had Thomas.

Shutting out the noise, Callum turned the notebook over and back again, like the answer would reveal itself—

And it did.

On the inside back cover was a small insignia he had not noticed before. *F&F.* He could not read, but he recognized the symbols well enough: they stood for Finn & Fianna, an apothecary in Edinburgh. Brice's maids had often taken the trip when the pantry needed restocking; he had been once or twice himself. Rumors swirled of darker magic being practiced there, too, though Callum had never given it a second thought until now. It seemed like no coincidence that Thomas might have been a customer.

Certainty took hold of him again, fierce and swift. The

answer to the riddle of what had happened to Thomas in Kelpie's Close—of what was happening to Callum now, of what had sent him forward in time to Klara—was within reach. He was sure of it.

Callum stared into the flickering flames. If The Black Hart had survived all this time, there was a sliver of hope that Finn & Fianna might have as well.

Edinburgh was no easy journey, but no grueling one, either. It was possible on foot. The road that Klara and he had traveled to The Black Hart may have looked different, but it traveled in the same direction as the road out of his Rosemere all the same.

Callum stoked the fire with his boot, sending a spark skyward. First, he would rest while he could. Then he would leave for Edinburgh at first light.

Edinburgh was bigger than when Callum had last seen it, but that wasn't the only thing that was different.

The buildings towered above, most as tall as church steeples, and others soared twice, or even three times the height. But this surprise was nothing compared to his shock at the people who flowed through the streets. All were dressed differently, and in myriad colors. The women dressed much as the men did, and their beauty was undeniable: teeth white, skin clean, and hair of all lengths and colors. Many had their faces painted, some with red lips, some with purple and blue and black the likes of which Callum had never seen.

Callum tugged at his own clothes, feeling out of place and self-conscious. But no one made eye contact with him. No one seemed to notice him at all.

The moving throngs parted and re-formed like schools of fish, somehow avoiding walking into each other, even as they stared at those strange machines in their hands. They were not all speaking Scots, Gaelic, or even English. Languages he had never heard before flowed around him, as did people of all different skin colors.

The future was wonderful and strange and unlike anything Callum could ever conjure. Though why anyone would want to have blue hair was beyond him.

He liked it.

He wished desperately that Thomas were here to see it.

Someone jostled him from behind and he stumbled forward. Callum whirled, fists raised—but it was only a black-and-gray-haired man. He lowered his hands.

"Pardon me," the man mumbled. His eyes darted over Callum, lingering on his still-clenched fists, before he sped off again into the crowd of people.

Though many of the streets were unfamiliar—and packed with loud horseless carriages, much like Klara's—it did not take Callum long to reach the center of the city using Edinburgh Castle as a polestar. Seeing the grand castle rise above the city buoyed him with confidence. Five hundred years had passed, but something of his time still remained.

Even more to his excitement, the tarred roads soon turned into stone-paved streets and twisting, narrow alleys. And, like magic, he found that the squat apothecary still sat where it had five hundred years ago, at the end of a row of old shops, its curtains pulled. Callum wrapped his cloak around himself tighter. He caught a whiff of rose—Klara's perfume, lingering in the fabric.

The bell above the door chimed as he walked into the store. An aroma of lavender and myrrh immediately filled his nostrils. The interior was even dimmer than the street. The walls were lined with shelves that held colorful vials, each filled with liquids, spices, and substances that had lined the shelves of Brice's pantry. Dried herbs hung from the rafted ceilings—sage, thyme, an assortment of pale flowers. All were connected by the thin clouds of smoke that drifted through the small room. The door swished closed behind him.

The young man leaning over the counter didn't stir or look up. Callum approached and rested his hands on the gnarled wood surface. Nothing. "Pardon me—"

The young man jumped, hand flying to his chest. He pulled a white object out of his ear. "Can I help you, sir?"

Sir. The word rang strangely in Callum's ear. He shifted, taking Thomas's notebook out of his pocket. "I'm looking to learn about this notebook. It belonged to my friend—"

The young man cut him off. "We appraise antiquities, if you just fill out this form." He opened a drawer and slid a piece of paper in front of Callum without glancing up.

The confidence flowed from Callum all at once, a tide rushing out. Frustration filled its place. This man did not believe him, just like Klara hadn't. He was not even listening.

"My friend was killed," he said, more urgently this time.

The young man looked at him now, brown eyes round with shock. "Killed?"

"Yes, five hundred years ago, but for me, it was just yesterday, and all I have left of him is this, which came from this shop." The words spilled out of Callum before he could stop them. "I think the man who killed him may have been en-magicked somehow—"

The young man got up and took a step back. His stool screeched against the floor. "This isn't my area of expertise." He turned over his shoulder and called out, "Aion!"

A man emerged from behind a thick curtain, where Callum glimpsed bottle- and box-lined shelves. Dark hair fell over the man's forehead, partially obscuring a pair of mischievous but wise eyes. Though he looked quite young—older than Callum, yet younger than Brice—he exuded an air of authority that made Callum straighten his shoulders.

The young man scurried out the front door, throwing the man a look as he did. "You really don't pay me enough for this, you know," he whispered, and then, louder: "I'm going on lunch break, you can handle this…customer…and the courier delivery later."

The man—Aion—turned to Callum and smiled. "Don't mind him. He has an imagination the size of a hazelnut." He paused, examining Callum's face. "Have we met?"

"'Tis not possible."

His gaze still lingered skeptically, but he recovered himself. "How can I help you?"

Aion's piercing eyes made Callum feel even smaller—even more foolish, even though he knew he spoke the truth. He pushed Thomas's notebook toward him across the counter, leaving one protective hand on it.

"I've come with a strange request, as I told your man…" Callum paused, unsure how much to tell *this* man—this stranger. Would it earn him more ridicule? But if he shared nothing, he would learn nothing of his friend, nor the force that brought him here, nor the murderer that had killed Thomas and may be coming for Klara.

"Strange requests are our business," Aion said, as if he knew Callum's thoughts. He smiled again, glancing down at the notebook. He raised an eyebrow.

"This belonged to my friend. I believe it came from this shop." Callum gestured to the F&F insignia. "I believe it has something to do with the reason he was killed." He paused to let his words settle, to gauge Aion's reaction. Unlike the boy, he did not betray any emotion. "I wondered if ye could tell me anything about it, or what's inside."

Aion stared at Callum, unblinking. His eyes moved down to Callum's clothes, then traveled down to the notebook. "May I?"

Callum drew his hand back, allowing Aion to pick up the notebook. He inspected the insignia. "We haven't used this seal in quite a long time—since about the middle of the seventeenth century, in fact."

"Aye, the notebook is older than that," Callum said cautiously.

Aion gave no indication that he found this strange. "It's very valuable, then. And in such perfect condition."

"I will not sell it," Callum said quickly.

"There are more ways to count value," Aion replied.

Callum paused. Aion's words felt heavy with meaning, but the meaning evaded him. "I was hoping it might help me figure out the truth behind who killed its owner."

"Was he killed over the possession of this notebook?"

"Well—not that I can tell," Callum said.

"Then why does it interest you? Are you a historian?"

Callum shifted from foot to foot. He wanted the man to

meet his gaze—he wanted to take measure of him—but Aion kept his eyes fixed on the notebook. "'Tis the only record I have left of him, and I suspect he or the man who killed him was involved in something. Something not of our world, but another." His heart skipped. "I thought ye may know about supernatural matters, as I surely dinnae."

Aion looked up now. Callum could not read his closed expression. "Would you like me to look inside?" he said, his voice neutral.

Callum nodded, eager for someone to make sense of it, to harvest Thomas's secrets from it.

Carefully and slowly, Aion turned the pages, reciting names as he inspected the drawing on each. He passed the ones that had been exed out. "Looks like your friend didn't like what he found in these spots, but the others..." He pointed to the one of the mound. "The tomb of Maeshowe." He rotated the notebook to better inspect the sketches. "Fairy Glen in Skye." This was the pool in the highlands. "I'm not familiar with this one—" he said, indicating the fairy ring in the Elder Forest that Callum had already identified. "And the Ring of Brodgar. All mystic centers."

"Mystic centers?" Callum repeated.

"Spiritual sites, where mystic energy is said to gather and flow more freely than elsewhere."

Energy. Klara had used that word to describe what they encountered in the Elder Forest.

"Why might one seek out these places?"

Aion shrugged, but the move was too casual, too quick. "Belief itself is a kind of energy. It connects us with the gods as well as realms beyond our ken. It cannot be seen, tasted, smelled, touched—but humans try to make it so. They build and visit monuments, recite prayers and incantations."

Callum waited for Aion to say more, but he did not. "Why these places in particular?"

Aion tilted his head. "Some say energy flows at these sites because—at these mystic centers, or thin places—the barriers between our world and the next are thin, especially at certain times of the year, or with specific celestial events, the power of which is beyond our understanding."

"What's wrong with the ones he crossed off?"

Aion sighed, like he was speaking to a child. "I don't know, boy, he was your friend, wasn't he?" Still, he continued: "Different centers are thought to be closer to different gods, or different locations in the Otherworld."

Callum nodded. "So he sought a certain one."

"All faith seeks certainty."

Aion's way of dancing around making a clear statement gave Callum pause.

"Humans have visited these sites for centuries. Thousands of years, in some cases. They seek connection."

Was that what Thomas was doing, and nothing more? "Do they still?" Callum asked.

Aion raised an eyebrow. "What do you think, laddie? Don't ya' ken anything of your own country?"

Callum shifted, trying to hide his misstep. "Ye are the expert on the matter."

Aion eyed him, but continued nonetheless. "Much of humankind has lost contact with those worlds, as well as the gods once worshipped on this land—but that does not mean they have gone," he said. "You're a Scotsman—surely you know how easily the *aos sí*, descendants of fallen angels, can pass into our world at Samhain." Callum's face darkened at the mention of the mythical race. Aion smiled then, his grin fox-like. He half expected to see a flash of teeth. "I see you believe in that kind of thing."

"Aye," Callum said carefully. Brice had been strict about Callum's upbringing in the church, but even he carried salt in his pocket to appease the *aos sí*.

"Not many these days recognize them." Callum paused— had he made a mistake?

Still grinning, Aion resumed turning the pages of Thomas's notebook. When he reached the illustration of the knot—the one carved into the killer's skin—he stopped and ran the pad of his pointer finger along it.

"Do ye ken it?" Callum asked.

"Arianrhod's mark." Aion lifted his eyes to Callum, his expression as smooth as stone. "It *is* you."

How could he recognize Callum when he had never seen this man in his life?

The bell rang out behind them, making his tensed muscles jump. He whirled. Men carrying large boxes were backpedaling in through the open door.

"Damn delivery," Aion mumbled.

"Wait, what do ye—" Callum turned back—but Aion was already in motion, walking toward the men at the door. His chest froze. The notebook was no longer in Aion's hand, nor on the counter.

It is *you*. Did Aion know him?

Heartbeat quickening with confusion and fear, Callum cast his gaze around the room in search of the notebook. The curtain to the back room swung gently, as if recently disturbed. Had Aion hidden the notebook back there, just out of sight? His skin prickled again with mistrust.

The men lifted crates on their shoulders and followed Aion into an adjoining room. A towering stack of crates stood in the street, just outside the propped-open front door.

"Stay there," Aion barked over his shoulder. He softened his voice, adding, "I'd really love to finish this conversation."

Stay there. Aion might as well have instructed him to pry. Throwing a glance behind him to make sure he was not being watched, Callum slipped behind the curtain.

Lined with shelves on either side, the narrow room extended several paces back, stopping at a stone wall. It was dimmer and damper than the room he had just left. Dust motes floated in the air, clouding his vision. Callum let his eyes adjust and spotted Thomas's notebook tucked in between two boxes.

Triumph singing in his veins, Callum slid the notebook out with a finger and clutched it to his chest. He was about to leave the way he came when he noticed something strange at the far end of the room—a bright light filtering up from somewhere below.

He crept toward it.

To his surprise, there was an open hatch in the floor. A ladder led downward into a room below. A lit torch must have been flickering there, bouncing its light off the walls.

Suspicion—and curiosity—stirred thicker in him. He crouched low and reached out a hand to test the ladder that made its way down. The cool metal rung felt steady under his grip.

His mind whirred. It could have led to a storage room, perhaps a wine cellar—and if it was only a storage or wine room, there would be no harm in trespassing.

Callum glanced back toward the curtain. It did not stir; no voices rose up from the other side. Carefully, he eased his body into the passageway and climbed slowly downward, dropping onto the stone floor with a small thud.

The chamber he stood in was circular. Just as he thought, a torch burned steadily on the wall. The room and walls were mostly bare, save for an opening at the far end shut with a large gate. A cell? Shuddering, Callum stepped closer.

A noise echoed above him. Callum froze, listening. It came from the shaft that led to the shop above.

Callum hurried over to the ladder and looked up. Aion's head loomed in the space above, a grim smile on his face.

"Your destiny beckons, boy."

A scream resonated from beyond the cell door.

But not just any scream.

Klara's.

CHAPTER TEN

KLARA

Callum embraced Klara, and their closeness burned a fiery trail to her core. Heat and lightness wrapped around her body in a pair of strong arms.

She pulled away and looked into his eyes. She imagined the softness of his lips, the roughness of his stubble against her skin. His face was so close to hers she could count the flecks of gold in his differently colored irises.

Her heart pulsed. What if she got even closer?

The world around them seemed to slow. He held her.

Wait—why was he holding her?

Klara shot upright. Her room came into focus around her: the forest green walls plastered with family photos, last night's muddy clothes hanging over the lip of her hamper, makeup jars strewn across the vanity.

A dream. A dream about Callum. A *sexy* dream about Callum.

At least she had actually managed to fall asleep after tossing and turning all night.

She sighed. She collapsed back into bed and lifted an arm to shield her eyes against the sunlight that streamed in through her window. But Finley wasn't having it. He barked and nudged her arm with his wet, cold nose.

"Finley, did you watch over me?" She patted his head. "You didn't let any murderers in? Good boy."

After Finley was sufficiently pet, Klara flung off the duvet and got dressed. She stretched her arms and legs and wiggled her toes, feeling thankful that she was alive at all. The realness of the dream evaporated—but it was replaced by fear as she remembered what had happened the day before. Shame skipped right alongside it: Klara had left Callum out there, to fend for himself. Alone.

After throwing on a T-shirt and cardigan, Klara pulled the curtain aside to peer out the window. Was the cloaked man waiting for her somewhere out there? The sight seemed so...*normal*. If one time traveler seemed highly unlikely, two seemed downright impossible...

Her dad's voice floated up the stairs. "Klara! Breakfast!"

"Coming!"

Klara let the curtain fall closed.

Downstairs, she found a bowl of Coco Shreddies and a carton of milk waiting for her on the kitchen counter. Her dad was loading dishes into the sink.

"What a luxurious breakfast. Remind me to leave a five-star review," she said, even though she would love to eat Coco Shreddies and nothing else for the rest of her life.

"You can expand your palate when you get up early enough for the continental breakfast," her dad said dryly.

Spoon in one hand, Klara checked her phone. Her open tab was The Black Hart's site, reminding her of last night's research on Callum. Her thumb hovered over the X to close out the window, but she couldn't bring herself to tap it.

Klara was torn. Mostly, she wanted to forget what happened forever but her rational brain—her scientist brain—craved an explanation. She wanted closure.

A little more research couldn't hurt, she decided.

"Your cereal's getting soggy," her dad said.

Klara's head snapped up. "Yeah. Sorry. Distracted." She absentmindedly scooped up mushy cereal. Something occurred to her. "Just thinking about some research I need to do."

Her dad cocked an eyebrow. "You're doing research?"

"It's just a little personal project," Klara said quickly. *I think I met a time traveler* was not a conversation you had with your father before breakfast. Or ever, really.

He squeezed her shoulder and nodded approvingly, which made her feel even worse instead of relieved. It was so easy to lie when he believed her lies so easily. "Well, say hello to the Doctor for me. Watch out for those Weeping Angels." He said, chuckling at his *Doctor Who* reference.

"I don't think that episode takes place at the National Library of Scotland."

"Just don't blink," he said, giving her a wink.

"Noted." Klara laughed as she pulled up the online catalog for the library. She went to the search bar and tried every combination of search terms she could think of, falling down a rabbit hole of digitized manuscripts—they had thousands, some of which dated back to the ninth century, some side by side with English translations.

Just when she was about to give up, an entry jumped out at her. *Magic and Mystic Centers.* There was no digitized copy; the physical was in a special collection at the library.

Her dad handed her a steaming cup of coffee. "You know, if you drive to Edinburgh, you could always pop by your Grams's…"

Distracted, Klara nodded, turning her attention half-heartedly back to her soggy Shreddies. A quick trip to Edinburgh wouldn't kill her. After yesterday? Going to the library would be a cakewalk.

Pulling her sunglasses down slightly, Klara scanned the bustling city streets. Her nerves were still jangling from parallel parking, and the sea of strangers did nothing to calm her—could that man be here, looking for her?

I'll find you by Samhain.

She pushed the words out of her mind.

Unless the man was wearing a furry costume, she probably wouldn't be able to spot him in these crowds anyway. The only people that stood out were a group of dark-clothed kids about her age in front of a Starbucks. One of them had bleached tips and was wearing what appeared to be a home-made cape. No threat detected. She let her glasses fall back onto her nose.

Klara urged her muscles to relax as she tried to enjoy the walk to the library. In a few strides, her forced smile turned into a real one. She hadn't been to Edinburgh since she and her dad had moved back to Scotland. When they got off the plane, it was straight to the manor for them. Kingshill was only an hour from the city, just outside of Culross, and though it was close, the manor had them pretty wrapped up in its dusty spires since they'd gotten here, so seeing Edinburgh's steepled buildings sent a thrill through her. The feeling reminded her of when she'd moved to the United States when she was seven. She hardly remembered the move but the feeling was one she could never forget—just like now, everything was thrilling, even the stuff she already knew.

A prime example: the National Library of Scotland.

At least once a month, when Klara was young, her mom would bring her here and rummage through the stacks, playing hide-and-seek and making up tales of far-off lands. Though her day job had been as a consultant to big investment firms, her mom could've easily been a writer.

Klara stopped in front of the towering granite building to admire it. The larger-than-life stone figures carved into the facade peered down at her: Medicine, Science, History, The Poetic Muse, Justice, Theology, and Music. The Pillars of Civilization. When she was little, she used to pretend they came to life at night and walked around the city, like her own personal *Toy Story* but with Scottish statues.

It reminded her of Callum. She marveled over how many thousands—millions—of people over the centuries had stood looking at these very books, admiring the same sight.

Another wave of nostalgia hit her as she walked inside.

While Klara had changed in the last eleven years, the library was as magnificent as ever. Grand cathedral ceilings arched overhead in the main room. Rows of oak desks fanned out across the floor, sprinkled with people nose-deep in books. Two stories of shelves rose above the main floor.

A calm fell over Klara like a heavy blanket. In here, it was as if the world outside didn't exist. She was safe. Confident, she strode to the reception desk across the room.

"Can I help you?" the librarian asked as she approached. Surveying her imperiously from above her horn-rimmed glasses, she was the dictionary definition of a librarian. Her graying hair bun was even held in place by a pencil.

Smiling, Klara rested her elbows on the high counter. "I need help finding some information."

The librarian narrowed her eyes skeptically, either at Klara's American accent or her question, she wasn't entirely sure.

"It's called—" Klara pulled out her phone. *"Magic and Mystic Centers?"*

The librarian turned her attention back to the computer to her right. Keys clacked as she typed. "That would be in the archives' manuscript rooms. Special collections."

"Okay." Klara waited for the librarian to explain where that was. She didn't. "Where is that, exactly?"

"Restricted," she replied.

"Restricted?"

"Off-limits to the public."

"Yes, I know what 'restricted' means," Klara snapped. Seeing the librarian's affront, she smiled as sweetly as she could. "Can I make an appointment to take a look?"

The librarian smiled even wider than Klara. "Are you a student? If you are, you can look in our digital archives."

Klara paused. She considered lying, but she looked like the type to ask for credentials. "No."

"Either way, only a qualified specialist can handle it, and we only have one." Her voice dripped with venom-laced sweetness. "They're currently on vacation."

"When—"

"Why don't you send an email and we'll respond to your query as soon as we can." Her smile fell and she returned to her computer without another word.

Before walking away—she was clearly dismissed—Klara glanced at the book's location on the librarian's computer. She walked all the way to the door before she stopped to pull out her phone and brought up a map of the library. All of the public areas were up the broad, grand staircase, but beyond the reception desk and down a level was a large room labeled Special Collections.

Slipping her phone into her pocket, she did a slow spin and headed toward the staircase at the other end of the floor, taking a wide curve around the front desk to avoid detection. She descended the narrow staircase down into the depths of the building.

The air cooled as she went down. She made her way along a long corridor and stopped to drink at a water fountain when she spotted two library employees walking toward her from the opposite direction. They were too absorbed in a conversation about the newest Laura Sebastian book to notice her.

Finally, Klara reached a glass door labeled Special Collections. The inside was dim, not a soul to be seen. She turned the handle. To her surprise, it gave.

Rows of shelving were crammed into a poorly lit room. She wasn't even sure if she could call it a room—it seemed endless, conforming to the shape of the building, broken only by a few particle board partitions. The air inside was stale, but cool against her face. The door shut with a soft click behind her. She paused, waiting for the other shoe to drop—but no one came to drag her away.

"Hello?" she tried. No answer.

Pulling her jacket around her, she made her way down the first row. Unfortunately, the books there seemed modern, with laminated covers and labeling on the side, all piled onto metal shelving. Signs with letters and numbers hung from the ceiling. She followed the letters and numbers she'd memorized from the librarian's computer.

Klara ran her finger across the spines of the dusty books. She reached the end of the room and found a partition wall. Beyond was the section she was heading for, and she was relieved to find the door there unlocked, too.

It opened with a slight hiss, cool air escaping.

It was an older section—the stone ceilings were low enough that Klara had to duck beneath a hanging light bulb. The sight reminded her of how old the original building was. *At least as old as Callum*, she thought. Though the main building was modern, underground was another story. She imagined the room as it must have been once, with carriage wheels clattering overhead. Somewhere above, an air-conditioning unit chugged away. The sound brought her back to the present day.

The light bulb flickered. A shiver shot up her spine. Really, it made a better haunted house than a library.

"A whole lot of nope," Klara whispered.

She laughed at herself, but the sound quickly died, leaving her more ill at ease. They just kept it cold so the books stay preserved, she thought, though deep down she knew the goose bumps on her skin weren't entirely caused by the cold. This place gave her the creeps.

She shook the worries from her thoughts. The only thing to fear was getting caught by a stern librarian. Or worse, by a rogue spiderweb. On she walked, weaving between shelf after shelf of tomes, her eyes roving along the labels and signs above. She passed a barred wooden door that looked like it belonged in a prison, not a library. Display cases stood in the middle of the room, ancient tomes housed under the glass.

"Aha!" Even at a whisper, her voice echoed throughout the room.

Her finger found the spine she was searching for. The reference number matched. She gently pulled it from the shelf and eased it onto a nearby table.

It was only loose pages collected in a protective binder, its margins illustrated with green vines twisting along their edges in simple yet beautiful Celtic knots. Klara breathed in their earthy scent. Her chest filled with reverence and a twinge of grief—her mom would have loved this.

Lowering her face to the book, she inspected it delicately, her finger hovering above the page to trace the tightly packed script. Her whole body tensed, feeling suddenly heavy with the weight of the moment—then fell with disappointment, foolishness. What had she been thinking? She couldn't read Gaelic. If this even was Gaelic...

Klara turned the last page. Instead of script, there was an illustration that took up the whole space. She tilted her head. It looked almost like a family tree, with space for names under several branches—some filled in, some not.

The names under the branches were twisted in an almost illegible font. But a name caught her eye, maybe it was just her dyslexia playing tricks and trying to make her see something that wasn't actually there but toward the bottom was what looked like her name…but it couldn't be. She shook her head.

Definitely just her brain twisting words on a page as it usually did.

She moved on, roving over the intricate lines, her eyes caught on familiar-looking Celtic knots that were nearly hidden in the illustration. It took her several seconds to process what she was seeing, but then it hit her all at once: it was the mark that was tattooed on the man's neck.

Instinctively, her hand flew to her own neck. Light-headedness swept down her body.

Nerves crackling, she took out her phone and began to take photos of the pages. Through the screen, she looked at the heavily slanted script on the page, feeling even more distraught and frustrated. The text was one hundred times more illegible than deciphering *Beowulf* in literature class when she was fifteen.

Snap.

Somehow, she doubted Google Translate would be able to help. It helped her with *Beowolf* at least…that, and SparkNotes.

Snap.

An illustration caught her eye. It was unlike the others in the book, drawn in muted tones of gray and black. It easily could've been overlooked in the shadow of the much more colorful, ornate illustrations, but she noticed it. Something about it almost pulled her eyes to it like a magnet. It featured a trio of individuals who were stepping out from a dark mist. The first figure was a woman with a raven on her shoulder, then a man with wings set atop his head like a crown, and lastly a second woman standing before a faded sun. They looked equally eternal as they did intimidating.

Klara snapped a picture.

She took photos one by one, the only sound the occasional snap of her phone and the careful rustling of centuries-old pages. Somewhere behind her, a door creaked open.

She spun in the direction of the sound—back in the direction she had come. For a moment, she stared into the dark, a blinking red exit light the only illumination.

"Hello?" an authoritative voice called out. "Who's there?"

Just one more second, just one more second, almost done...

"Shit," she cursed and hurriedly snapped a few more photos, then jammed her phone into her pocket. She replaced the binder as quietly as possible and ducked behind a glass case just as the door opened.

The timing was almost too perfect. A second longer and she would've been seen. She smiled to herself. Maybe it was magic. Or maybe time and luck seemed to be on her side... for now.

From her vantage point, all she could see was a pair of feet in polished black shoes hovering by the open door—the only exit. They were the shoes of a security guard. They began to shuffle in her direction.

"I know someone's in here," a man's voice said.

Klara backed up on all fours—right into a shelf. The clang echoed.

The feet picked up speed.

Staying as low as she could, she scrambled around the other side of the case and down the nearest aisle, then pressed herself against the stone wall—but the guard was still between her and the exit. To her left was the ancient wooden door she had spotted earlier. She sidled over until she was crouching in front of it. She would never make it past the guard, so if she could just hide somewhere, wait him out and hope he didn't find her...

Reaching up, Klara felt for the handle and pushed as hard as she could without making a sound. Mercifully, the door gave way. She slipped inside and closed it behind her.

Klara scooted back, expecting to hit a wall, or even a bucket and mop. But this space was way bigger than a broom closet. She stood fully and stretched her arms wide, letting her eyes adjust. The only light came in through a grate above. Its pale slivers barely illuminated the darkness.

"Hello?" she whispered. Her voice echoed, then faded out slowly.

Crap. The security guard...she hoped he didn't hear her. After a moment of silence, she mustered up the courage to take out her phone and shine her light down what was definitely not just a broom closet or storage room...actually, she wasn't in a room at all. She was in a tunnel.

Its cavernous stone walls arched upward no more than seven feet above her, cobwebs connecting across the curvature of the tunnel.

She shuddered at the thought of running into a low-hanging web.

The door rattled behind her. She jumped. *Shit.* The guard. Klara lunged for the door and found a latch which she quickly dropped into place. The door rattled again, harder this time. Deciding it was best not to wait around to see if the latch held, she took off down the tunnel, brandishing her phone flashlight in front of her.

"Whoa," she whispered. A memory resurfaced suddenly: her mom had once told her of the abandoned tunnels under Edinburgh, where illegal markers and secret societies thrived. A thrill rippled through her.

Then, the quiet turned thick. The hairs on her neck stood up, as if someone had run their finger down her back. She slowed her pace.

A low snarl rumbled from the darkness.

She froze. The last thing she needed was an encounter with a rabid sewer dog or whatever else lived down here.

The air grew hotter, seeming to curdle. A smell, one she could only describe as that of rotting flesh, hit her like a ton of bricks. Her hand flew to her nose. She suppressed a gag.

Another growl emanated from the shadows. Closer this time.

"Go away, go on," she said through her shaking hands. The words were strangled and soft and unconvincing. Scared.

Backing up, her fingers only met the cold stone wall. She crossed her fingers and held her breath, listening.

As if to answer, an enormous creature slithered from the darkness, slinking into view with the slow confidence of a predator with its prey cornered.

Just another dream, Klara told herself.

But then it lunged straight for her, yellow fangs bared.

She screamed.

CHAPTER ELEVEN

CALLUM

The scream for help rang off the walls. Callum looked up again at Aion, but the man had vanished.

Strength will come on swift wings.

Callum had always believed the words when Thomas spoke them. They won him countless fights, allowed him another strike when his body burned and only defeat seemed possible. But when he *needed* it to be true—like when his friend lay dying in front of him—it had proven false. Or rather, strength had come, but not enough.

Still, he called upon it now.

He searched for the source of the sound; there, behind the crates: a small doorway, half-size like the door in Brice's root cellar, with an iron grate sealing it shut. There wasn't anything he could use against the iron door to get out.

"Damn it!" he hissed, turning and hitting his fist against the stone, nearly striking a rusted torch sconce that jutted out from the wall. His hand fell to his side as an idea formed.

He looked back up at the torch sconce. Though old with age, it could possibly be of help to him.

Careful to avoid the sharp rusted pieces that jutted from the sconce, he grabbed the base and pulled. It groaned but didn't budge so he tried again. Nothing.

He needed more leverage so he planted his foot against the wall, and yanked. Nothing.

"Come on!" He groaned, biceps flexing.

The wind was knocked out of him as the sconce pulled free from the wall sending him toppling backward into a pile of crates.

He took a wheezing breath. "Should have seen that coming." Though half of the sconce was still securely fastened to the wall, a curved bar the size of his forearm lay by his side. It would have to do.

Callum spared only a moment to catch his breath, then grabbed the rusted iron and headed to the small door. He wedged the bar under the grate, pulling upwards with all his might, worried it might not be enough. The grate lifted and *clicked*, then fell forward, leaving an opening to what lay beyond. Still gripping the bar, Callum leaped over the mess and through the gate. He emerged into a tunnel that extended in both directions. A strangled roar sounded to his left. Another scream. He ran in the direction of the sound, turning a corner when the path in front of him ended abruptly—and stopped.

He watched as the shadows thickened, congealed, and took the shape of a beast: standing as tall as a horse and twice as wide, it bore the head of a snake, the form of a panther, and the cloven hooves of a demon.

On the other side of the beast stood Klara.

His heart skipped, shuddered.

Their eyes met. Hers, terrified, then unbelieving.

"Callum?" she said.

The beast swung its head around and spotted him. It swiveled to face him, swaying hypnotically as it approached until it got so close that Callum could see the venom beading from the tips of its fangs. Close enough that he felt its hot breath. It stepped into a pool of light that filtered in from above, revealing smooth scales that seemed to melt into dark fur.

Klara stood frozen with terror, her only movement the trembling of her hand clutching the small box she carried everywhere, which was now their only source of light. Time seemed to slow as he crept backward. He could draw the beast away from her. He felt his own pulse in his mouth.

The creature lunged at Callum.

He threw all his strength at the beast, ducking down and ramming his shoulder into its stomach. It took the creature by surprise, as it stumbled back just enough for Klara to round them and slam her phone into the beast's snapping jaws.

It reeled back with a hiss, a fang catching with a *snap*. Callum leaped back and landed clumsily in front of Klara. She helped him up quickly. Gripping the bar with two hands, Callum swung at the head that shot toward him. His hands exploded with pain as the bar made contact and rang out against the creature's skull.

The monster's neck whipped side to side in pain, its tail tearing the bar from Callum's throbbing hands, and slamming it into the wall of the tunnel with a terrible crash that echoed around them. After a split second of silence, stone began to fall from above in large pieces, breaking apart upon hitting the floor. Dust bloomed in the small, dark space.

"Klara, move!" Callum shouted.

Recovered, the monster lunged forward again with awful speed. Klara fell and Callum darted to help her up, even as the teeth snapped shut a hand's length away from her face. She screamed.

Callum grabbed the dirk hidden in his clothes and fumbled. He watched helplessly as it skittered along the floor just out of reach.

The creature lunged again.

Dirk abandoned, he leaped forward to meet it, attacking the monster with his fists. His hands caught its jaws as they tried to close on him. Muscles rippled along the beast's mouth and neck, its haunches straining against the ground as it pushed against Callum. Yet by some miracle, Callum managed to hold it back.

"Run," he managed through gritted teeth.

Instead, Klara fell to her knees and scoured the ground with her hands. "Where's your dagger?"

Slowly, ever so slowly, the jaws were closing, the fangs inches from Callum's face. "Run, Klara—"

The monster swung its neck like an unbroken horse, throwing Callum head over heels into the nearest partition wall.

"Callum!" Klara screamed.

His body exploded with pain. Ears ringing and splayed on his back, Callum watched helplessly as the monster turned its blazing red eyes on Klara again. She held up her bag like a shield.

It was happening again.

He was going to watch someone die.

His body stiffened like it had been gripped by an invisible force. Panic tore through him, wresting the strength from his limbs, stealing the breath from his lungs. He gasped to refill them as the edges of his vision darkened. Chest heaving, he rolled to his knees.

Klara's cry broke through the haze.

His head snapped up. The monster lumbered toward her, its tongue lashing the air as its hideous head darted and swayed. Its monstrous skull smashed into Klara's side and sent her sliding along the floor.

Callum struggled to his feet, even as the monster jerked forward and wrapped its tail around Klara's leg, dragging her limp body into the depths of the darkened tunnel.

"Klara!"

A scream rang out in response.

Callum blinked again and he was running, his feet slipping on the wreckage of stone and dust. Rock crunched under his boots. He skidded to a halt, eyes catching on a long shard that remained whole. He tore off his shirt, wrapping it around his hand before snatching up the shard and wielding it like a weapon.

"Come on, beastie," he snarled, cutting diagonally across the space as the monster pulled Klara along the tunnel. Her head lolled to the side, making his stomach turn.

Breath thundered in his lungs now, fear driving him forward. He mounted a leaning shelf and vaulted toward the creature, shard raised. He met his target with his full physical force, landing askew on the creature's neck.

Callum slammed the rock into the beast's spine, the spot on the neck where scales met fur.

The monster shrieked in pain. The shard broke where it impaled flesh, causing Callum to lose his only point of purchase. He fell down its scaled back, now slick with dark blood as the monster fell on its side, pushing the shard in deeper with a horrible squelch.

Klara was only a few paces away. Relief flooded Callum when he saw that she was no longer limp—she was kneeling, emptying the contents of her stomach onto the floor. Callum felt his own gorge rise, but forced it back down and turned back to the beast.

A rasping breath rattled from its throat. Then, it fell silent.

Callum watched as its dark blood pooled on the ground, reaching toward him like growing shadows.

Klara struggled to her feet, wiping at her mouth with her shirtsleeve. He ran over to help her, nearly slipping on the blood still spilling across the floor. Even in the dim light, he could see that her face was leached of color.

"Are you all right, lass?"

"Look," she said breathlessly, pointing.

Her eyes flicked to the beast behind him. Callum turned, only to see the creature's body darkening—not with blood, but with shadow. When it was fully draped in darkness, its misshapen form began to crumble, like a sand sculpture on a beach.

Within the space of a breath, the monster was nothing but a pile of dust on the floor.

CHAPTER TWELVE

KLARA

"How? Just...*how*?"

Klara wasn't sure if she was talking about the beast or Callum's appearance—or both, or everything that had happened in the last cursed twenty-four hours. Standing in the dim light of the tunnel, Callum stared at her, his mismatched eyes full of wonder. He looked just as surprised as she felt. But certainty and determination burned in his gaze, too, so intense she had to tear her eyes away.

When he first appeared as the beast charged her, Klara didn't have time to think. She had been pure fear, pure *survival*. But staring at him now, as the dust literally settled around them, made her heart flap wildly behind her ribs.

Callum approached her and grabbed her elbow, his grip

gentle but insistent. His other hand swept away a tendril of hair that had fallen across her face. The motion sent a flurry of shivers down her spine.

"Do ye believe me now, about everything?" he said in a low voice. His eyes roved across her face as if looking for her answer before she even spoke it.

The truth was that she did believe him now, including time traveling and Thomas—and that scared her more than anything.

Klara dropped her gaze. "Well, getting attacked by a monster makes this whole time travel thing a lot more believable."

Callum let go of her arm. The tilt of his chin was a little prouder than before.

"How did you find me? Did you follow me?" Klara asked.

Callum shook his head. "We were fated to meet," he said, pushing his hair away from his face. "There's no other reason for it."

Tipping her head back, Klara leaned against the wall and breathed out, her whole body trembling as the air left her. She kept one eye trained on the mound of dust that only minutes ago had been a yellow-fanged monster. "There's always a reason, an explanation."

Callum pushed the hair away from his forehead. "I dinnae ken the reason, but does it matter?"

"It matters to me, considering I'm the one being attacked and all," she said.

Something had drawn them together—*again*. That something was beyond her understanding, beyond her control. Her body squeezed, like she was trapped in an invisible net that was being pulled tight around her. "Okay, fate aside, how did you get here?"

Callum glanced behind him. "I'll explain, but not here. We shouldna linger."

Klara pulled her cardigan tighter around her shoulders. The fabric was splattered with dark dust that matched the large pile of dust on the ground. *Beast parts*, she thought with another shudder. "I can't argue with that."

Finding a way out was easier said than done. Going back through the library seemed out of the question—the thought of the wreckage they were leaving behind gnawed at her chest with a thousand tiny bites. The tunnel was destroyed. Dust motes hung in the air and dark streaks were smeared across the flagstones. The monster had slammed into the ceiling when it reared its massive head. A slanted pile of rubble and stone led upward to a narrow hole at the top of the tunnel, where light streamed in—daylight.

Klara squinted. If these were the ancient tunnels under Edinburgh, that opening must lead to the streets.

"Come on," she said, gesturing to the opening.

Callum picked up his dirk from the ground and slipped it into his waistband. His own shirt was hanging on by a thread. Literally. His eyes roamed over her, as if searching for injuries again. She was suddenly aware of how she must look, and blushed. "Are ye well enough to climb?" he asked.

Klara nodded curtly, determined to prove that she was okay, and tested out the pile of rubble with her one shoe. A few pebbles rolled down, but otherwise, it seemed sturdy enough for them to scramble out. Naturally, this was the moment her balance decided to fail her, and the first rock she stepped on slipped from under her. She wobbled, arms pin-wheeling backward; *of course* she'd survive a monster attack only to die by gravity's hand.

Callum's hands caught her shoulders, and her back fell into him with a *whoof.* At his touch, it was like the tension of the fight just poured out of her into a puddle. Relief surged through her to be with him again. Because of it, she didn't step away immediately. She sighed, feeling her shoulder blades move against his ribs. "Thanks."

"It is my pleasure, lass," he responded quietly in her ear. She shivered, but recovered quickly.

"Turns out that fighting for your life twice in twenty-four hours is exhausting. Let's get the hell out of here."

"To where? Back to the manor?" Callum asked.

"I don't know, Callum, we'll figure it out—"

She stopped. The message her grandmother had left yesterday surfaced in her mind. *My door is always open.*

A chill ran down her spine. Had she known that Klara would need a safe haven? Grams was the only person in the world who might not bat an eyelash if Klara appeared on her doorstep covered in beast juice with a time-traveling stranger. And she knew more about mysticism and magic than anyone Klara knew. Not to mention Gaelic.

"I know a place," she said, adding, "and someone who might be able to help us."

Back on the streets of Edinburgh, Klara led Callum through winding roads without pause, gripping the straps of her back-pack until her knuckles were white. Why was disaster fol-lowing her everywhere? Her eyes darted to every passing face and shadowy corner, muscles jumping and twitching with paranoia.

Crowds swelled around them, and it soon became clear that the passersby were clearly more concerned about them. She was a wreck. Her jeans were torn in one knee. Hair clung to her cheeks, stuck to her skin in patches of dirt and sweat. She was limping from missing a shoe and smelled rotten, thanks to her new beast blood perfume.

Sure enough, a man wrinkled his nose at them as they passed. Callum glared back.

They rounded a corner, where the crowds thinned. "What *was* that back there?" Klara asked.

"I wish I knew," Callum said. "A beast straight from hell itself."

"Now will you tell me how you got here?" Klara asked.

Callum glanced around. Satisfied that they weren't being watched, he began to speak. "I went to Finn & Fianna, the apothecary. Thomas's book came from there, and he used to visit from time to time. I thought they may know about the supernatural, something that might help us."

Us. Against her better judgment, she was starting to get used to the word. "I always thought that place was a tourist trap."

"The man there, the shop owner—Aion—said Thomas's illustrations were of mystic centers. I think that he was searching for certain ones."

"Mystic centers? That was in the title of the book I almost got killed for. Why was Thomas drawing them?"

"Aye, that's the word he used but I dinnae ken why Thomas was compelled to do so."

Klara felt for her phone. Good thing she'd taken photos. The ancient book was still in the library basement, hopefully not with any of her traceable fingerprints on it. "Did he say anything about pillars?"

"No. I didnae get to ask much before I heard ye screaming for help. The store connected to the tunnel that led me to ye."

"The library isn't far from there," she said. "The tunnels must connect them."

His brow furrowed. "I'd like to go back, I have more questions—"

Klara cut him off with a glance. "Let's skip that stuff for now and get somewhere safe. After that beast, we don't know what else is waiting to kill us."

The beast attack loomed in her mind, blood going cold as the memory sharpened. The beast seemed to find her when she hadn't even known where she was going—just like the man in the Elder Forest had appeared from nowhere, reaching for her...

She shivered, wishing she could yank the invisible target off her back.

"Do you think the man sent that thing after me somehow?" she whispered, as if saying it would summon the killer.

Callum waited for a family to pass before responding. "I dinnae believe it is chance."

Why did everything want to kill her? She tucked her arms around herself as if that alone could ward off the cold that seeped into her limbs.

Klara had just started to turn the corner when she noticed that Callum was no longer by her side. She reeled sharply to see him crouched on the pavement staring wide-eyed to the sky.

Klara rushed to his side, kneeling beside him.

"What's wrong?" she asked, touching his arm but he still didn't bring his eyes to hers.

"That!" He pointed to an airplane's tail, just as it disappeared over a building, leaving contrails in its wake.

She looked at him, bewildered. "The plane?"

"What monsters live in this world of yours?" he groaned, "It could have snatched us up for supper."

Her face loosened into a grin.

"It's nothing to be scared of. It's called an airplane." She helped him stand. "People use them to travel faster. Think of them as large carriages, but instead of traveling on ground, they use the sky."

"Magic," Callum whispered. "Only birds can fly."

"Not anymore," Klara said, giving him a wink.

Callum chuckled. "What's next, the stars?"

"Actually..." She paused, considering. They had both had enough new experiences today, no need to overwhelm him with more.

"Come on." She tugged on his hand.

Silence fell between them as Klara navigated to her grandmother's flat. There was so much hiding within the city she thought she knew. Edinburgh transformed around them, turning from old stone buildings to smaller houses, ones that seemed far more similar to the cottages and establishments of an older world. *Callum's world.*

It was obvious he felt it, too—he relaxed as he walked, clearly more at ease in these narrow streets. The area was beautiful, with the houses facing out along a calm, tree-lined canal. Clothing was set out to dry on thin lines, drifting lazily in the breeze.

"We're almost there—Dean Path."

Klara stopped in front of the familiar pale green facade. Had her Grams really known that she would come?

After waiting to make sure no one—or no *thing*—was spying on her, she fumbled for the skeleton key under a flowerpot. She slipped it in the lock and opened the door, then led Callum up a creaky staircase to the second floor, where the door of her grandmother's flat was already ajar. The force of her knock inched it open farther, allowing the scent of frankincense and bubbling tomato sauce to escape.

"Grams?" Klara called through the opening.

Her grandma stood at the stove, yellow shawl flowing behind her like a cape. She always looked incredible, even when she was just at home cooking. She turned, clapping her hands over her mouth at the sight of Klara and let out a muffled, excited cry. "Darling!"

She beckoned them inside with one hand while she covered the pot and turned off the stove top with the other. Klara shut the door behind Callum, jamming it with her shoulder when it refused to close all the way.

"I've been telling her forever to get this fixed." She smiled with affection.

With an air that was stately and whimsical at once, her grandmother strode toward them, arms wide. Grams's white hair was streaked with pale red—but it was the cool blue eyes, lined with crow's-feet and dancing with mirth, that always made a smile creep over Klara's face. They were striking and sharp, even at her old age.

Klara let herself be engulfed into a bone-crunching hug.

Grams drew back, nose wrinkled. "Oh, you smell something dreadful, dear. And look even worse."

Not waiting for a reply, she turned to Callum once more, meeting his gaze with a soft but still suspicious frown. Callum bowed.

"Callum Drummond."

"Of course you are. Adele Westwood," she returned, warmly.

"Klara tells me ye are a witch," he said plainly.

Klara's mouth dropped open. "Callum!"

Her Grams's expression broke. She tipped her head and laughed. The movement set off a chorus of musical clatter as her bangles knocked up against one another. "I like you, lad."

Her grandma looked back and forth between the two of them, settling on Klara with a tight-lipped smile. There was a distant, wistful cast to her face—like she was watching a sad movie—that made clammy gooseflesh spread up Klara's arms, followed by a cold sense of unease that nagged at the corners of her mind.

Confirming her thoughts, Grams waved away whatever Klara was about to say. "I sense that we have a lot to discuss. First, to the showers with you both."

Klara was more than happy to strip off her dust and blood-crusted clothes and spend the better part of an hour in the blissfully hot shower. After scrubbing her hair, careful to avoid the bleeding welt she discovered on her head, she'd washed off not only the rotten scent, but at least four layers of her skin. That was one new perk of having red hair: it masked blood.

If she weren't so exhausted, she'd have laughed.

Wrapping a soft cotton towel around herself, Klara stepped out of the tub and into the steam-filled room. A pile of clothes were folded neatly on the toilet seat; Grams must've sneaked in while she showered. She was shockingly stealthy for a woman of her age.

With the heel of her wrist, she wiped the condensation from the full-length mirror and assessed herself. Her green eyes stared back at her, stark against the dark circles beneath. Exhaustion was visible on every inch of her face.

She dropped the towel to the ground. Bruises, cuts, and bumps adorned her body. But aside from the gash across her collarbone and the bleeding head wound, most seemed minor. Her fingers glided over the injuries, pressing and poking, and found they were bearable. No broken bones or punctured lungs or anything else that might land her in the hospital.

Her mind was a different story.

A car horn outside sent Klara jumping out of her skin. She stumbled back, meeting the edge of the tub with her heel, and just barely kept herself from falling by grasping the rim of the sink with one hand.

"Jesus!" she hissed. She took a few deep breaths, trying to calm her pounding heart.

"The monster is dead," she whispered to her reflection. "It disintegrated into a pile of sand."

But there *was* a monster.

First a time traveler, then a murderer, then maybe seeing her name in that book in the library, then a monster.

Her heart sped up again. Running to her Grams's apartment had made her feel safe for a minute, but that didn't mean she actually was. The scaly, furred creature slithered through her mind, bringing along with it paranoia that gnawed at her like a trapped fox at its own leg.

Realizing she was soaking the pink tile, Klara grabbed the fallen towel off the floor and dried herself off with shaking hands. The folded garment that Grams had left for her caught her eye: a familiar periwinkle satin short-sleeve dress that cinched at the waist. She'd left it behind the last time she had visited.

Considering the state of her other clothes, Klara slid on the dress, pleasantly surprised by how refreshing it felt against her clean skin. She ran her fingers over the hem, suddenly remembering the night she'd last worn it: two Christmases ago, homemade apple pie, the warm burn of whiskey in her throat.

It was the last holiday they had spent together as a family.

Without warning, tears spilled onto the dress, darkening the fabric alongside water droplets from her hair. Klara let the tears flow. It felt good, freeing.

With a deep breath, she straightened her dress, preparing herself. Whatever her skill as a seer, Grams always saw right through Klara. No fooling her, unlike her sweet, oblivious dad.

Out in the sitting room, Klara found her sitting in an overstuffed armchair, hands clasped in her lap—waiting, it seemed. Klara sunk into the claw-foot sofa perpendicular to the armchair. A golden tray of tea and biscuits sat on the oak table between them.

"Your friend seems to enjoy that bath. He's been in there for ages." Grams leveled a gaze at Klara. "You'd think he'd never had a proper one before."

Klara flushed. She wasn't sure if she should spill the fact that Callum was a time traveler right away when she was still processing it herself. "We've had a long day."

Taking the warm tea into her hands, she peered out the bay window that overlooked the street. Brown-gray buildings followed the curvature of the road, only stopping as it met the river that flowed through Dean Village. A pair of old men wandered down the lane, hands behind their backs and tartan hats atop wisps of white hair. Even though the scene was perfectly normal, she felt deep in her bones that nothing was normal any longer.

Was Klara putting her grandmother in danger by being here? She fought the sudden urge to flee. If there was someone who didn't need protecting, it was probably her Grams. The woman was afraid of nothing and could wield a pair of knitting needles like deadly weapons. But then she thought of Callum being locked in that basement and the beast with its yellow, dripping fangs. The invisible net tightened around her again. Who knew what other dangers might be lurking, lying in wait for her?

It would be safer to keep the truth from her Grams—at least as much as she could.

As a kid, she believed Grams's visions to be true and took all of her clairvoyant wisdom to heart. But as she got older, Klara found magic elsewhere: everything could be explained by science. Or at least Klara had thought, until yesterday. Now her whole world was turned upside down, and she needed help. But she couldn't ask for it—not without putting her Grams in danger.

Klara ran a hand through her damp locks, which were beginning to curl. She spotted a familiar oversize bright yellow raincoat draped over a chair. "Where's Granny Laura?"

"You just missed her. Her sister is visiting from Mumbai and she went to a spiritual retreat with her for the weekend."

"Oh." Disappointment panged through Klara. She hadn't seen Grams's wife since the funeral. She lifted the teacup to her lips and drank. The delicate liquid glided down her throat, tasting of raspberry and honey.

"Taste familiar?" Grams asked.

"How did you get this?" Klara asked, remembering the small tea shop she, her mom, Grams, and Granny Laura went to in Paris when she was just a little girl and still living in Scotland, just before Klara went to the Louvre for the first time.

"It wasn't easy, but it was worth it. I tracked it down when your father told us you were moving back, after your mother passed on."

Grams smiled warmly, her voice as level and pleasant as if she was talking about what nice weather they were having. "Are you going to tell me why you decided to drop by so suddenly?"

Klara shifted, setting the cup down with too much force, causing it to clatter against the saucer. "Don't you already know?" she said playfully. Grams winked, and Klara's smile faded. "I'm sorry, it's just… I've had a rough day." She swallowed. "I know we haven't talked in a while, but Callum and I were in the neighborhood, and I thought you might be of some help."

"Oh?" Grams surveyed her.

"We fell down a rabbit hole about mysticism and the supernatural after watching a documentary," Klara said quickly, hoping her explanation was good enough.

Based on the slight arch of her eyebrow, she knew Grams could see through her. No matter. She still was not going to put her grandmother in harm's way by telling her the truth.

"I thought you wouldn't mind because you're always so on top of giving me mystical advice, even when I didn't know I needed it. Today, I definitely need it," she continued, tears springing to her eyes unexpectedly. She hadn't realized till now how much she craved the comfort of her grandmother.

Just when Klara thought she wasn't going to be able to hold in her tears any longer, the bedroom door burst open and Callum strode into the room.

Now Klara's eyes flew wide.

"What *is* that?" she said, trying to hold back laughter.

Callum was wearing the most ridiculous outfit she had ever seen. It looked as if a lava lamp had exploded on an oversize asymmetrical Hawaiian shirt. Splotchy reds, yellows, and greens mingled together like colorful vomit. But it was the leather pants that pulled the whole outfit over the edge. Ironically, he looked the part of the time traveler—if he came from the 1970s.

She no longer had any qualms about her barely-out-of-fashion dress. None at all.

Grams gestured casually for Callum to take a seat with them. "Those were Albert's old clothes. I'll have you know he was quite the rake in his day."

Albert. It was a name Klara had to blow dust off of. He was the last guy Grams dated before meeting Granny Laura.

Callum sat, looking almost small in the baggy hippy clothing. Grams pushed the tray toward him, nodding for him to take the third still-steaming cup.

Klara never realized there was a way to drink tea voraciously, but Callum was living proof that there was. She watched as he drank and smiled secretly into his cup, completely in his own world.

Grams leaned over and whispered, "That's the first time I've seen you smile in a long while, dear."

Klara made a show of dropping the grin. "I'm not smiling."

Callum's shaggy head popped up from his cup, the spell dispersed.

Klara took a deep breath. "Callum and I shouldn't stay for long. We were hoping…could you tell us what you know about mystic centers?"

Her Grams shifted, making the armchair squeak underneath her. "I've never heard quite that term exactly, but there are many sites throughout Scotland where the boundary between our world and the Otherworld are thin. 'Thin places,' I've always liked that term. It's quite descriptive."

"The Otherworld," Klara said. "The realm of the gods? The one that you always said opens on Samhain?"

Her Grams nodded.

The word bubbled up in Klara's memory. Of course she was well aware of the tourists who came for Samhain, wanting to experience one of Scotland's most ancient traditions. But she had childhood memories, too. Bonfires burning bright on the hillsides, their acrid smell carried on a chill wind. The pull on her hand as her grandmother led her through a wood flickering with firelight. Legend said it was a day that the dead and mythical creatures could go between worlds, as if passing through a doorway.

"According to some beliefs, the Otherworld is comparable to the realm of the dead, but it's more than that, too," her Grams said. "Our world, the human world, is mostly severed from that of the gods—that's why there are so many stories of gods using animal familiars to visit earth, and why certain people are conduits—" she smiled "—like seers."

Klara stilled. If it was possible—really possible—to travel from one world to the next, would it be that different than traveling through time?

"What do you know of Arianrhod?" Callum asked.

"Goddess of the Silver Wheel?" Grams looked at Callum, then Klara, for recognition. Finding none, she continued. "She is not as well-known as other deities, though she is said to be extremely powerful, a primal figure of female strength—often associated with the moon, she had dominion over the sky, reincarnation, and even time and fate itself. In Celtic mythology, her silver wheel symbolizes the past, present, and future. All gods have an item like this, just as they have an animal familiar. Hers is an owl, said to send comfort to those in death when she cannot herself come to our mundane world. Though she once walked the earth, she is thought to reside in the stars with her female attendants." Grams winked at Klara. "Better known to budding astronomers as the Corona Borealis."

The hairs on Klara's arms stood on end. The face she saw in the night sky through her telescope, the one she thought she imagined—she was looking in the direction of the Corona Borealis when she saw it.

"Dear? Are you all right?"

Mind racing, Klara pulled out her phone. She looked at the screen, certain the guts of the phone would be hanging out after that impact, but the screen wasn't shattered at all from the encounter with the beast. In fact, it just had two spider hair cracks reaching it across it— *A+ for modern technology*, Klara thought. Or... maybe she should thank dad for insisting on a screen protector.

"Can you tell me what this means? I think—that's my name, isn't it, Grams? Do you know what this document is?"

Grams took the phone from Klara, slipping on a pair of reading glasses that dangled from a chain around her neck, and studied the screen. The longer she read, the more she seemed to shrink into herself. Klara pushed away a feeling of guilt.

After a long pause, Grams spoke. "The lineage of the Pillars of Time," she breathed softly.

Pillar. An electric pulse ran along Klara's body, forcing her to sit back in her chair.

To think that the final Pillar is only a little girl. That's what that man had said to her.

Grams placed Klara's phone in her lap and clasped her hands over it. Her eyes unfocused, her gaze wandering to the space between Klara and Callum. She looked suddenly exhausted.

"Are you okay, Grams?" Klara asked.

Grams started, snapping her head to Klara like she'd forgotten she was there. "I always knew you were special."

Callum and Klara exchanged glances. "Special how? What do you know?" Klara asked.

Grams plucked off her glasses and rubbed the red irritated skin of her nose. "Oh, sweetie. I don't know." Her voice wavered. "I pride myself on knowing answers but this is one that I do not have the answers to."

"So you don't know what this Pillar thing is?"

"From these illustrations, and what you say—it looks like individuals, including you, are associated with Arianrhod. And you've been known to be part of this for a long time, based on the age of these documents."

"Callum's friend Thomas—he was killed, and his name is also on this list," she said. "Is the same thing going to happen to me?"

"No!" she said strongly. "You cannot run away from destiny, it will always catch up with you in the end. Rather than be caught unprepared, you must turn and face it." She looked at Callum. "Do you mind giving Klara and me a moment alone?"

Callum shifted in his seat, his gaze darting between Klara and Grams.

"It's okay, Callum," Klara said, giving his arm a squeeze.

He looked down at her hand then up at her, a slight smile gracing his lips.

"Of course." He nodded, touching her hand briefly, then got up and left the room.

Grams picked up the teapot and poured more fragrant liquid into her cup, hands trembling. Tea spilled over the edge of the cup and onto the table. "We don't choose our family, do we? But we love them all the same. For the most part." She smiled weakly. "Our destinies are the same. We have to make what meaning we can of what we're given."

Klara tried to quell the frustration rising in her. "But how do I find out what I've been given?" Grams handed Klara's

phone back. It was open to the picture of three beings stepping out of the mist.

Grams put a hand on Klara's knee, bangles clinking musi-
cally as they fell to her wrist. "Dear, all of my life I felt like
I had been blessed with a connection to another world—the
world that is all around us, that some remain blind to and
others simply refuse to see." Her voice cracked. "But lately I
realized how foolish I've been, and how little I truly understand about the powers of this world and the next. Sometimes,
knowledge is a curse. It hurts us.

"But I know this. And that young man you're traveling
with, he may not know much, but he can guide you—and
maybe your heart—in the right direction."

"But why me? I don't understand." A desperate feeling
raked against Klara's chest.

"You don't know how incredible you are. Of course you
feel this way, anyone would, but remember that fate chose you
for a reason. The reasoning may be uncertain now, but know
that as you go forth on this journey, the path will clear and
you will be able to unearth all these answers." Grams's eyes
clouded with tears. "Look at me. I always suspected you had a
touch of the Otherworldly to you. And now, I *know* you do."

She reached for Klara's hand and squeezed. "I promise you
will find your way."

CHAPTER THIRTEEN

CALLUM

Twilight fell in sweeps of gray outside the window of Grams's office. Pleasantly lavender-scented, the interior resembled the interior of Kingshill Manor: polished wooden shelves stacked with books lined the walls beside instruments and framed portraits. The portraits were the most lifelike Callum had ever seen—like the figures captured within the frames would move and speak at any moment. Many of the portraits depicted Klara, and others he assumed were her family. All smiling. As if he was stung by a serpent, envy swelled in him like venom at the sight of her loving family, though the feeling subsided quickly.

Gently, he took a portrait off the wall and held it in his hands. A lovely, grinning woman stared back at him.

"They're photographs."

Klara's voice made him jump. He turned to see her standing in the doorway. Her face looked more peaceful than when he'd left the room. Confident. It made her even more beautiful, if that was possible.

"Photographs?" he repeated.

She walked to him. She gave him a curious smile—an expression he was getting accustomed to seeing on Klara's face. "Images, captured from life. Here, I'll show you."

Leaning toward him—so close she brushed his upper arm with hers—she took out the object she called a phone and held it in front of them with an outstretched arm. *Snap.* When she brought the phone away again, there was an image of them, standing together, exactly how they had just been. Warmth rose to his cheeks.

"It's…" His voice dried up in his throat.

Callum had never had a portrait painted of himself, and never expected to. Especially at the side of a woman as beautiful as Klara.

"What is it?" she asked.

"Nothing," he replied quickly.

Klara's questioning gaze lingered on him, sending sparks along his skin, before she finally turned her attention back to her phone. "Don't ask me to explain how it works. Call it magic. There's enough of that going around lately," she said with a wry grin.

Klara took the framed photograph from Callum, running her thumb along the frame.

"Your ma?" he asked.

She nodded. "On the Faroe Islands. She found peace there after some pretty rough teenage years."

He looked into the smiling, carefree face—so like Klara's. The dainty nose, rose-touched cheeks, the mischievous glint in her eyes. The wind lifted strands of her hair and framed her face. The serpent stung again. *What had his ma looked like?*

He pushed the thought away. No use in asking what cannot be known. "What were her troubles?"

"She had undiagnosed ADHD—a disorder that means she learns in a different way from most people. I'm dyslexic, which is different, but also means I learn differently from others," Klara explained. "At that time, not much was known about it. So instead of helping, her classmates all called her stupid, which only made her try harder."

Callum's heart tweaked. He had no education himself, but he knew how cruel children could be. "She sounds like an incredible woman."

"She was. That's why she wanted me to go to college so badly—to feel that purpose to succeed even when hurdles were stacked in front of me. She told me to leap past them." Klara frowned. "I haven't told anyone this yet, not even my dad, but—" she bit her lip "—I decided not to go to school. With everything happening, it doesn't seem like that should matter at all. But it still does, somehow."

"Ye're already the smartest person I ken," he said easily.

"Thanks, Callum, but you only know, like, four people from the twenty-first century, and one of them is my dog. It's not exactly a lot of competition."

"'Tis good ye have a portrait of her. All I have of Thomas is his notebook."

Klara turned away to hang the photograph back on the wall, taking time to straighten the frame carefully. When she turned back again, she was transformed, her gaze eager and blazing rather than soft and affectionate. "Enough trips down memory lane. We have work to do, before we get ambushed by a unicorn or something."

"I'd take a unicorn over a monster any day," he replied with a sly smile.

Klara sat on a sofa and gestured for him to join her. "If studying science has taught me anything, it's that you do not need to understand a phenomenon for that phenomenon to occur. Let's treat this as a phenomenon we don't understand, like ghosts." She fixed her stare somewhere over his shoulder. Concentration made furrow lines on her brow. "Let's start with the mystic centers. Why was Thomas drawing them?"

Callum considered this for a moment. "I think he was visiting them," he concluded.

"Are you sure?" Klara asked.

He nodded. There could be no other explanation. "In the months before the night he was killed, he disappeared for long stretches. He had no kin to visit, no other business to attend. He was utterly consumed by his own thoughts before he died." His blood chilled, and shame followed, thinking of Thomas facing this alone. A lump formed in his throat.

"So what next?" she asked.

His voice roughened. "There's something I have to show ye." Callum stood and walked into the guest room, emerging with Thomas's notebook in hand.

He sat down next to her and opened the book to the drawing of the fairy circle. Klara leaned slightly into him, eyes squinting at the worn pages. Landscapes, all of them. Some crossed out.

"Thomas drew these?" she asked.

"Aye."

"May I look?"

Thomas put the notebook in her hands and for several moments Klara turned the pages slowly, before going back to the beginning.

"See here," she said, pointing at the inner spine. "Some pages at the front have been torn out."

Thomas frowned. "I noticed that too. But see inside the cover, where he wrote his name? The writing is different—a child's. He must have had it for many years. I don't remember a time when he didn't carry it around with him."

"So you think Thomas might have torn out the older pages?"

Callum shrugged. "If they no longer meant anything to him..."

"Maybe." Klara didn't sound convinced. She flipped a few pages and pointed. "But this one? It's the fairy circle...we were just there. This can't be a coincidence."

"No. The alley drawn in the corner, there? That's Kelpie's Close. Where I...fell through. And there are other sites like this one..." He trailed off. "There is also one more sketch." With a look in Klara's direction, he flipped to the last page where her face stared back at them. "'Tis ye, lass. Thomas must have known ye. Somehow, somewhere."

Klara took a breath, leaned back, and closed her eyes, sweeping her hair over her shoulder with one hand. "*We have to make what meaning we can of what we're given,*" she whispered, as if she were steeling herself for what came next. The scent of her perfume filled his nose. *"The lineage of the Pillars of Time,"* she recited. She took out her phone and brought up the photographs she had taken of the manuscript at the library. "Look, here's the mark—Arianrhod's mark," she said, using her fingers to make the symbol on the page bigger. "My Grams said Arianrhod had dominion over time. And here are Thomas's name and mine, connected." She traced the line between them.

Though Callum was never a strictly religious man, he believed in the worlds of heaven and hell—and though forbidden in Brice's theology, it was no great leap to believe worlds beyond that existed, like the Otherworld. Old gods were still worshipped in his land, and they lived in worlds only great men and heroes dared to enter—according to the bards' tales. Then there was the realm of man, which held its own worlds within it, just like a tree trunk held nested rings. There were the rich and poor, disparate worlds that rarely met.

He thought of Klara, her speech and dress, her intellect and education and her beauty. Even here and now, she seemed to walk in an entirely different world than he did. Thomas, too, now inhabited a different world, Callum thought with a lurch. The world of the dead.

"He spoke of men leaping between worlds. I thought he was going mad, but—"

"Leaping between worlds," Klara repeated. Her gaze drifted as she lost herself in thought. He recognized that look. "If we're looking at this scientifically, and if the rules involve anything close to physics in our world, you would need a huge amount of energy to do that." Her eyes widened.

"What is it, lass?"

"When we were in the Elder Forest, I felt something."

Callum recalled the word she used. "Energy?"

"Kind of, but it was coming *from* me. Almost like… I was the one sending the man who attacked me back into the mist." She looked at him, meeting his eyes with a blazing look. "Did you feel anything like that, when you traveled from your time to mine?"

Callum was familiar with a similar sensation—during his worst fights, he had pulled himself out of near defeat by a miracle of muscle and desperation, a sudden rush of power that coursed through his limbs to animate him. He scoured his memory but remembered no such feeling came over him in the alley—at least not when the white light had enveloped him. If anything, he had felt completely helpless. Though, of course, he did not want to admit that to Klara. "No."

"What about the man? What did he do before he—" She paused, searching for the word. A visible shudder ran over her body. "Jumped?"

Though it pained him to do so, Callum closed his eyes to recall more of that night: The iron smell of blood filling the alley, thick as the man's sinister voice filling his ear; the scrape of cobblestones against his back as the man tossed him as if he were made of straw. Details came back to him, water pouring into a wheel well.

"I couldna see him well in the dark, but the man was laboring over something," Callum said. The memory sparked Aion's words about magic and intention. "He was acting with intention, like a witch over a cauldron."

"Maybe he was opening a door." Klara folded her hands into her lap. "Did Thomas ever mention anything like that?"

Callum shook his head. "I dinnae believe so."

"What about…feeling like he had some kind of…power?"

He had such a dearth of knowledge of his friend's mind. "No, but I'm not sure he would have told me if he did. He grew so distant in those last months, and I couldna save him in the end."

Klara's fingers flew to his forearm and squeezed gently— a gesture of kindness and comfort so unfamiliar to him that he flinched. "Don't be silly. From everything you've told me, you tried your best."

Callum tried to smile, though he knew she was only trying to make him feel better. For a brief moment, he was grateful for the lie—at least until the truth raged in his chest again, burning away all doubt as to who was truly at fault for his friend's death.

He vowed to do better by Klara.

"Thomas was never the largest fighter, nor the strongest— he could never put muscle on, no matter how many bannocks he wolfed down," Callum said. "But he was the cleverest. He always sniffed out his opponents' weaknesses like a hunting dog on a scent. If he was visiting those mystic centers, there was a reason for it."

A spark seemed to flow between her mind and his. He sat up eagerly, a new idea animating his limbs. "Maybe he went to those sites because he was searching for a weakness in his enemy—if he knew he had one."

Klara nodded. Callum continued.

"If he was cunning enough to ken he was being pursued

before he was killed, he was cunning enough to find a way to defeat him. Or at least, he would have tried."

Klara's face resolved into a mask of determination. "We don't have a choice, then."

Callum raised an eyebrow. "We dinnae?"

"Of course not." She grinned, and it set a match to Callum's heart. "Just like Thomas, we have to go to the mystic centers ourselves."

"I'll tell her, Dad. And while I'm gone, *please* don't give Finn any more hot dogs. I'm going to have to put him on another diet, and you know he hates that."

Klara's father's voice rang out weakly from the object she held to her ear. *Her phone,* Callum reminded himself. The wonders of this new world made him dizzy—it took everything in him to resist leaping from the sofa to press his ear against the other side of the phone so that he might better hear his words. But even without being able to hear his words clearly, whatever her father was saying was causing Klara to bite her bottom lip. When she spoke again, the pressure of her teeth left red marks on her skin. "I will. I love you."

Klara slipped the phone away from her ear, then sighed. "I hated that. If we survive, we are going to have to come up with the most amazing excuse of all time to justify all these lies to my dad."

Callum nodded. "It's for the best, lass. Ye'll be safe. Ye'll return to him."

With each word, he renewed his vow to her. *He* would keep her safe. *He* would return her home.

"In how many pieces?" she mumbled.

A terrible force moved in Callum's veins, an unfurling viper in his chest that propelled him *up*. He sprang to his feet. "The man will not harm a hair on your head."

His voice came out loud—louder than he intended. The words stung his mouth like molten iron.

Klara stared at him, eyes wide in shock. "I was only joking, Callum. Kind of." Her look of surprise turned to one of affront. "You're not my keeper. You don't know you can protect me because we don't know what we're really up against. We can't survive this if we don't work together. So don't put all the burden on yourself. You can't get *killed* for me. It's so—" She puffed out air and shook her head. "It's just too much."

Callum clenched his jaw, knowing why she said it, but he knew that he had his own destiny. And if that means protecting Klara, that's what he would do.

After surveying him for a moment longer, Klara relaxed her shoulders. "I took a look at the map. The closest mystic center is the Fairy Glen in Skye, then Maeshowe, then the Ring of Brodgar—luckily those two are close to one another. I'm going to go tell Grams that we'll leave in the morning."

Callum only nodded. Shame grew into him from the floor below, rooting him to the spot.

Klara suddenly reentered the room, Grams trailing in her wake, hand on her back.

"You have to go," Grams said urgently.

"But why?" Klara asked, confusion lacing her words.

Fearing the worst and with visions of the beast rearing in his head, Callum rushed toward her.

"Sweet girl, trust me on this. Take my car—" She handed Klara a set of keys.

Klara had a bewildered look on her face, but her hand grasped the keys regardless. "And this—"

Grams disappeared for a moment just to come back with a long object covered by a sheet of fabric.

"Our family heirloom. Something feels right about giving it to you now. Know, always, how much strength you have within you."

"What—" Klara started, but her grandmother stopped her, "Know, always, that I love you."

The tender words moved something in Callum's chest—a soft beating of wings that helped dissolve the tension in him. It was then that he noticed a gleaming point poking from beneath the fabric.

"Is that a...a sword?" he said.

Grams puffed out a laugh, eyes crinkling. "Not just any sword, a very old and special one. It's been passed down through generations of our family."

Klara took the sword from her grandmother, the fabric slipping down to reveal an ornate hilt—and nearly dropped it, her eyes going round with surprise.

"Heavy then, is it?" Callum thought he recognized glints of gold and brass in the fine metalwork.

Klara hurriedly laid the sword down on the table, flustered. "No, it's just—I mean yes, it's heavy, but—"

"It knows you." Klara's grandmother was studying her with a sly smile. "Just as when you were a little girl."

"But I've never seen it before." Klara pulled back the fabric and tentatively stroked the flat of the blade. It must have been a trick of the light, but the sword seemed to blur and shimmer at her touch.

"You have, though. On one of your visits, when you were only three or four. It was the gems that caught your eye, the way they sparkle. The minute you touched it you jumped like you'd stuck your finger in an electric socket. Your mam rushed to pick you up but you were laughing. You would have played with it all day if we let you."

"You said it knows her…?" Callum couldn't take his eyes off the beautiful weapon. The blade was as long as Klara's arm, the hilt formed like a Scottish thistle. Spiny leaves twined its way up the cross guard, which flowed into a handle made of twisting stems that bloomed into an amethyst-studded pommel in the shape of the prickly flower. Though it was a prickly flower, the handle looked comfortable, smooth even just enough for a hand to fit comfortably around it. Excitement welled in him at the sight of such a finely made weapon. He could not tear his eyes away from the gorgeous blade."

"Perhaps I did." But it was clear she meant to say no more about it.

"May I?" Callum asked, pulling the cloth all the way off and noticing something he'd missed—an object woven into its handle.

Pinching it with two fingers, he pulled it out gently from the latticed metal until it broke free.

He held it up to the light. It was a worn ribbon, woven from strands of red and white. He offered it to Klara.

"What's this?" Klara took the ribbon from him. The far-away look reappeared as she gazed at it.

"It's yours," Gram's answered for her. "From when you were a girl. I used to weave it into your hair before taking you to the Samhain bonfires."

"I didn't know you still had this, we haven't celebrated Samhain together in years."

"We will again," she said softly, coming up and stroking her cheek.

Callum remembered Samhain celebrations as if they were yesterday. The villagers in animalistic masks celebrating the veil of the living and the dead thinning for the night. He never truly believed in such things but now...after all they had been through, he might just.

CHAPTER FOURTEEN

KLARA

Three days.

Three days until Samhain.

The warning played on repeat in her head. It was like a dark shadow that slowly crept closer, just as the man who tried to kill her did. She hoped, at the very least, this meant they had three days before anything came at them. At least the beast that had attacked them was a big pile of dust in the tunnels under Edinburgh.

After packing all the clothes Klara could find, and messaging her dad that Grams signed her up for a five-day spirituality trip in the Highlands (which he believed, to her surprise), they piled into the old red Fiat and left Grams's flat.

First stop: mystic center, the Fairy Glen in Skye.

Normally, when she wasn't careening toward possible murder by a supernatural entity, Klara loved driving at night. She loved the bright splash of headlights across the pavement, the flashing animal eyes that peered out from the edge of a dense wood. The loneliness of the empty, winding Scottish roads was the polar opposite of the teeming streets of Manhattan, but she found them just as thrilling. As she and Callum drove farther from the flat, her dad, and everything familiar to her, she was doubly thankful for the veil of darkness that made it more difficult to see what she was leaving behind.

If only she could see where she was heading toward.

She gripped the wheel harder. The five-hour drive to the ferry then to the Fairy Glen, where who knows what awaited them, was almost over. She had been to the nearby Fairy Pools with her mother, but something told her this trip was going to be quite different than playing hide-and-seek. For the millionth time since she'd started driving, she wondered what Thomas had discovered there.

Whatever it was, it hadn't helped him survive.

In any case, she was five hours closer to her destiny: Pillar of Time. But she felt like the same old Klara, only twice as groggy.

Eventually, the road curved and grew narrow as she turned off the highway. Klara took a sip of the cold, bitter coffee she'd taken from her grandma's. Another close call with vehicular homicide was *not* what she needed right now. God forbid another time traveler appear from nowhere. Mental note: *Do not rescue.*

From the way Callum kept glancing down at himself, she got the sense that he actually liked his seventies attire. He had insisted on packing more of Albert's clothes. He tugged at the shirtfront, looking almost small in his oversize hippy clothing. Not at all like the guy who just yesterday had stabbed a mythical beast to death. Callum couldn't stop staring at the light bouncing off his shiny faux-leather pants, like a cat mesmerized by a laser pointer. He still managed to look incredibly good in something that should've been very, very ridiculous. Klara tried to keep her eyes on the road and *off* the deep V of flesh she could see under his silk shirt.

Not that Callum noticed her gawking. When he wasn't gazing in wonder at his clothes, his eyes were fixed outside the window, where the light of the nearly full moon revealed the outline of a jagged northern coast. From memory, she knew there was an expanse of angry gray sea just beyond. She rolled down the window and breathed in the salt-laden air, letting it flow into her body and perk up her senses.

"Have you been to Skye?" She had to raise her voice to be heard over the wind now rushing into the car.

Callum perked up, too. "I havna seen it with my own eyes."

"You will soon."

Klara had been to Skye with her mother when she was little, but when she finally reached the car park, she realized her memory did the sight little justice. Drenched in moonlight, the rolling, ridged hills seemed to undulate within the valley. It was like standing on the back of a great beast. (*The good kind*, she thought to herself.) Waterfalls flowed freely down the mountains, spreading life across the land until they escaped into the endless ocean.

"We should head to Castle Ewen, it's at the highest point in the glens," Klara said, recalling the site her mother had taken her to. Squinting, she located the outcropping of rock in the distance and pointed.

Callum followed where she pointed. "Why there?"

"My mom always said that's where the fairies hid. Maybe there's something to it," she said. Normally, saying something so kiddish would have embarrassed her. But now that magic had begun to permeate her life, the weight of it pushed in at every seam and corner of her. She felt the weight of it. Suddenly, it didn't seem so silly.

Callum nodded. "To Castle Ewen, then. We have a few hours before dawn, when spirits can better cross the threshold."

"Right," Klara said.

After getting out of the car, she slung the sword over her shoulder and walked through the grass toward the Fairy Glen, Callum trailing closely behind. Her gut tumbled and roiled, pulled from either end: she felt guilty at the danger Callum was putting himself in; at the same time, she liked having him close.

"We won't need a flashlight—a torch," she clarified for Callum's sake. "The moon's bright enough tonight."

Klara liked to think that in Scotland, people wouldn't have balked at a young woman carrying a sword. Luckily, no one was on the path that led to Castle Ewen at this ungodly hour. Just in case, though, she'd put the weapon into one of Granny Laura's old hockey stick bags. It wasn't like there were any guns handy in bonnie old Scotland, not that she would have wanted to use one anyway. The bulky weapon banged against her back with every step toward their destination.

Before she lived in a world with monsters, swords were

things of the past and fantasy. Now, she hoped the one at her back was as deadly as it was beautiful.

Callum strode ahead of her and whirled around, walking backward to speak to her. "Do ye ken how to wield a sword, lass?"

The flirty, musical lilt to his voice made the butterflies in her stomach stir, but she knew it was only an act—the tension plain on his face revealed the truth of what was lying underneath. *Fear. Danger.* But if she thought of what actually might lie in store for them when they reached the mystic center they were heading to—another scaled beast, the flash of fangs, or worse, the man who'd tried to kill her, or *even worse*, some unknown threat—she wasn't sure she'd be able to keep going.

"If you can travel through time, I can figure out how to use a sword," she said. "Have you ever heard of *mansplaining*, Callum? Maybe you can take the concept back to your time and spread the word. It would spare womankind a lot of trouble."

He grinned at her. How could Klara take anything seriously when Callum was parading around in faux leather pants? *No one gets killed by a magical beast when they're wearing faux leather,* she told herself.

After a few minutes' walk which grew steeper with every step, Klara and Callum reached Castle Ewen. Klara stopped, trying to hide how her chest was heaving with exertion, and pretended to admire the view. The land undulated out around and below them—litcrally rippled in small rolling ridges, as if someone had dropped a pebble into calm water or pulled up the rug of earth and given it a sharp tug. It would have taken her breath away if she'd had any to spare.

Next to her, Callum breathed in the night air in one deep

breath. Then, he tipped his head back and let it all out, yelling at the top of his lungs.

His voice wrenched the air open. For a second, the goose bumps on Klara's skin had nothing to do with the cold. The next second, the noise echoed and faded despite how hard Klara wanted to hold on to it.

Callum turned to her, looking slightly shy. "Something Thomas and I used to do." He smiled. "Give it a try, lass."

But suddenly, Klara wasn't feeling so bold. Going to meet your destiny was understandably nerve-racking. Still, he looked happy, so she took a deep breath and whooped into the silence.

As her voice echoed back at her, she realized: she *did* feel better.

A gust of wind shot straight through her sweater. She pulled it tighter and craned her neck upward. The sky above was uninhibited by a single cloud. But she knew better than to trust the weather in Scotland, where it changed with the slightest breeze. One moment it would be clear skies, followed by a sudden downpour with a dusting of hail.

Klara used to think there was something poetic about it: nothing was certain, and everything was subject to the whims of unseen forces that guided the universe. Mother Nature called the shots.

Now that she was subject to those whims—caught up in the drama of time and gods—the fickleness of the weather didn't seem so poetic. It seemed cruel.

Bent over, Callum milled around her. Picking up sticks, she realized. She watched as he motioned to a relatively flat patch of ground sheltered by the outcropping of rock.

"What are you doing? An offering to the gods?"

"Ye're cold," he said. "Might as well keep warm while we wait for dawn. Got a few hours yet, no use wastin—"

"Energy?"

Callum glanced up at her, smiling. "Aye."

He clashed two stones together. A spark jumped out and into the sticks. Within seconds, the fire was blazing.

Klara wasn't about to argue. Exhausted, she let the bag drop onto the ground with a clatter and knelt near the fire. After hesitating for a moment, Callum crouched next to her. Their knees brushed. Even though the contact was brief, she found it hard to ignore.

He turned his head. "Wind's coming from behind us. Better if we block it out like this." He stared straight into the fire, but Klara saw the tension around his eyes. Was he trying not to look at her?

She cleared her throat, rubbing her pinched shoulder with one hand. "Who knew a sword could weigh so much? It's wild to think people used to carry these around all day."

Callum chuckled. "Not everyone in my time uses swords, lass."

Klara lowered her voice, teasing. "So you don't know how to use one?"

That wiped the smirk off Callum's face. He bristled, looking at her now. "Aye, *I* know how to wield a sword. I was taught to protect my Master Brice, on occasion. Ye could learn, too."

"Are you sure? I took an archery class at summer camp and almost impaled my instructor with a rogue arrow." Her face scrunched up. "He cried."

Callum gently grabbed her arm. His eyes were full of concern. Klara stopped breathing.

"What?" she said breathlessly.

He gingerly touched her hairline. "Your bruises. I hadn't noticed them before."

Klara caught her reflection in her phone camera: under the flickering firelight, she looked like death incarnate. Everything looked worse on pale skin. Veins, bruises, pimples. And that's not even taking sunburn into account. Self-conscious, she pulled her hair in front of her shoulders, letting strands fall over her face.

"They'll go away."

Meanwhile, Callum wore his beat-up look like a natural. His tanned face bore cuts and bruises, too, but on him, they blended into his features. He was a fighter, she reminded herself. Rugged was clearly his uniform. The way he carried himself suggested he fought off ravening beasts every night before bed. "You look..."

"Handsome?" he quipped.

Yes.

Klara didn't say it aloud. She said the second thing that came to mind. "If you're such a master swordsman, why don't you teach me?"

Klara hadn't really been serious. But Callum was.

She had a handful of talents. Crashing essays at the last minute. Executing a decent cat-eye. Making a perfectly bitter cup of iced coffee. Fighting was not one of them.

Growing up in New York, it was a rite of passage to learn how to defend yourself from a bag thief, or worse. Unfortunately, aside from knowing not to tuck her thumb in her clenched fist when throwing a punch, the self-defense class she and her mom had taken together at the Y was a hazy memory. She had been just surprised as Callum was when she knocked him down in the grove days earlier.

Even though his face was deadly serious, Callum was clearly having too much fun with her sword, which he had already withdrawn from the bag. Once again providing ample evidence to support her thesis that boys hadn't changed much since the sixteenth century.

He stood, offering her his hand. She stared at it.

"Can't we start off with sticks?" she said, her voice a few notes higher than usual.

He raised his eyebrows. "Why would we do that?"

"So I can work my way up to the scary pointy stuff?"

Callum tilted his head. "This is grave, lass. Are ye with me?"

"If I say no, does that mean we can use sticks?"

"No," he said sternly. "Learning to protect yourself is vital."

Still, she said, "But we killed the beast."

He bent low over her, until his lips were practically brushing her ear. "There's never only one."

Klara didn't want him to think she needed saving, but a quick tongue and a right hook would only go so far. She took a deep breath and pulled herself up. Their chests bumped, and the impact seemed to wipe the bravado off Callum's face.

Widening his stance and crouching slightly, he lifted the sword, both hands securely gripping its thistle-shaped hilt. His arm muscles strained against the fabric of his shirtsleeves. Her lower belly stirred.

"Ye froze in the tunnel," he said.

It wasn't easy for her to admit her fears. She'd rather keep them buried deep. "And?"

Callum came up to her, leaving only a foot between them. He looked her deep in the eyes. "I used to freeze, too, when I first started fighting."

"Really?"

"Really. I would get pummeled. My master, Brice, would be so mad that the beating wouldn't stop until I did better in the next fight."

Her heart squeezed. "He hit you?"

He looked away from her, but not quickly enough to hide the pain in his eyes. "I will never make ye do anything ye dinnae want to do, but all I request of ye is that ye try. For me."

She swallowed. There was that feeling again, a powerful *swoop*, like a dip on a roller coaster. "Okay. But if I draw blood, you asked for it."

He rounded her so her back was to his chest. The breath she had just taken hitched in her throat.

"Open your hand." He slid the hilt of the sword into the crook of her open hand. "Feel the weight."

"'Kay," she said quickly. She found it hard to feel anything but him behind her. As if reading her thoughts, he stepped away and moved back into her line of sight. "Stick it straight out before ye."

She did as she was told, holding the heavy blade outward. The sword felt incredibly balanced in her grip, the handle growing warm in response to her touch. "Not bad, right?"

He smiled at her mischievously. "Now, hold it there until I say stop."

About thirty seconds in, her arms started to tire and shake. Klara glanced at him from the corner of her eye. Callum smiled but shook his head. She groaned but stared down the blade and into the distance, taking sudden interest in a lonely cloud that blew across the sky.

"Stop," Callum said. She dropped the tip to the ground.

"How will this help me fight?" she asked, shaking out each arm.

"Ye need to understand the strength it takes to wield a sword for a prolonged period of time."

Over the half hour, he made her do strengthening exercises. Moving the blade up and down, side to side. Only when her arms felt like they were going to fall off did he start with technique.

But instead of working with the sword, he disappeared over the other side of Castle Ewen, only to return with two sizable sticks.

She rolled her eyes.

"Why couldn't we start off with sticks?" Klara asked, taking it into her hand.

"Ye also need to ken what 'tis like to fight when ye're tired."

"Wow, Callum, nice to see you coming out of your shell finally. Sword master becomes you."

"I dinnae take your meaning, but I hope 'tis meant to be good." He stood before her and moved into a wide stance, raising his own stick aloft. "Do as I do."

She mirrored him, following him as if they were dancing. It was hard not to laugh. Impossible, actually. A giggle escaped with every other step.

His arm shot out and gripped her waist, swiveling her around so her back was against his chest. He rested his stick just below her neck.

"Do ye think this is funny, lass?"

"Yes, actually," she said, flicking the stick, trying to ignore the rise of his chest against her back.

He let her go and she missed his momentary closeness.

"You're right," she said, turning to him. "It's just hard to take myself seriously, that's all. I'm not a fighter, Callum. I'm not like you."

"Ye are. Believe me, I ken. I can see it."

Clearing her throat, she moved back into the stance. Feet planted hip-width apart. Left leg one step forward. Callum nodded approvingly.

"Where ye place your feet is almost as important as how ye hold your weapon."

More than once, she fell on her back as Callum jostled her back and forth, a shoving match she was destined to lose but that taught her how to plant a back foot, or dodge to the side. In the dancing light of the fire, he showed her when to block, and when to step away. How to back away while staying balanced. How to press forward without overextending. Then, he showed her how to strike. To follow through on a swing, and how to bring the sword back to defend should she miss the first.

She was surprised by how easy the movements came to her. It felt like the stick was an extension of her body and maybe the weight of the sword would prove her wrong but for now at least, she felt pride in this new skill.

When they began to spar, he went easy at first, then harder

as she improved so that she could barely tell she was improving at all. He lunged low, swiping at her ankles. The first few times he tried this, she fell on her butt. But the third time, she expected it.

Swipe.

Klara leaped over the swooping stick, twisting around before sweeping her stick down toward the base of his throat.

"Dead!" she cried triumphantly.

Callum ducked the blow, whipping out a leg as he dipped. Her ankles swept from under her, and she collapsed on top of him.

"Not dead yet," he said, grinning.

Klara leaned forward and suddenly, their lips were millimeters apart. She twisted her body, straddling him in one smooth motion, and held the stick to his throat. Callum stared down the blade at her, eyebrows raised in surprise and approval.

"Leaving aside my distraction, that was finely done."

Klara removed the stick from his throat, heart pounding in her throat. "Maybe I was a champion swordsman in another life."

"You've got the basics down, I'll grant ye, but ye still must practice. Men train lifetimes to learn swordcraft. The muscles need to learn, too, and that takes time."

"Time is exactly what I don't have." Klara laid the blade flat against her palm, staring into the shining metal. Her muscles already felt easy and loose, recovering quicker than she'd expected. Still. "Like I could ever stand a chance against that guy."

"He will get what's coming for him. Evil men like him always do," Callum said.

His body stilled, but she could practically hear the desire for vengeance whirring inside him. He ran his fingers over the blade of the sword. The weapon brought something out in him, and she wasn't sure she liked it.

"I feel different with ye, like I have a purpose in life other than to earn my keep," he said softly.

She snorted. "Protecting a helpless maiden?" Her words were laced with sarcasm.

"'Tis more than that. I feel…" He met her eyes, and the look in them stilled her completely. "Free."

A crackling quiet settled between them. He pressed his palms into the ground. Settling next to him, she did the same, laying her hand so close to his that their fingertips almost touched. Before she could move, or breathe, Callum's eyes fixed on the rock formation in the distance.

"Look," he said, pointing up the inclining thin path at Castle Ewen.

A mist was curling around the rock. It grew thicker, almost opaque, and curled into undulating fingers of gray that reached toward the sky. Twisting and spinning, the strands rose, rose, rose—until it collapsed suddenly, pooling at her feet. The mist flowed down the ridged green hill like water down the drain.

Klara froze.

They were no longer alone.

CHAPTER FIFTEEN

CALLUM

The mist enshrouded Callum as they climbed toward Castle Ewen. Around them, the land moaned as the wind whipped over it, rattling the rocks like the bones in a soothsayer's cup.

A woman stood before them.

He blinked.

The woman remained.

She was lithe, with an elegant, tall frame, and her face was the color of the moon. Catlike golden eyes peered out above full lips. Long tendrils of silky golden hair framed her pale, angular face, and as Callum's gaze lingered, the moon set them aglow. Her delicate neck disappeared into a dark cloak which billowed around her, yet somehow left no curve to the imagination.

Klara's arm went limp on his shoulder, a look of shock splashed across her face. Her knees crumpled as she stumbled over a protruding rock. Callum stood as confidently as he could in the presence of a goddess, helping Klara to her feet alongside him.

"I know you," Klara whispered. "I saw you, in the stars."

"And I, you," the woman replied.

Klara took a hesitant step forward, squaring her shoulders, but Callum held on to her fast. He was afraid of what might happen if she got too close. "Who are ye?"

"The Silver Wheel," she said simply.

Callum and Klara exchanged another glance. He could almost hear the words that rang out in her head. They were the same swirling inside him, transporting him back to Grams's home.

Goddess of the Silver Wheel. She is often associated with the moon, and was thought to hold dominion over time and the sky.

Callum's hair stood on end. With a lurch of recognition, he realized he had seen those golden eyes before, belonging to the owl perched on the alley wall when he searched for Thomas in Kelpie's Close—now that he recognized them, they were unmistakable. He recalled Grams's words, about gods visiting the earth in the bodies of animals.

The realization of who the woman was struck Callum harder than any punch.

"Arianrhod?" he breathed.

"I have many names, and that is one. And you…" She paused, letting her eyes settle on Callum. The mist swirled around his feet in milky tendrils. "You are a warrior. Yet you have lost your way and your fight."

Callum swayed on his feet. Though her gaze betrayed no emotion, it pierced clean through him, leaving a white-hot trail of shame in its wake. He wanted to argue. To fight and scream and demand that she take it back. But he could not—because in his deepest heart, he knew she spoke the truth.

Klara broke the heavy silence. "You're wrong." Her voice was sharp, but he detected a quiet tremble lingering just underneath the edge. It seemed the goddess did, too. A shadow of a smile danced across her lips, though her mouth remained unmoving.

"My child. Whether you recognize me as I am here, in front of you, you know me, just as I know you. I will show you."

Arianrhod lifted her hands. In response, the fog gathered around them again, spiraling upward at the behest of her fingers. A familiar form took shape in front of Callum's eyes. His chest wrenched open with disbelief and wonder.

When the goddess's hands stilled, Thomas stood before them.

Without thinking, Callum stepped forward, hand outstretched. Klara moved quickly into his path, pressing her palms into his chest to stop him from going any farther. "It's not real, Callum."

Irritation whipped in his chest. He may not have been from Klara's time, but he was not such a fool as she thought him. "I ken, lass. I—"

Callum glanced over Klara's shoulder, where the conjured shape hovered. His voice cracked at the pale white visage of his friend, brought to life with light and shadow, standing only a few paces away. "I just want to look upon him."

With only a slight hesitation, Klara moved to his side, hooking her elbow in his as she turned.

Arianrhod dropped her hands, dispelling the likeness of Thomas back into thin mist. She shifted imperceptibly—*as the wind does*, Callum thought—to address Klara.

"You are both right and wrong about reality, child. Only humans think in this way. Only they consider what is real, what is imagined. Your vision is as a rodent's vision to that of a hawk. You only perceive a sliver of the world as it truly is."

"I'm beginning to realize that," Klara said. "I wish you would explain how it *really* is to us, because of our puny mortal vision and all."

Arianrhod looked back upon Klara. "You understand so little, child." Callum thought the goddess was wrong there—there was so much Klara knew, and to see her stand tall in front of this Otherworldly being only strengthened his belief that she was indeed made for something great.

"Tell me how I can protect her," Callum demanded.

The goddess stirred. "The man who attacked your friend knew that Thomas's life was precious—more precious than most of the humans who walk this earth. There was a power in his blood more valuable than any mortal treasure, more valuable than the wealth of any queen or king who has ever lived."

Time seemed to slow as he listened to the words unfurl from Arianrhod's lips. He was caught in her gaze. It made him feel like an insect suspended in amber. If the woman in front of him were human, she would have blinked. But she only continued to appraise him as she spoke, her honey eyes aglow—the night sky aflame, encircled in two sockets.

I tried to protect him. The words screamed in his head, but they wouldn't leave him. They lay in his stomach, heavy and rotten.

"He…" Arionrhod's voice caught and a darkness flashed in her eyes, and was gone. "He spilled Thomas's blood to steal this power from him. He sought to use it—to *corrupt* it, to bend it to his will—for his own purposes."

One hand still hooked around Callum's elbow, Klara addressed Arianrhod. "Did he use the power to travel in time? To attack me?" Her tone volleyed between wonder and disgust.

Callum recalled Klara's words. *A great deal of energy.* "Why Thomas?"

Arianrhod dipped her chin. "Thomas was *chosen* to be a vessel."

Beside him, Klara sucked in a breath. "To be a Pillar of Time?"

"Yes. Just like you are, Klara," she affirmed.

Face taut, Klara shook her head weakly. "I don't understand how that's possible. I—" She stopped, looking suddenly pale, though her cheeks were pinched bright red. "I'm not a vessel."

Arianrhod shifted, and the mist shifted around her. "Before the realm of man and the gods fully diverged, I grew weary of being pursued for my powers—dominion over the sky, the moon, and even of time itself—and so I divided them amongst ten human souls that would be born into your world, a place no god may ever enter themselves without great sacrifice, great power, and great risk to both worlds. Spread across the centuries, each of the ten chosen ones became a Pillar of Time, with my power sealed within their blood."

The mist shifted and re-formed into the silhouettes of ten faceless people, each with a swirling orb at their heart center.

"It was unknown to them, buried deep. Dormant to their use, so that none would know. Once the last Pillar dies, my power will be transferred into the earth. Though, in order for that to come to pass, it has to gradually be given over, which is why I transferred it to the Pillars."

The light danced on Klara's wide-eyed face. "That's ir-responsible. Giving them something like that, without their knowledge."

Arianrhod's gaze took on a hollow emptiness, and Callum had the sudden impression that she was looking not at, but through him. "It was meant as a blessing," she said, almost bitterly. "If I allowed them to have that knowledge, even the well-meaning may have been corrupted. Sovereigns have de-stroyed entire kingdoms for less."

Callum could not tear his eyes away from his friend's face smiling out at him from among the faceless. The memory of Kelpie's Close came back to Callum: the killer's blood-splattered skin, his cruel laugh, his unnatural strength.

"But ye failed," he insisted, frustration and anger rising within him. "Thomas figured it out, as did someone else, and he was killed for it—killed for your power, like a lamb to slaughter. He was in danger, and ye did nothing."

Too late, Callum saw that his bold words had provoked the goddess. She seemed to swell before him, the mist at her feet igniting into silver flames that formed a white-hot corona around her. "Do not speak of what you do not know," she thundered, her cool veneer falling away to reveal the sheer, raw power underneath.

Callum stumbled back a step as, with seeming effort, Arionrhod lifted her hand and quelled the flames. She stood before them as before, but now he sensed the danger hidden beneath her beauty.

Seconds passed as she stared unblinkingly at him with her eerie golden eyes. When she spoke again, her voice seemed sharpened like a blade. "The man who has corrupted this power uses it to travel through time. He has been flitting in and out of human history, killing the Pillars with a weapon stolen from the gods long ago in order to better harness the power of the blood he spills. He gathers my powers unto himself, growing more godlike—and powerful—with each death."

Klara and Callum exchanged a glance. "A beast attacked us. Was that his doing, too?" Callum asked.

"He has taken his power unnaturally, used it unnaturally, and so it manifests in unnatural ways. With every perversion, he disturbs the boundaries between worlds, each time producing a wilder magic than anyone can control or contain."

Arionrhod's shoulders seemed to sag as she considered the two of them. "What he refuses to understand," she sighed, "is that he can never fully possess the abilities he so desperately seeks. But that does not mean he cannot do great harm as he tries."

"But why would someone do this?" Klara demanded.

Ariaonrhod didn't answer right away. She gazed past them at the ancient rock formation rising from rolling verdant landslips, its stark beauty undiminished by time.

She finally turned back to Klara, a challenge in her voice. "You would not want to assume the power of a god, child? To break the barriers of time itself and bend it at your will?"

Klara was undaunted. "Not every human is a megalomaniac."

Arianrhod lifted one silver eyebrow, granting her the point. "But this man is no human."

Another pause, longer this time, until she seemed to come to a decision.

"This man...he was not always stained with evil. Once, he was the most beautiful..."

Her voice trailed off, but then she shook her head almost angrily and began again. "He was born with an aberration within him, one that would reveal itself in time to have consumed him from within, leaving behind a hunger that could not be contained."

She seemed to summon some power from deep within her, the mist encircling her flickering and stuttering.

"He is a demigod, and his name is Llaw," she said, her voice eerily empty. "He is my son."

It took Callum a second to absorb what the goddess had said. Beside him, he sensed Klara's shock in her sharp intake of breath.

"Millennia ago, the gods you know now lived much as humans do—we fell in love, satisfied lust. We hurt others, and we were hurt."

Emotion stirred in Callum. He was familiar with the tales of the gods, of course, but it was another thing entirely to hear it directly from the lips of a goddess.

He thought of Klara's grandmother, who still maintained a connection to the magic seeded into this land and its people. Thomas, too, had been constantly slipping away in search of the gods.

"A connection between worlds is created when divine energies, relegated to their realms, seek and find one another across an otherwise uncrossable chasm. Usually, the connection is as weak as a single thread, and easily snapped."

Arianrhod stepped closer. Something had changed—her features had sharpened in her lovely, shimmering face, her lips twisted in a mockery of a smile. Any tenderness, any weakness he might have glimpsed in her had vanished, and Callum felt a surge of fear. A gentle pressure on his elbow told him that Klara wavered where she stood, but remained in place. "But Llaw would disrupt the balance of our worlds by harnessing this power, undoing this careful balance."

"But how can I enter the Otherworld without disrupting the balance?" Klara asked.

"Because the power within you is meant to be, but Llaw's acquisition of the power is tainted, impure, whilst yours is pure. Meant to be."

The goddess took another step closer. At this distance, Callum could see the goddess more clearly. She wore her beauty like a mask, but there was something unearthly swimming just beneath her features, as distant and magnificent as the moon itself.

"Llaw must be stopped, before he takes your life, and I lose my power. He has already taken the power from the other nine vessels, but my power can all be restored as long as you live past Samhain. He wants more than anything to be a god, and live in our realm. Killing you is the only way to gain my power, and step into our world—colliding two separate worlds, so delicately connected now, into one aberration." Arianrhod stared coolly at Klara.

"So I'm a means to your end." Realization seemed to dawn on Klara. "If I can't stop Llaw from killing me, you lose."

Arianrhod nodded. "Yes, but humanity loses, too. If he succeeds, the consequences will be unlike anything your world has ever seen. He could usher in a new era of god and man—and undo time itself."

"And what exactly *happens* when time unravels, pray tell," Klara asked, crossing her arms.

"For me? Nothing at all. For humanity, space and time will fracture. Eras will crash into each other, all scientific theories disproven, a chaos will erupt that cannot be mended," Arianrhod said. "But Llaw, he's determined...dangerous, and I cannot allow him to move forth with his plans."

Callum caught Klara as she fell against him. Fear worked its fingers into his body, too, mercilessly gripping his stomach, throat, chest until he could scarcely breathe. Still, he forced the words out of his throat. "He will not succeed."

"I've seen your world throughout the ages, many succeed when they believe what they are doing is just," Arianrhod uttered, and her voice seemed weaker, as if speaking was taxing to her. Callum looked above her golden crown of tresses. Behind them, the sun had crested the horizon. The goddess was fading. Confirming his suspicion, she paused, closing her eyes as if collecting her strength. "I am confined to my own world and can only reach into your world where the barrier is thin. To do otherwise would be to risk destroying the balance of your world and mine. The balance I have so carefully constructed is now tipping."

"Then—what do we do now?" Klara asked.

"You Klara, must deepen your connection with what lies

within you. You must seek out the mystic centers and by doing so you will be able to unlock your powers with each one."

Klara shook her head. "But you'll help us defeat him, right?" she asked.

"I can no longer cross worlds without dire consequences. Llaw has made it so. I come now to offer you this message—my warning—but nothing more for the sake of all that's at risk."

Klara's mouth fell open. "*What? That's it? Why*—"

The question went unanswered, because with a tilt of the goddess's chin, a tendril of mist rose and encircled Klara's head. Her mouth parted slightly. She touched her ear. As she did, the mist lost its form and came at her like a wave.

She flew back, hair whipping around her before landing on her back staring up at the sky.

Head spinning, she loosened a long groan.

Taking a deep breath, she picked herself up just as Callum reached her. "I'm fine," she said, warding him away with her hand. "Arianrhod—"

Their heads snapped around, searching for her. Morning light flooded the Fairy Glen, illuminating everything in the lush landscape.

He searched for Arianrhod but the goddess was gone.

CHAPTER SIXTEEN

KLARA

Klara was about to be sick.

A time-traveling murderer and an actual goddamn *goddess*.

Throwing up was the only thing that made sense right about now.

Next to her, Callum fumed. His whole body was animated—chest heaving, hands working through his hair, legs working to stand. "Llaw." He spit the name out like poison and leaped to his feet.

He looked down at Klara. The new sun burned in the sky behind him, framing his body and weaving trails of light along his mussed hair. "This man cannot live. We will find a way to kill him, Klara."

He extended his hand to help her to her feet, but Klara

didn't move. She couldn't even process the simple task of standing up, let alone *killing* someone. A demigod. Her stomach revolted at the thought. She squeezed her eyes shut to push out the nausea. It didn't work.

Then there was what Arianrhod had whispered to her. Whispered but not whispered, putting the words directly into her head. *You can send Callum home.*

"Klara?" Callum's voice from above. "What is it?"

She brushed the goddess's voice in her head away. "Nothing."

"'Tis obviously something," Callum said with concern.

"I—I don't want to be here anymore." The rippling hills, which glowed green in the early sun, might as well have been ashen. "Can we please go back to the car and get the hell out of here?"

"Where shall we go?"

Her head ached. She hadn't slept in twenty-four hours and she was beginning to feel it. "I don't know yet, Callum, I just need to drive."

"But Llaw—"

"You can't just go around *killing* people, Callum," she said, trying to force confidence into her voice. If anything had been true in her life until two days ago, it was definitely that.

Callum didn't back down. His expression softened. She swore she felt his heart beating, only inches away from her. "But you heard Arianrhod. This man will slaughter ye if we do nothing."

She turned and began to walk the way they had come. "I know."

"Llaw is coming for ye. To kill *ye*."

Callum's voice caught. The emotion in it made her stomach swoop until the reality of his words cut through her butter-flies. *Kill.* His fingers wrapped around her throat again, cold and unfeeling. She shuddered. Llaw had murdered the other nine Pillars for Arianrhod's power—the power that, accord-ing to the goddess, flowed through *her* veins. Through her very much *alive* body. A power that she never asked for and definitely didn't want.

Klara was the only Pillar left.

But she wasn't a hero. She wasn't a *murderer.* Was she?

Callum's silence scorched her all the way to the car. She shoved it into Drive and pulled onto the main road, wheels shrieking. Callum said nothing, though a quick glimpse be-trayed a greenish tint to his skin.

At first, the groaning roar of the car beneath them loosened the tightness in her chest. But less than a mile away, her body squeezed back in revolt. The edges of her vision blurred. She slammed the brakes and gripped the wheel, shaking.

Callum peeled her fingers off the wheel and held her. She looked at his hand in hers—his bruised knuckles, his scarred skin. She imagined the bones that had broken underneath, the blood his blows had spilled. Had *he* killed a man? Was it that simple?

"The world is in danger, so it's up to me, right? But I'm not a killer." She meant it to come out as a statement, though it sounded more like a question.

Frustration clouded his features. *"Klara—"*

Her chest clamped shut. Heart beat wildly under her ribs. *Breathe.* She needed to breathe.

"Please give me a minute, Callum. I have a lot on my mind

with this whole 'it's on you to save the world' thing," she begged.

Avoiding Callum's intense gaze, Klara pulled over and got out. She had only walked a few steps when she glanced back to see that Callum had stayed rooted to his seat, though from the way he held himself in place it was clear his entire body was in revolt. She knew how much he wanted to help her, but he couldn't help her with this.

She walked along the tree line without seeing. Grass cushioned her footfalls. Twigs cracked under her shoes. The sharp *snap snap snap* quieted her screaming head and pounding heart. Soon, she found herself weaving in between trees, the road long gone behind her.

Stomach heaving again, she doubled over.

But nothing came, aside from that pressing feeling in her chest. Why hadn't she just hopped behind the wheel, blasted Metallica, and driven as far away as possible when she'd found Callum in the middle of the road?

No matter how much Klara wanted to, she couldn't push away the knowledge that she would have still ended up here. Alone.

Or dead.

She sucked in a breath. Then another. The idea of her holding the power of a goddess in her freaking *blood* scared her even more, not to mention the whole "you're all that's standing between a supervillain and the destruction of time itself" tangle.

If Helen of Troy's beauty started a war, then Arianrhod's powers could start a worldwide extinction.

Klara looked to the pale blue sky, overwhelmed by all the

questions she hadn't asked Arianrhod. Though it was impossible to see in the bright of day, Klara pictured the goddess's glowing constellation puncturing the dark night sky. Its fiery light traveled billions of miles to reach her eye. Just thinking about it made her breath slow and calm.

Callum might have said that sounded like magic.

Maybe it *was* magic. Was that why she had always been drawn to the universe—because she had a piece of Arianrhod inside of her?

You can send Callum home. She knew he had to go back. The past was his home…not the future. A light-headedness swept over her, making her sway harder, though she was already unsteady. She looked at her palms. Was it that simple? Though she hadn't realized it at the time, she had used her powers to push Llaw backward in time when he had tried to kill her in the Elder Forest. This had started with Callum. Maybe it could end with him, too.

"Come back," she whispered, thinking of Arianrhod.

Something inside her *pulled*.

She clasped a hand to her chest. It was the same feeling she'd gotten two days ago, when she'd been drawn back to Callum at the edge of the Elder Forest, same as the one she felt moments before in the car. Before she could wonder, really, if she was imagining things, the nagging pull became an urgent and sudden tug behind her rib cage.

"Not imagining things," she said aloud.

Or was it something else—the powers flowing through her blood? Arianrhod's words came back to her. *A connection between worlds is created when divine energies, relegated to their realms, seek and find one another across an otherwise uncrossable chasm.*

The planets and stars were held together or pushed apart by their smallest, invisible components—invisible to the human eye, at least—creating fields of attracting force that radiated from within. Klara thought of the earth below her feet, the planets and stars circling each other like hungry animals but never touching, just like the moon that Arianrhod governed, the same celestial body that caused the tides and so much more. With an invisible *pull*.

Too bad she had no idea what to *do* with it.

She cast a glance backward. Then, trying to let the tugging in her chest guide her, she stepped toward the direction she was being pulled. The force led her to a nearby section of woods that sprang up from the grass.

Inside the woods, it was difficult to imagine that this place existed outside of a fairy tale. Though she had traveled a lot, she still found the simplest of sights the most enchanting— and the forest was the simplest of all.

The scene bloomed with lush greenery, from the mossy floor to the trees that jutted up into the sky. Rays of sunlight cast beams through the canopy from above. The air felt thick, alive. She moved through the trees, and the feeling seemed to respond in kind, thumping in her chest alongside her heart.

The sun faded as she trekked deeper into the forest, adjusting her course in response to feeling, which was constantly shifting within her. Glistening specks drifted in the air. They reminded her of dust that filtered through a room, only visible when a ray of light shone upon them.

Klara paused, allowing the specks to land on her arm. The particles made her skin shine like a million tiny stars, as if it held the universe.

"What are you?" she breathed, wishing fiercely that she had her microscope on hand. She'd always loved microscopes, which were so much like telescopes: each examined worlds that could not be grasped by the human eye.

Movement flashed in her peripheral vision. Her breath hitched.

She'd almost missed it. A stag, standing in trees. Half in light, half in shadow. His branching antlers seemed to meld with the tree branches. The pulling feeling inside Klara settled low in her gut, as if to anchor her to the spot.

Majestic and unafraid, it began to approach her.

The animal strode toward her with soft, thudding steps. A stream of sparkling motes drifted in its wake, swirling and growing thicker, making the air behind him shiver with light. Its black eyes remained on hers. The longer she stared into them, the larger and darker they seemed to grow, until Klara felt they would swallow her whole.

Something far in the back of her mind told her to be afraid—but no fear came. Now standing in front of her, the stag felt as pure as the forest she entered. The invisible pull tugged at her again, drawing her forward.

Klara moved without thinking. She walked toward the animal with her hand outstretched, driven simply by the desire— the need—to make contact with it. To see whether or not it was real.

The beast lowered its great head, a hoof scraping back as it knelt in the soft leafy soil. *Was it kneeling for her?* Klara placed a hand on the side of its proffered neck.

The scene around her faded and blurred.

The sudden pull of the Otherworld dragged her into its realm.

The feeling was familiar, Klara expected Arianrhod to be on the other side, but instead she saw something—someone else.

As the mist subsided, she emerged into a grassy plain. Rolling hills went on as far as the horizon stretched, though her gaze was drawn, not to the landscape, but to who was in front of her.

She watched in awe as the stag fell away, its body transforming until the only thing that remained of the beast were its antlers, velvet-covered angles sprouting from long yellow hair. The antlers crowned a man—he stood in front of Klara, proud in his nakedness, his golden body lean but muscled. His modesty, covered by a simple cloth.

He was beautiful. Ethereal.

And then, just as suddenly as she entered the Otherworld, she was thrown out, landing back into the Mundane Realm.

The man who had just morphed before her was once again a stag, and started retreating back into mist. Attempting to re-orient herself, Klara watched him, when suddenly something went flying past her, almost knocking her to the ground. By the time her eyes landed on what it was, she barely had time to comprehend what lay before her. The stag was crumpled before her, his neck in the jaws of another beast. Familiar teeth sunk into the animal's furred flesh.

One of Llaw's beasts.

A sickly flush swept through her body. She had come to know that feeling all too well in the past few days.

Fear. Panic. *Run.*

The beast, similar to the one from the library, snapped its head up from the stag's neck, blood dripping from the pearly points of its teeth. She met its serpentine eyes. The stag, still breathing, was long forgotten to the creature—now, its full attention was on Klara.

Her relief for the stag was instantly replaced with terror.

The beast lunged at her.

The last time she encountered one of these creatures, she had frozen—but now, she allowed her instinct to take over. Her legs carried her away, as if working on their own. She darted between trees, forcing the beast to slow as it wove through trees less quickly than she did. When it was far enough from her, she swooped behind a tree and pressed her back to it. Seconds later, the beast growled a horrible, predatory rumble and stopped on the other side. Spit flew from its mouth and landed with a heavy smack on the tree, acid sizzling where it met the bark—right next to her face.

Klara struggled to still her heaving chest. The sword was back with Callum. All she had was her jacket and her phone and a weak left hook. She waited and tried not to breathe, taut as a wire.

When her heart slowed, she peeked around the tree—and saw nothing. She leaned farther out, daring to peer back to the spot where both creatures had just been. Neither the stag nor the beast was there.

No relief flooded through her body. Deep down, she knew she wasn't safe. She'd seen enough horror movies to know that when the killer disappears suddenly, it's never a good sign.

Out of sight, out of mind, my ass, Klara thought. *Just get to Callum.*

Careful not to make noise, she crept to the next moss-covered tree, but just as she darted behind its trunk, a sound split the air. A breaking branch.

Another growl sounded.

Another branch snapped and this time, she could pinpoint its location: directly above her.

Unfortunately, she made the mistake of looking up.

The beast's tail came first, swinging at her like a pendulum. The impact threw her back against a thin tree. Klara tried, and failed, to breathe through the pain as the beast descended like oozing slime, serpentine and slinking down the trunk.

She steeled herself and snatched up a branch that had splintered off when she hit the tree. It felt reedy in her hand, easily snapped—but it was something. She sure as hell wouldn't go down without a fight.

"I know you can't kill me," she tried. "I know Llaw will want to do it himself."

The beast, identical to the one that had attacked her in Edinburgh, slunk up to her. Acid spit dripped from its mouth. It brought its face within an inch of hers, a strange, intelligent hunger in its yellow eyes. Furious and trapped and desperate, she took the branch and swung. The branch cracked across its skull and broke. The beast did not flinch.

It growled.

Its leopard-like tail came around and pinned Klara against the tree. Splinters cut through the back of her jacket and into the soft flesh of her skin. She convulsed with a full-body shiver as its jaws opened.

This couldn't be it.

"Callum!" She screamed, then yelped. The beast's spit flecked onto her clothes, burning through her jacket and scorching flesh. Her shoulder burned, *smoked*. The pain was so harsh, so searing, that Klara barely registered the stag.

The stag charged from the left and slammed his antlers into the beast's side. The beast reared, its long neck flailing, releasing Klara, who slumped to the base of the tree. Gripping her shoulder, she forced herself up again, even though her body begged for her to just lie down and close her eyes.

The stag sunk its horns deeper into the beast's chest. A thick black substance oozed from the punctured skin. Her stomach clenched violently as she heard a *snap*, then watched as a piece of the stag's antlers fell to the ground.

Klara tried to forget about her burned shoulder, grinding her teeth against the pain. Callum wasn't here to save her. She had to save herself. She had to save the stag, even though she knew she should run and run and never look back.

The familiar magnetic feeling burst within her body. It magnified everything around her, loping out of her and around, connecting her to the trees, the ground, even the molecules of rain-dampened air.

The wind, once still, now howled. All the light around her was sucked away, leaving the stag and beast veiled in darkness. The world blurred, and she released, and the light burst back into it.

The energy that flowed was like a key unlocking a forgotten door. Two parts made whole. It was overwhelming but at the same time, comforting. She was in control.

And just like a key in a lock, the world clicked, too.

The wind ceased to howl and the forest came back into focus. But it was different now. The beast and the stag were interlocked and unmoving, completely still.

No—not still.

They had stopped completely.

Time had stopped.

She gasped, froze. The magnetic feeling that had been so strong flickered, then faded with a *whoosh*.

The beast blinked.

"Shit," she said.

Her heart sped up with the scene around her. Whatever she had done, whatever hold she had, was draining rapidly.

With the last of her strength, Klara grabbed the broken antler from the forest floor and rammed it into the beast's eye. The black pupil sunk like putty around the shard, which shuddered violently in her hand the deeper she plunged it. Her fingers vibrated and the force echoed back into her body, but the more she shook the tighter she held on, refusing to let go until she was sure the thing was dead or disappeared, pushing until the antler burst through the creature's eye cavity and into its brain. *Or whatever passed for its brain*, she thought with a lurch of her stomach.

The beast shrieked then collapsed into darkly shimmering dust, like the one had in the library.

She released the antler from her trembling hand and fell backward against the stag as adrenaline loosened its grip on her. His side rose and fell evenly against her back. Then, the heat shifted, and she felt comforting arms—human arms—wrap around her. *Safe*.

Barely able to open her eyes, she let go of whatever power she held.

The last thing Klara heard as the world faded around her was her name, half-spoken, drifting on the wind.

PART TWO

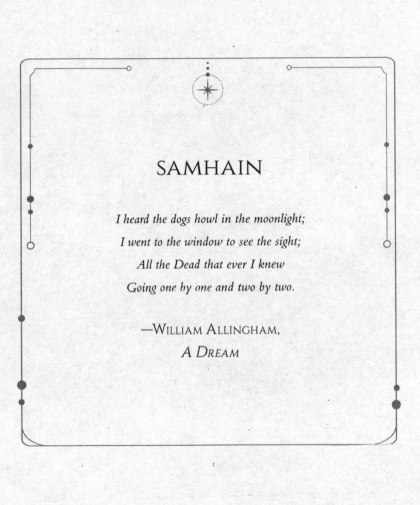

SAMHAIN

I heard the dogs howl in the moonlight;
I went to the window to see the sight;
All the Dead that ever I knew
Going one by one and two by two.

—WILLIAM ALLINGHAM,
A DREAM

CHAPTER SEVENTEEN

CALLUM

As he waited for Klara to return, he felt that the carriage wrapped around him like an iron cage. Callum pressed against the door, trying to spring it open. Finally, with a tug of the handle and pressure of his arm, it fell open—him with it. He breathed in fresh air, hoping it would calm his racing mind.

But the quiet outside did not help. There was nothing to drown out the memory of Arianrhod's speech, which echoed in his mind even though the goddess had returned to her realm.

Callum had not been chosen by a goddess. He was an accident of fate.

But his body—his very soul—screamed to be there, to be *worthy* of being there.

Klara's destiny had come to her. Thomas's, too, with deadly force.

Where was his?

Exhausted all at once, Callum sunk to the ground. Even after only a few days together, Klara's sudden absence left a pit in him. The memory of their near kiss at the edge of the fire—only hours ago—slammed into him all at once, a wave washing him away from shore and out to sea.

His cheeks flushed. Callum could face the assassin—even the goddess herself—with a relatively steady pulse, but the thought of their lips touching sent his heart racing. For a flash of a moment, he was glad she had gone. If she were there, she would witness how he fell apart in her absence.

An unearthly roar split open his thoughts.

Klara.

Grabbing the sword bag from the carriage, Callum ran. His legs carried him so far, so fast, that he wondered if Arianrhod had blessed him before she disappeared.

The sight of Klara lying prone on the forest floor sent panic charging through Callum. Her body was still.

He knew how to fight. He knew how to heal cuts and scrapes and calm a mild fever. He did not know how to heal this.

What had Klara done for him, when she'd found him in the road and brought him back to life?

Hands shaking, he knelt by her side. Carefully, he lifted her in his arms and curled her torso into his chest to keep her warm. But despite the chill in the air, her body was on fire, so hot that her flesh burned his skin. Shocked, he released her too abruptly, and winced as her body hit the ground with a soft thud.

She groaned, eyes shifting beneath lids. "You oaf."

He laughed with relief, running both hands through his sweat-slicked hair. "Are ye all right?"

She nodded without opening her eyes, and it seemed to take all the strength she had left. "Is it—is it gone?"

"Aye. For now," he said, casting a wary glance over his shoulder. "But I dinnae ken when it will be back."

She raised an arm. "Let's get the hell out of here, then."

Callum pulled her searching arm over his shoulder and lifted her to her feet. Her legs immediately gave way and she stumbled into him. This time, he did not let her fall. "Easy, Klara. We should take you to a healer."

"Callum, trust me, a modern doctor is not going to be able to help me with this. I'll be okay, I just need rest." Her head lolled. "It feels like seasickness, but all over. I can't—I can't—"

He pulled her more tightly to him. "I've got you."

Her hair hung limply over her shoulders; her face was alarmingly pale, though she managed a weak smile that tweaked his heart. "Good. Because you're going to have to drive."

Callum had no idea how to drive a carriage—car—but he did his best not to harm Klara further as he guided the juddering thing toward shelter.

Mercifully, they reached a small town. There were only a few buildings on either side of the compact road. One was a pub, another a market, and the last was a small inn. A thatched roof, thick with moss and vegetation, crowned the building; a billow of smoke puffed through the brick chimney and spiraled into the sky. Callum guided the carriage to the side of the road and followed Klara's instructions for parking it. The engine went silent. He wiped the sweat from his hands.

Careful to ease her from the car, Callum guided them through the door and into a small, cozy sitting room, where she sunk into the couch that stood near the door. Some of the color had returned to her cheeks, but a faraway look still lingered in her eyes. Though her gaze was peaceful—almost dreamlike—it cut another notch of fear in him. What had she seen in the forest?

"Wait," she said, just as he turned. She handed him a thin hard rectangle. "Give this to them. They'll know what to do with it. If they call you my dad's name, just go with it."

An old man stood behind the counter. His skin was weathered, and bore deep creases and sunspots, but his blue eyes were sparkling and youthful. He tipped his faded tartan flatcap to Callum, partially revealing wiry white hair beneath. A warm feeling swept over Callum: the man resembled Riley, Rosemere's baker, who had always slipped him and Thomas extra bannocks every Sunday—which they wolfed down, though his bannocks were honestly shite.

The man raised his brows, angling his head toward Callum expectantly. "Can I help ya, son?"

"I hope so, sir," Callum said. "Do ye have a room for the night?"

"Aye, lad." The old man pulled skeleton keys from the wall behind him. He pressed them into Callum's hand. "You're in luck—there's not many open sites around here, with Samhain comin' up."

Once inside the room, Klara collapsed on the bed, not even rousing as he lifted her legs to slide them gently beneath the blankets. In the sunlight that filtered in through the window, he noticed that a light dusting of gold had settled on her, giving her skin and clothes the appearance of shining marble. Her hair fanned out like flame on the soft pillow beneath her head. If it were not for her chest rising and falling with shallow breath, Callum might have thought her a statue.

Callum swallowed. Give him a man and a handful of coin, and he'd fight until his knuckles were bruised and bloodied. But it was hard to know what to do in this world—in this time. Callum considered his scarred knuckles, his rough palms. From his years with Brice, he knew he was only as valuable as his body, only as good as his strength. But his strength was nothing against Llaw's.

Klara slept. He knew not what she dreamed, but her chest rose and fell steadily—even peacefully. That, at least, was a temporary relief.

A thought pinched him in the dark, insistent and sharp. He would have preferred it were him. That way, Klara would have been safe. But he had not been chosen. Thomas had.

He had failed Thomas, but he wouldn't fail her.

It made him question if his friend met with the goddess, too? Or was it the bean-nighe that delivered news of his fate? The wind whistled through the cracks in the windowpanes. He imagined the bean-nighe singing to Thomas of his death. If everything else that Callum doubted had been proven real, so must the bean-nighe walk the earth.

Anyone who looked upon the bean-nighe was destined to die. But the spirit was not only a harbinger of death. If one could catch her by surprise, the bean-nighe was obliged to give him his most ardent desire.

The stories of his childhood came back to him now. *Gille-*

cas-fliuch, a washer boy, went gently and quietly behind bean-nighe
and seized her in his hand. "I will not allow thee away," said Gille-
cas-fliuch, "till thou promise me my desire."

Callum knew his deepest desire. He imagined demanding
that she grant him one gift—

Strength.

With strength, Callum could spill the blood that needed
to be spilled.

But there was no way to call the bean-nighe to him, even
if he dared to seize her—at least none that he knew of. *Aion*
could ken, he thought. But Callum certainly could not walk
to Edinburgh from Skye in a single night.

Standing again, Callum looked out the window. The
view of the village below was blocked by the thick, tangled
branches of a yew tree. If any threat were to appear, he would
only see it coming when it had reached them first. He imagined swinging the door open, met with the hot, putrid breath
of the beast—or worse, the blade of a demigod. Klara was
certain he would come for her on Samhain, but he did not
trust the devil not to have tricks up his sleeve.

Feeling for the dirk in his pocket, Callum pulled the blankets up to Klara's chin and left her to sleep while he descended
to the streets below.

"Laddie!"

Callum whirled, one hand on the front door and the other
immediately clenching into a fist. But it was only the man behind the counter calling to him. The generously browed gentle-
man held Klara's card aloft. He waved the black card in the air.

By now, Callum knew better than to ask why his money

was being returned to him—it was another part of Klara's world he couldn't hope to understand. Instead, he offered a smile as kindly as he could muster through his exhaustion. "I thank ye, sir."

The man offered a grin and a wink. Just as Callum was about to turn, something on the desk caught his eye. A shining black object similar to Klara's.

Callum cleared his throat. "Is that a phone?"

The man's brows flew up. "It is. Need to make a call?"

"Aye," he said slowly.

He was not sure yet what people of Klara's time would make of a time traveler. His gut told him to be careful. But an idea struck him, like a rope thrown to a drowning man. Maybe there was a way after all to find the information he needed about the bean-nighe without putting himself or Klara in danger. "Can I call anyone of my liking?"

"Well, that depends." He smirked. "Long distance will cost ya extra."

"I have no coin," he said.

"I'm only joking, lad." The man laughed and shrugged. "Ye look like a lost soul, but a kind soul. Who is it ye need to call?"

A moment later, after the innkeeper made the call, Callum pressed the object to his ear. Before he'd breathed a single breath, a gravelly voice answered.

"Finn & Fianna," Aion said.

"Hello, Aion—" Callum stopped abruptly when Klara's voice rang in his ear, a warning. *Don't.*

Callum opened his mouth, but regret gripped him immediately, stealing his words. He handed the phone back to the man before Aion could speak again.

CHAPTER EIGHTEEN

KLARA

The stag appeared in Klara's dream.

The animal glided toward her through a sparkling mist. Relief rushed through her as she took in the sight of it—his neck was whole and unblemished. Then, with a shifting of the mist, the stag's body transformed from beast to man. A golden aura surrounded him. It was the same man that had come to her in the forest.

She stepped back instinctively, expecting fear to come, but it didn't. Instead, a wash of warmth spread through her body. Something about the man's presence made her feel safe. Cared for. *Like Callum does*, Klara thought distantly.

He stopped a few feet away from her. She had to crane her head upward to meet his kind, grass-colored eyes. "You're alive. I thought—"

The man tilted his head to the side. His blond locks swung, brushing his shoulder. "I am not so easy to kill."

The softness of his voice shocked her. But what did she know about how stag-men spoke? His words blended with the sounds around them—the birdsong, the shifting of branches in the wind, the chirping insects—into the song of the forest itself. By his tone, he seemed almost disappointed in her question. "Humans think of death in such strange terms," he continued.

"So I've been told." Klara had obviously asked the wrong question. "Who are you? *What* are you?"

"I am Cernunnos, to some, though I am many things to many people. What am I?" he asked thoughtfully. "That depends on who you ask."

"*I'm* asking," she said simply. "Me, Klara."

A broad smile lit up his face. "To you, I am the god of the wilds. Of nature and, in a way, of life itself."

Two gods in two hours, she thought. "I thought the gods couldn't come into the realm of man?" That was what Arianrhod had told them, though she'd come to them anyway. "But I'm dreaming, so—you're not really here, are you? Just like Arianrhod wasn't there…"

"My essence is connected to the soil, the leaves, the trees, the oceans. In that sense, I never truly left the realm of man. Arianrhod on the other hand is tied to the sky, which is why you might've seen her there." His smile faded. The sadness that lurked in his dark eyes rose to the surface. "Though your oceans are polluted, your trees cut down, your animals slaughtered and starved to extinction. It is not much of a world to exist in."

Shame coursed through her. "Why are you here?" *Clearly not to give her a cheerful pep talk.*

Cernunnos tilted his head again, now as if she were something curious. "You called me to you."

"Call you?" Klara balked. "I didn't call you. I didn't mean to, at least." She looked at her hands again. They shimmered with the gold dust that she'd seen in the forest, though it was thicker here. The sight undulated as though she was looking at her hands underwater.

"I felt a connection to you. You felt a connection, too. Otherwise, you would not have had the power to call me to you, in the forest."

Was he talking about the persistent tugging in her chest, the pull that drew her into the woods? But Klara had no control over that—it had control over her. Right now, she felt like she didn't have control over *anything* at all.

Cernunnos lowered himself until his eyes were in line with hers. "I have heard whispers," he said. "Of a girl who walks my earth with the powers of a god in her, as others have. And you deny that you called me here?"

"Let's say I did call you. If I called you to me, does this mean I'm unlocking my...powers?" she asked. The words came out slow and halting as she fought the impulse to deny the truth of what lay within her.

"Arianrhod's power is rising within you, that much is certain."

"Certain?" She shook her head. "My whole world was just turned upside down, along with everything I thought I knew. *Nothing* feels certain anymore."

The stag god seemed to consider this. "There is certainty

in the world. Life, death, and rebirth. Cycles and change are the only things we can truly be certain of."

"That's exactly what I'm afraid of," she said. "Arianrhod told me that Llaw can undo time and space, causing catastrophic change."

Cernnunos only nodded, as if this were just another day in the life of an ancient god. *Maybe it was*, Klara thought with a jolt.

She considered the god carefully. Already, she'd interacted with gods long enough to know that they did not speak directly, but roundly. She would have to sift through his words if she wanted to get anything useful out of their meeting. Though it felt like they'd been pulled out of time itself, Klara might wake up in the real world at any moment.

"God of the wilds," Klara repeated, thinking. "The beast that attacked you, it's been attacking me, too. I thought we'd killed it, but it came back. Unless there are more than one…" Klara shuddered, sincerely hoping that was not the case. "Do you know how to destroy it?"

Cernnunos flinched at the word *destroy*. "It comes from the breach between worlds. It can only be destroyed by the powers of a god."

"Then why can't you destroy it?" she asked.

Cernnunos lowered his head. His grass-green eyes clouded over in thought. "I am a companion of journeys, I have helped usher souls to the places, traveling between the layers of our existence, the Otherworld, the Mundane Realm, and the Underworld. I help where my guidance is needed but my powers are no match for this."

Adrenaline coursed through her, making her light-headed,

even in her dream state. "There was someone else like me, in another time, and I think he was trying to figure out a way to stop Llaw. But he was killed before he could see his plan through. Can you help me talk to him? Or the other Pillars?"

"I cannot tell you of another's journey," he said sternly. "That is their knowledge, and theirs alone."

"What about Arianrhod herself?"

He shook his head. "Souls pass to and from the Otherworld, not messages."

"But that means I'm really the only one left." Klara's voice broke slightly, but she forced her way through the emotion climbing into her throat. "Arianrhod told me I have to kill Llaw, but I don't know if I can kill anyone."

The wilds shifted around Cernunnos. "And what if I told you that true death is impossible—that the soul never dies?"

She puffed out a breath. "I would still have to kill his body, never mind his soul. That's the part I'm not too pumped about." She mumbled the last part to herself.

Desperation rankled in her at the thought of Llaw's strength. Even if she wanted to kill him, she didn't know if she could. *Callum could.*

The last thought came suddenly, and she pushed it away just as quickly.

Cernunnos remained silent, and his silence was another infuriating riddle to be answered. Klara thought of souls, and her mother's face surfaced in her mind. It was her name on her tongue. Could the stag god see into her mind? Was that what he wanted to hear? Klara's grief, her pain?

Callum had talked about mortals being tested by the gods. Was *this* some kind of test?

The god stared at her. He stared *through* her, with his eyes like dark emeralds.

Another idea occurred to her. "What if I went there—to the Otherworld?"

"It is true that mortals have entered the Otherworld," Cernunnos's voice was measured, purposeful as he spoke. Klara felt a flood of relief until he continued. "But I cannot guide you there."

Disappointment extinguished the spark of hope. "Why?"

He held up a hand. Deep grooves swirled on the skin of his palm in intricate, interlacing patterns.

Her mouth went dry, the image of her mother flashing again in her mind. *No*, she thought, though the word refused to leave her lips. Under his unblinking stare, she averted her eyes to her feet. She was supposed to be figuring out how to hone the powers of a god. She was *supposed* to be following the path that Thomas had begun to forge and making sure she didn't die in the process, to complete the mandate of a goddess. But that wasn't her.

She was a girl who missed her mom more than anything, even with so much at stake.

Klara gritted her teeth and pushed the thought of her mother into the back of her mind.

"The solstice will soon occur in your world," Cernunnos said. "It is a time of shifting power, great change, a time where the fae can walk freely amongst the humans without detection and gods can be called to earth," he said. "If you want to seek the Otherworld, now is the time to seek. You must not look without, but within."

"You sound like someone I know," Klara said, missing her

grandmother. "Someone I trust." Tears welled up. They were tears of anger, tears of exhaustion.

Cernunnos reached out and placed a hand against her cheek. His skin felt like a breeze against hers, hot and cold at once. Her body flared in response. She stepped away from him, taken aback. The man's presence stirred something in her: a scorching desire, but not for the god. Instead, another face filled her mind. A man with midnight hair and eyes like the line between land and sea.

Klara's cheeks blazed.

"Do not be ashamed, Klara. Such feelings are normal for humans when they encounter me in my true form. I am not only the god of nature, but of fertility and life. The earth resides in flesh, and flesh in earth—all is perfectly natural. But my presence does not inspire anything that is not already within you."

Klara gathered herself, letting the sensation be drawn away on the breeze that fluttered her hair. A breeze that, she reminded herself, only existed in her dream.

Her dream.

"You do not need my help, Klara," he said. "But know that I am always here."

She took one last look at the stag god. "Then I think it's time for me to wake up."

Klara woke to darkness and a sharp inhale of breath. Her breath. The liquid shadows that surrounded her were a stark contrast to the brightness of her dream.

She blinked, letting her eyes adjust. An unfamiliar room came into focus. There was a stone fireplace, a wooden rocking chair, an antique dresser. The lush, blooming trees and

golden light of Cernunnos's world were gone. The god was
nowhere to be seen. But traces of his world lingered. Feelings clung to her—awe, excitement, frustration, confusion.

Desire.

Klara brushed all away, except the last.

"Callum?" Klara threw the covers off and stood up quickly.
A digital clock blinked 19:00. Too late to catch the boat to
Orkney. The next mystic center, Maeshowe, would have to
wait until morning.

Klara took stock of herself: she was still wearing the outfit
she'd faced the beast in but aside from grass stains and a few
minor scrapes, she was unscathed. The sick, woozy sensation
that permeated her body after the fight was gone, too. She
felt whole again, restored.

But Callum was nowhere to be seen.

She opened the door to the hall. No sign of Callum. Her
heartbeat quickened. Padding down a set of creaky wooden
stairs, she set out to search for him. A man in a tartan cap sat
behind the desk, reading a worn paperback. "Have you seen
a man about my age, tall, dark hair—"

His eyes danced. "The broody dobber?"

Dobber? Klara hadn't heard that particular term before, but
she was pretty sure it wasn't a compliment. She didn't know
whether to laugh or defend Callum's honor. "…Yes?"

The man gestured outside. "'E's bein standin out there for
hours, just staring like this." The man pressed his lips into a
thin line, furrowed his brow into a serious expression. "Firs'
I thought he was trying ta take a—"

"Thank you."

Klara charged out the door and into the night, savoring

the fresh sweep of wind that lifted the hair away from her face. At the sight of her, Callum pushed away from the tree he was leaning against. His taut muscles shifted beneath his thin cotton shirt as he closed the distance between them, stopping just short of her. The heat of his body filled the space between them.

"Ye're awake—ye're shaking," he said, his voice shifting from relief to worry. He pulled his jacket off in one fluid motion and moved to ease it around her shoulders.

"Don't." She stopped his hands. "It's not the cold."

Klara's voice was husky. Callum's brows dipped. Tender concern flashed across his face. The look twisted in her belly, melting her in the core of her.

"I hope I didnae frighten ye, Klara. I thought t'would be safer if I watched over ye from outside. And I…"

"What?" she breathed.

"I didnae ken if I should stay in the same room with ye, alone." His eyes darted to hers, shy and uncertain. "I didnae want my presence to dishonor ye."

What he left unspoken made the desire gathering in her throat thicker. It was as if her encounter with the god unlocked a feeling deep inside her. She knew the feeling—her want for Callum. It was as if the walls she had raised within her were broken down in one fell swoop.

"I had a dream—but I think it was real. It was the stag who came to me at the Fairy Glen. Only it wasn't a stag at all, it was a god."

Callum gripped her shoulders. "A stag god?"

"Yes, a god." She breathed out, letting her own words hang thick in the air. "He said I called him to me."

A look of pride washed over his face, visible even in the weak light given off by the inn. "Ye are getting stronger, connecting with your powers. Ye must be." He rubbed her shoulders. The roughness of his palms sparked against her skin. She leaned into his touch, not even bothering to be subtle about it. He asked, "Are ye all right?"

A soft *mmm* escaped her throat. Callum's dark hair swooped over his brow, tousled from running his hands through it. *It could be my fingers running through it,* she thought. Pulse racing, she lifted her hand to his hair and curled a lock around her finger.

He froze. "What are ye doing?"

Klara withdrew her fingers. "Touching," she answered, as if that answer was enough.

"I can see that, lass," he said quietly.

She stopped. "Is that okay?"

He brought his hand up to hers. "Definitely."

Shadows danced on Callum's face; the tree branches above them swayed and whispered in the breeze. The whole of Klara's dream came crashing down on her again, washing away the knot of stress, fear, and confusion her life had become, at least since Callum's arrival had torn everything she knew to pieces. Right here, right now, all Klara wanted was him.

It was simple—the one simple thing—and she clung to it.

"Positive?" she asked for good measure.

Callum paused, and the moment stretched until the heat gathering in Klara's belly felt like its own star, with its own gravity, threatening to pull all of her inward. The look on his face was wild, his eyes alight with desire—and hesitation.

"Klara." He paused, taking a shaky breath. "Dinnae stop."

Callum dropped his hand and took her waist between his strong hands, pulling her close. In a swift movement he turned Klara so that her back was against a nearby tree. His body flush against hers.

She could feel every inch of him.

His eyes stared hungrily into hers, their color bright against the night sky. She watched as his tongue moistened his lips, slowly. She wanted that tongue to do that to her.

Callum dipped his head, his breath against her neck.

"Beautiful." He whispered, his voice rough with lust. His hand trailed from her waist to the base of her back…then lower, leaving a trail of electricity in its wake.

Her core ached for his touch.

She ran her hand up his chest, reveling in the ripple of his hard stomach. Her head fell to the side, welcoming his lips. The moment they connected to her exposed neck, they sent a jolt through her body.

She moaned.

Klara felt him smile against her neck, then the slight flick of his tongue. She gasped but it was cut short as his lips connected with hers.

It was euphoric.

His lips pressed hungrily against hers, and she grasped the nape of his neck, wanting him closer still. She needed him to touch every part of her. As if he could read her mind, his hands roamed over the side of her leg, up her thigh and under to grasp her behind.

"Callum." She panted.

He pulled back suddenly, murmuring, "Did I hurt ye?"

She let out a slight laugh. "No!"

Klara pulled him back to her. Their lips danced. She willed him to move faster, harder against hers. Her tongue dipped into his mouth and he moaned at the contact. They ground their bodies against one another in perfect unison, and—

"Oi! Who's out there?"

She stopped and her hands fell away, as she turned sharply to see the innkeeper looking out into the darkness, though he didn't see them.

Callum laughed, pulling her to the other side of the tree. Face flushed with embarrassment, she began to turn away but he grabbed her wrist and pulled her back. Heat rose between them again, and Klara could feel her pulse against Callum's thumb.

"There is a band playing tonight," he said.

She laughed. They'd gone from one hundred to zero very quickly just now.

"A band?" Only two days since she'd left, and the idea of anything remotely normal seemed like it existed on a different planet.

"If we are going to be here overnight…will you accompany me?"

Klara raised her eyebrows, which made him drop her wrist and quickly add, "After the time we've had, I reckon we deserve it. A wee respite before ye grow too powerful and forget all about me." He grinned. The roguish, pink tint that lingered on his cheeks only made his smile grow brighter. That was one hell of a make-out…and she hated that it had to stop, but it was probably for the best. Though, this acknowledgment didn't help calm the flurries in her chest.

"We better hurry, then." Klara smiled. Joy crept into her chest, and the light sensation felt more miraculous than anything else that had happened. "It's a date, weirdo."

CHAPTER NINETEEN

CALLUM

Callum adjusted his new clothing, courtesy of the gift shop, in the mirror in the parlor downstairs.

His hands, which usually were stilled in moments like this, couldn't stop moving. Nervous energy buzzed through his veins at the thought of seeing Klara.

His body was still warm in all the places she had touched…

Whatever had come over them outside was something he had never felt before…but desperately wanted to feel again. The intensity was almost too much for him.

The want, the desire. It had come on so fast, and now he was left with uncertainty.

What should he do when Klara came down to meet him? Did she feel the same way he felt, a rolling desire muddled with uncertainty?

He had only kissed one girl before, Isla Fraser, one of the maids who tended to Brice's house. Thomas had been the one to tell Callum that Isla had taken a liking to him. Later, he learned that he had told her the same.

Isla had been sweet to him, kind.

The night they'd shared their first kiss—Callum remembered, a "chance" meeting again contrived by Thomas—had been their last. The next day, he woke to find that she'd been sent to work in a house in Edinburgh, in part due to rumors that she was a distraction to Master Brice's best fighter.

But Isla didn't make Callum feel the way Klara made him feel—like he was falling from a great height, like losing her would mean losing everything.

Callum had never known true desire before Klara sparked it in him. His few dalliances with women had been pleasing, but unlike Thomas, he'd yet to find one who inspired more than a passing attraction before he grew bored.

Though Thomas's ladies seemed to change with the seasons, he spoke of soaring passions and triumphant conquests, a feeling like eating fire and dancing with flame as it consumed you from the inside. Of course Thomas had been given to exaggeration and boastfulness, but Callum still wondered if his own heart would ever catch fire.

But with Klara, Callum could not deny how he felt. His lust for her ran like a river through his body, one that grew stronger every waking minute and changed the landscape inside him. Deep and powerful, it nourished him at the same time it threatened to sweep him away.

Callum wanted to get swept away, to lose himself. But he couldn't, not while Klara's life was in danger and the future filled with thunderclouds. Perhaps one day—but one day felt like an ungraspable dream, a peak far in the distance with plenty of obstacles in his path.

The eighth chime tolled. He listened until the sound faded out completely, leaving only the heavy silence in the parlor. She would be coming down those stairs any moment. Why did that seem more frightening than the thought of facing that beast again?

Klara stood at the top of the stairs in a green knit dress. Her hair was loose from its bun. Soft, shining strands tumbled down her shoulders.

"Take heart, man," he whispered to himself.

"Not bad for gift shop outfits," she called down. Even from their distance, he could see the bright blush upon her cheeks.

Callum approached the staircase. In the bright light of the entry hall, he could clearly see the light freckles that blossomed across her nose as she walked down the stairs.

She tilted her head. "What?"

"What?"

"You're staring."

Now his own cheeks burned. "Your freckles. I like them."

Her hand flew to her face. Maybe his nervousness was just anticipation since the ease of which he did this was as if it had been done a thousand times before.

"Oh." She laughed. "Thank you."

Gently, he lifted his hand to hers and brushed it away from where it covered her cheek. "They say freckles mean ye've been touched by one of the wee folk."

"God, that's the *last* thing we need." Klara laughed.

He took her hand and gave it a squeeze. Her eyes met his.

"You make me nervous. In a good way."

He chuckled. "Aye, ye make me feel the same."

"Really?"

He nodded.

"After what happened outside…" She trailed off.

He smiled knowingly, as his cheeks pinkened.

"Shall we?"

He offered his arm.

"Sounds good, my lady," he said, tilting his head.

She curtsied in return just whimsically enough to take the edge off the moment and then took his arm. "You look good. Handsome." She leaned in and whispered into his ear, leaving a trail of heat along his neck. "Though I kind of miss the seventies look and the leather pants."

A strangled *aye* was all he could muster.

Muffled voices hummed through the door as they got closer to the pub next door. Inside, the dim room was aglow with pulsing candles. Groups of people huddled around tables and threw their heads back in laughter.

"The whole town has come out for the show!" He shouted, feeling the energy of the place seep into him. *Energy.* He liked that word.

"I think a lot of them are tourists." She scrunched her nose, until a more serious expression usurped her disdain. "They're probably all visiting for Samhain."

As he listened more closely to the chorus of voices, Callum could discern that not all were from Scotland. Callum felt a bubbling excitement at the thought of people from so many lands in the same space.

Emotion pulled in his chest, chased by a dangerous thought:

If he and Klara found a way to defeat Llaw, could he make a life here?

Klara tugged on his arm. "I see a table over there. Come on."

The innkeeper waved to Callum from behind the wood top as he passed a balding patron a beer. A three-person band was setting up on a small stage at the opposite end of the room. She pulled Callum with her to a rafted alcove at the farthest side of the room and plopped down hastily. They sat close enough that their shoulders touched.

Callum didn't dare move, remembering with a jolt how close they'd been earlier that evening—desire swelled in him at the memory of the heat in her eyes.

Just when he was imagining, in detail, the soft press of Klara's lips on his skin and her arms around his waist, a fiddle let out a whine as a player tuned up for the performance. A boyish grin spread over his face.

Klara smiled up at him. Now it was his turn to ask, "What is it?"

She shrugged. "You look so happy. It's good to know that in spite of everything, we can have a little fun."

"This place reminds me of home. There was always music at The Black Hart. I'm sure ye have many other forms of entertainment in your time, but music and tales are all we have, and we have plenty of it. It helps to sing through the hard times," he said. "Though these lasses are much prettier than any rogue who played in my time."

A wave of homesickness struck him. Though he was not eager to go back to his time, he felt a sudden gnawing in his chest at the thought of the loss of it—all those people he knew, gone. Rosemere was only ashes buried in the earth, scarcely a memory.

Klara's smile turned down. There was a touch of sadness in it and, as if she could hear his thoughts, she said, "All this time we've been talking about Thomas like he's some clue to a big maze we're lost in. But you must miss him as a friend, all the time traveling and goddess stuff aside."

He winced. "When I do have a moment to dwell on it, my heart feels like it will burst. I don't want to imagine a world without him."

"I don't want to imagine a world without anyone I hold close," Klara said. "It was hard enough to lose my mom."

Klara let out a soft laugh. "She always said I was destined for great things. Who knew my purpose had to do with finding a way to stop an evil demigod?"

"And here ye are," he said.

"Here *we* are. Both mourning those we've lost."

The barkeep swept by their table and slid two drinks before them. A finger of amber liquid ringed the bottom of each glass. "Cheers."

Callum nodded and raised the glass to his lips. The liquid burned his throat with hickory heat. Another reminder of home.

They sat in silence, watching as the band continued to set up their equipment.

"My dad would love this. The day I met you, he was trying to find a band to play at Kingshill Manor. I know this sounds terrible, but I'm almost glad not to be home, since I haven't been able to tell him about college."

Callum gestured with his chin to a nearby window, where

the night sky filled the windowpane. "The stars are there. Perhaps your father will feel better if ye study on your trip."

She shook her head, causing red ringlets to fall across her forehead. "It's not that simple. It's not really about the stars, it's about more than that. I don't want to disappoint him."

Callum shifted next to her, easing closer to comfort her. He recalled her words at Grams's house—about her mother's wishes for her future, how she hoped that Klara would have the opportunity to forge a different path than the one she had been given.

"Ye have a destiny now, Klara. That's the greatest thing a person can be given."

"Well, I'm not sure my dad will understand the whole divine will thing."

"Maybe not, but he seems to trust ye and that's what's needed now."

A few seconds of silence passed. Klara slid her hand over his and let it linger there. Grabbing on to his bravery, Callum squeezed back, running his thumb over her palm. The feeling of her skin against his sent his pulse racing.

"We're holding hands," he said plainly.

Klara's cheeks ignited. "Is that...okay?" She laughed nervously. "Does that mean I'm bound to you forever or something?"

He lifted his eyes to her. "Aye."

She snatched her hand away.

Callum burst out laughing. She shoved him.

"Dinnae worry, ye're not bound to me." He wiped a tear from his eye. "I would not subject ye to so cruel a fate."

"Like it would be so bad." She rolled her eyes.

Before Callum could respond, a bagpipe's haunting moan filled the room. Hesitantly, he laid a hand atop her thigh.

Gooseflesh rippled across Klara's exposed legs at his touch. Worried he insulted her by his brazen move, he went to lift his hand but was stopped by hers as she rested it atop his.

They both took a breath in unison.

The lead singer lowered her head to the mic. Her long blond hair was braided atop her head, adorned with blue flowers that seemed to spring from her head. She looked like a woodland nymph. When she sang, Callum wondered if she *was* a woodland nymph: the voice that filled the room was unlike anything of this world.

"Carry the lad that's born to be king.

Over the sea to Skye."

The song thrummed around them. Without having to think about it, his leg began to bump in time with the music, his knee knocking into Klara's on the beat. An amused grin on her face, Klara watched as he began to sing softly under his breath in Gaelic.

You know this song? she mouthed.

Despite every worry and grief that weighed on his shoulders, he allowed himself to get lost completely in the song— the melody bore his pain, his joys, and his thrills down the river of his body and washed him clean. The song clung to his skin and the notes danced along his limbs. *Speed bonnie boat, like a bird on the wing.* His voice entangled itself with the singer's words, two becoming one. *Onward, the sailors cry.*

As the song faded out, Callum opened his eyes, not realizing when he had closed them. The audience around them swayed along to the dying music in their seats. A few had stood to dance around the edges of the room. After a smattering of applause—and with a hearty wink to Callum—the singer thanked the audience and made to tune her fiddle.

Recovered now, Callum turned to look at Klara. Light danced in her eyes and a tear dropped down her cheek. His heart almost broke at the sight.

"What's the matter, lass?"

She sniffed. "I wish my mom were here to see."

She leaned into his shoulder. The fiddle struck up again, this time with a livelier jig. Boldness coursing through him, he wiped her cheek dry with his thumb. "I ken why ye're really crying," he whispered.

Klara straightened. She narrowed her eyes at him. "Why's that?"

"I didnae ask ye to dance."

She snorted. "I'm good, thank—"

He didn't let her get the rest of her sentence out. Springing up, he tugged her out of her seat and spun her in a circle. The world around them blurred, then stilled again as he pulled her against his chest. Titters of laughter and one cheer rang out in the crowd, but Callum paid them no mind. He could not take his eyes off Klara.

"Do you know how to line dance?" he asked.

Her brows shot up. "The only line dance I know was the kind people did at the rodeo-themed bar by my apartment in New York. So no, not the kind you're probably talking about."

"Follow me."

He tapped his right foot forward. She mirrored him, doing the same.

"Now do it with your other foot, adding in a wee hop."

Encouraged by the loudening cheers from the audience, Callum slung his left arm around Klara's waist so they were side by side. Her body seemed to spark at his touch, as if a surge of energy traveled from his fingertips to her skin. Callum moved them forward and she fumbled, trying to get the steps correct.

"Good," he said, even though it was *not* good. "Now lean forward and back up again in between the steps."

Soon, they spun and dipped. Their bodies moved in unison. Within a few steps, the rest of the audience was on their feet and swirling around them. Klara threw her head back in laughter.

"Did ye ken that the Scots play the bagpipes into battle to invoke fear in the hearts of their enemies?" Callum shouted.

Skirts flaring out around her, Klara leaned into him and pressed her face into his neck. Her warm breath and the light touch of her lips on his skin made him shiver. Strands of her hair brushed his cheek as she shook her head *no*.

"I'm not even the least bit scared!" she shouted back.

Callum gave her a sweeping dip. Time seemed to slow as she leaned into his arm, tipping back on her heels until the only thing keeping her from falling was Callum. He leaned in, his lips hovering close, close, closer to hers.

When their lips connected…it was slow, meaningful.

He almost forgot they were surrounded by others. He felt her sharp intake of breath.

"I understand what energy is now," he whispered against her lips.

And then, as he went back in for another mesmerizing kiss, the song came to an end.

Sweat dappled his brow. The sound of applause filtered through the pub and rose up around them—but somehow, it felt meant only for them.

Grinning from ear to ear, Callum looked around the room. A familiar pair of eyes made contact with his and turned his blood into ice.

Aion stood in the open doorway.

CHAPTER TWENTY

CALLUM

Callum dropped his hands from Klara's waist. The applause faded around them, then was swallowed completely as the band struck up another tune. No one in the crowd saw what he saw: the man who had somehow followed them from Edinburgh, his two piercing blue eyes set into a pale face, its bones sharp as blades.

Klara looked up at him. "What's wrong?"

"Stay here," he said.

Suddenly, Callum was on edge. How did Aion manage to find them? Was he an Otherworldly being as well? Callum's body responded swiftly, with neither thought nor hesitation. Blood surged within him, pushing against his flesh, animating his limbs with rage and heat. Aion's presence was as good as a challenge.

Callum charged.

"Callum!"

He shouted behind him. "Stay here!"

He ignored the rest of Klara's calls at his back, though the note of panic in her voice matched the feeling that was filling Callum now, flooding alongside the anger. He wove between the battlefield of square tables that lay between him and the door. He crashed into one with his hip, and glass shattered on the floor behind him. The smell of spilled ale blossomed in the air.

But none of that mattered to Callum, not now.

Aion flew into motion, retreating from the doorway and into the crisp night air.

Callum pushed past the final table and broke through to the doorway, pausing just outside. The chill air made him alert. Something flashed to his left.

"Aion!"

Aion darted around the side of the pub, deeper into shadow.

The man was a hand's length shorter than Callum, but fast. He only barely caught the fabric of his tunic between his fingers as Aion turned the corner, but it was enough to pull him backward, hard, before using his own weight to spin his body around and slam it against the wall of the pub. Callum pinned him down with his forearm, savoring the sharp *crack* that split the air as the body made contact.

Caught in Callum's grasp, Aion met his eyes. After a few labored breaths, he choked out a laugh.

"Ye have no right to laugh. Ye dinnae ken me." Callum pressed harder, muscles straining. Only three days away from home and the feeling was unfamiliar. It was like he was inhabiting another's body, a part of himself that had faded. Fixing his eyes on Aion's, he tried to summon the man he was before, the prizefighter who would rather bleed than break.

"Ye dinnae ken what I can, *and will*, do," he said.

Aion laughed again, tilting his chin to look up at the stars. Callum pressed the point of his elbow into his throat and cut the laugh short, into a wheeze. Aion winced in pain. Again, Callum took pleasure in it.

"But I do know you, better than you can imagine," Aion said. His voice came out dry, strangled, but his eyes blazed bright, as if they were absorbing the moonlight that streamed down from above.

"I know of your scrapping in the streets."

That gave Callum pause. What was Aion playing at? He recalled the day he met Aion in the shop. "A lucky guess, for one who knows such a great deal of history." Callum raised his free hand, angling his knuckles to display their scars in the moonlight. "Besides, I give myself away."

Aion raised his eyebrows in mild offense. "But I know far more than that. I know of your poor friend, lying bleeding in the alley of a long-lost town. I know of Brice, who raised you with no mother to love you, just a babe crying out for—"

Callum's knuckles sunk into Aion's cheek and nose, glancing off bone. His cry was muffled by Callum's fist. He drew his hand back, chest heaving. A line of dark blood trickled from Aion's nostril and over his lip.

The man smiled.

"I know how you fell out of time itself," he whispered. Callum lowered his fist. His eyes glowed again, dancing with mischief and something else Callum could not name. His stomach twisted itself into a knot. As if sensing his discomfort—Callum thought—Aion pushed against the weight of his arm and brought his face closer to Callum's. "You know nothing, lad. Nothing of what is to come. Do you want to know?"

The words drew a cold finger along Callum's spine, so unlike the heat coursing through his fingers. *Yes*, he wanted to say. But he found his lips would not part, nor the words leave his throat. His courage shrank within him, shriveling like a fruit under the baking sun.

"I only want to protect Klara," he whispered. He found strength in the truth.

To his left, the pub door swung open and the air bloomed with a swell of voices. A man stumbled out. Not Klara. For once, it seemed she had heeded his request that she stay away. Once the man stumbled away, Callum looked back to Aion. Aion, who shifted under his gaze.

Callum relaxed his arm, allowing Aion to move slightly under his hold. He took in a big, gulping breath. "I want to ken why ye are here."

He sniffed. "You *called* me, didn't you?"

"I didnae summon ye."

Aion persisted. "It's a bit rude to throttle a man you summoned."

Callum would not be distracted with Aion's twisted words. He decided to get right to the point. "What do ye ken of finding the bean-nighe?" If only Callum could find the bean-nighe, he'd have a much better chance of protecting Klara.

Aion flashed a wicked grin. "You wish to meddle with the world of the *aos sí*? Your mortal fate?"

"It has already meddled with me," Callum said easily.

Aion laughed in approval. "What do you want from her?"

"It does not make any difference to ye."

"No, I would just *like* to know." Aion flashed a roguish grin. "The bean-nighe appears to those she chooses, and those who will die."

"Aye, and I ken of the *geas*." The bean-nighe was one of the *aos sí*. The Fair Folk put conditions on their gifts as skillfully as huntsmen set traps for hares.

"And she's clever," Aion said, rolling his eyes like Klara did. "Are you willing to die?"

Callum considered this. Death had nearly touched him countless times. It had come for those closest to him, though not the ones it should have. For Klara? For the strength he needed to protect her? Callum would do anything. Compared to the thought of failing her, death did not scare him at all.

"Aye," he replied firmly.

Aion glanced in both directions. "You must go to a loch or stream, where she is known to frequent. Strip a length of cloth from your shirt, soak it in your blood, and leave it to the waters. With it, you must swear to leave your life—if the bean-nighe would so choose to take it." He tipped his head to the west. "There's a loch not far from here. Ten minutes' walk."

Callum waited, but Aion said nothing more. "Nothing more than that?"

"Nothing more than that? Nothing more than beckoning death itself to your doorstep?" Aion scoffed. "You *are* stupid."

Callum pushed Aion higher on the wall until only his toes scraped the ground. "How do I know you're telling the truth?"

"I suppose you'll have to try it and find out, lad."

Callum appraised him. Aion stared back. If the man was lying, he was good at concealing it. "Why did ye come here? Ye have nothing to gain, so far as I can tell."

Aion's eyes dimmed, leaving him looking far more like the man he'd first met in the shop. A hint of light burned low in his gaze. For a brief flash, there was sadness in his expression. It left as quickly as it had come.

"I have already meddled with my fate and lost. Now, I have my part to play, so I will play it. I had to be certain to play it correctly," he said. "This is the last time I'll see you, lad, though the same cannot be said of you seeing me."

Callum pressed him against the wall again and held him there. "Ye speak nonsense. What does that mean?"

"And if I don't tell you?" The man interrupted. "Are you going to kill me, with *her* just inside?"

Callum faltered.

"I didn't think so." Aion laughed and wiped the trail of blood from his nose. Eyes twinkling again, he glanced toward the door of the pub. "Does she know what you want of the bean-nighe? The omen of death?"

Keeping Aion pinned with one arm, Callum followed his gaze. Klara stood a few paces' distance away from them. Her brow was furrowed with worry, her arms slack at her sides, watching them.

Watching *him*.

"Dinnae concern yourself with us," Callum said sharply.

Aion snickered. "If you seek out the bean-nighe, your lady will know and she will find you."

He said it in a tone that puzzled Callum. Either with prom-

ise or pity. It unnerved him, but he pushed the feeling away...
for now.

Callum released Aion. Klara approached slowly, then picked
up her pace slightly as she came closer. "Mind telling me
what's going on?"

Aion straightened and addressed Klara, bowing his head in
deference to her. Or mock deference, Callum thought ruefully.

"I mean no harm. It was Callum who called me here," he
said, rubbing his throat with one hand.

"Called you here?" Her gaze snapped to Callum. "How is
that, exactly? And who is he?"

"Just a purveyor of wares," Aion said.

"Klara—"

Aion grabbed Callum's shirtfront, lowering his voice to
address him so that Klara could not hear. "My part is done.
Remember that."

Shooting a daggered glance at Aion, Klara pulled Callum
away by the elbow until they were outside of Aion's earshot.
"What is going on?"

Callum's mind spun with excuses and lies. Aion was right.
He could not confess the truth to her. She would only worry.
She would only stop him.

"If you're not going to spit it out, I'm going to make him
tell me," Klara said. "I've already tangled with a demigod, so
some shopkeeper does *not* scare me."

She whirled on Aion—but Aion was already gone. Only
shadows remained where he stood.

"You called him on the *phone*? Why didn't you tell me?"

Klara held a bag of ice—*ice*, Callum marveled, *ice* even

though the first snow had not yet fallen—against his raw knuckles. The skin had bruised already. It set purple under the cold.

"I didnae want to worry ye," he said lamely. "I thought he had more information. About Thomas."

Klara shook her head and pulled her hair over one shoulder then, readjusted the bag on her shoulder. He inhaled sharply through clenched teeth. "How bad does it hurt?"

"Nothing broken."

Klara stared at him. "But why did he come? What did he want?"

Callum averted his eyes, staring instead at the water pooling on the bar. Klara said nothing. Her silence made the air thick. He wouldn't tell her the truth—she was too proud, too kind, and she would never approve of his plan to trade his life spark for the strength to protect her. So he did what he had to: he lied. "He wanted the book back. I refused him."

The lie settled in his stomach.

Klara narrowed her eyes.

"Okay, but…we're not exactly supposed to be drawing attention to ourselves. Beating him up wasn't the best move." She lifted her hand from the bag of ice and pointed to herself. "Pillar of Time, remember? Big Bad ripping open space and time to murder me? Ringing any bells?"

His face burned. How was the one thing he was good at, the one thing she seemed to hate the most about him? It didn't matter. If he was going to protect her, he needed strength. He needed to be stone. Not something breakable.

She sighed, and softened. "It's okay. I know you're doing

your best. Not exactly easy being a time-traveling warrior, huh?"

"No, 'tis not," he replied solemnly, relieved at her olive branch.

Klara laughed, and squeezed his hand. "Always so serious. I'm going to bed." She stood up. "Oh, I forgot to tell you, I got the ferry schedule earlier. The boat to Stromness, the town where Maeshowe is, leaves at seven, so we need to leave before dawn. Don't be late."

With Klara safe in the room, Callum was free to wander, free to search for the bean-nighe. He left the inn and though the windows had darkened, he still felt Klara's eyes on him, watching. Winding down the path lit only by moonlight, he passed into the trees and approached the loch that hugged the property.

He waded into the stream, until he stood waist-deep in the cold sting of the water. Behind him, the inn stood at a distance. Smoke curled up from its chimneys, spiraling toward the moon above.

Withdrawing the dirk, Callum cut a strip of fabric from his shirt. It was the same he wore that night. Then, he clenched his jaw and sunk the blade into his inner arm, gritting his teeth as he drew the blade against skin.

It was over quickly. He had experienced worse pain. If the feeling in his gut was any sign, worse was still to come.

Gathering the cloth in his hand, he tamped the well of blood until the fabric grew heavy with it. He gripped it, squeezing until thread and blood and skin merged into one.

He submerged his fist into the water and let go.

With it, a vow of strength.

An invitation.

CHAPTER TWENTY-ONE

KLARA

The darkness around Klara stirred, as if it were alive.

She straightened up. A bolt of fear shot through her, ricocheting in her limbs. Her body was telling her to be afraid and her mind was racing to catch up.

A few seconds passed—she could hear the tick of a clock somewhere—but no sign of danger materialized. Klara touched her cheek. Her face was hot to the touch. Strands of sweaty hair clung to her skin. Blearily, she remembered waiting for Callum to come to her door. To knock, to hold her, to admit he wanted more.

Except he hadn't.

Klara tried to swallow her disappointment. She took stock of the armchair she'd apparently fallen asleep in, which was tucked in the corner of her room at the inn. Dad always said she could fall asleep anytime, anywhere, no matter what the circumstances. Considering she had been attacked by a monster, went on a date with a time traveler that was interrupted by a vindictive shopkeeper, all within the same twenty-four hours and while being pursued by a demigod, and still managed to doze off...well, she had to give him that one.

Klara blinked, trying to clear away her bleary vision. She reached for her phone to check the time.

That's when she noticed the dust.

She froze as it came into focus. The gauzy substance hung in the air in a shimmering curtain, shining in the dark. Only the specks hanging in the air weren't golden, like they had been when she first saw Cernunnos. They sparked between light and dark, devoid of the soft light that had bathed the forest.

The darkness shifted again and the room went suddenly cold. A figure stepped out from the shadows.

Llaw.

Klara's heart spasmed in her chest. She sprang up and lunged under the bed, scrambling for the sword she'd clumsily stuffed there earlier that night. Her hands met the rough wood of the floor and nothing else.

Klara drew back onto her heels. The sword wasn't there. Neither were her bag, her shoes, the dress she'd tossed away—

"I cannot hurt you here," Llaw drawled. Teeth flashed.

The horrible lump in Klara's throat loosened slightly, but she wasn't about to trust the words of a man who desperately wanted to kill her.

"That doesn't sound like you," she said bitterly.

Llaw titled his head, as if in thought. "Well, maybe I could hurt you if I tried really, *really* hard. Even then, it would probably be a scratch, nothing more."

He opened his arms. Klara flinched, but he was only gesturing to the space that surrounded them. The sleeves of his heavy cloak fell back slightly to reveal a swath of his pale arms. The dust seemed to cling to his skin, illuminating him in the nearly pitch-black room.

"This is neutral ground," he said.

Klara stood up from her crouch. She pushed down her fear while her mind clawed to gain purchase.

Llaw barked out a laugh.

Klara hesitantly glanced around the room, looking for the trick. The shadows were so thick now she could hardly make out anything besides Llaw and the bed she stood next to. She glanced out the window. Dark clouds had smothered the moonlight.

The gauzy substance in the air seemed to be growing thicker, expanding and shrinking with her every breath. It gathered on her clothes, her exposed skin.

"What is this?" she asked, fearing the worst. "Have you done something?"

"The matter between worlds." Llaw outstretched his hand. There was reverence, even awe, in the gesture. "One cannot travel between them without bringing something along, too. With enough discipline, it's like any other material."

Klara remembered her meeting with Cernunnos. An idea took hold. Her eyes snapped back to Llaw. "I'm dreaming."

He clapped his hands. He strode across the room and settled himself in the armchair Klara had fallen asleep in. "Now you're getting it, Pillar."

"I prefer Klara, thanks," she said easily. "If I'm dreaming, then why are you here?"

He shrugged, but the gesture looked unnatural on him. Inhuman. "It's your dream."

She scoffed. "It's a nightmare, then."

"A nightmare. I like that." He flashed his teeth. "In the flesh."

Her muscles tensed again. "But this is real—I'm not just imagining you," she said, not sure if she was talking to Llaw or herself. She thought about meeting Cernunnos in her dream. "This has happened to me before."

Llaw raised his eyebrows in mild curiosity. Klara scolded herself for giving away too much. "Then your powers are getting stronger." He paused, gaze lingering and hungry. "Do you feel it?"

"I'm not defenseless, if that's what you're asking," she bluffed.

He folded his hands in his lap. "Surely you've heard the old stories of men walking through their dreams in search of their destinies?"

"Some," Klara said cautiously. For the thousandth time, she made a mental note to thank Grams for raising her on the old stories and cursed herself for not studying them harder.

Llaw nodded approvingly. "They slept for days, their mortal forms neither eating nor drinking while they walked in the world of dreams, in search of truths they could not find in their waking lives.

"You will not be able to match your powers to mine in

only a few days." Llaw paused. Lingering in the air, his words sunk into Klara slowly, gnawing at the part of her that believed them. "Unless…"

"Unless what?" Klara said, too quickly.

Llaw seized on to the desperation that threaded through her voice. "Unless I help you. Unless we work together to—"

"What?" Klara balked. "Is that before or after killing me?"

"We are the last of our kind," he said. "The only people in your world capable of wresting the power of the gods, to restore the worlds as they once were."

"And who made it that way?" Klara's stomach turned at the thought of everyone who Llaw had slaughtered before reaching her. She saw the glint of the sword under his cloak. She started—the hilt was the same as hers, thistle forming the hilt and the pommel—an identical twin to her own. For some reason, it made anger flare up in her. He was an imposter, trying for the powers of a goddess. "You're wasting your breath. I'm the last of my kind. You're just a—a—"

"A what?" Llaw said simply.

"A thief," she said. "A murderer."

"Very well." Disappointment rang out in his voice. "I may not be able to reach you now—not fully—but eventually when I can, I will kill you *correctly*." He paused, and though she couldn't fully see his face now that he had reclined into shadow, she heard his smile in the dark. "That's the marvelous thing about bending time to your will. While you will be stuck in your world, rooted in time, I can just—" he snapped his fingers and the sound made her jump "—pop in. Not that it would matter to a dead girl."

Klara's heart skipped a beat.

Llaw stared at her, and the sharp glint in his eyes reminded her of a predator. As if sensing her thoughts, he softened his face and smiled—but the empty grin curling over his face only deepened her uneasiness, leaving a chill behind so strong that it reached into the real world, where her body lay asleep.

"You don't have to die," he said. *"Klara."*

"You don't have to kill me," she quipped. "See? Two can play at that game."

Llaw's smile faltered. For a moment, Klara glimpsed everything that was the human part about him—not the god half. The sag of his shoulders. The flinch of his mouth as he swallowed words. Klara wondered what he was holding back.

"I'm doing what I must," he said.

"What is that, exactly?"

"To pursue the life I am owed. To avoid death, in all its forms, forever." He looked away from her with a faraway gaze, considering something she couldn't see. When he looked back at her again, his eyes burned with their own fierce light. "You wouldn't understand, nor do I care to enlighten you."

"It's not so bad," Klara said. "I rather like the Mundane Realm."

"Then enjoy it while you can, because soon I will have it and the Otherworld."

Llaw raised his hand. Klara watched as the dust in the air gathered and swirled under his palm. While she watched in horror, a snarling hound took shape.

The hound lunged.

A scream ripped from Klara's throat as she thrust herself backward, anticipating the blow of its massive paws, the bite of teeth—

She shot up and sucked in a sharp breath. Blinked. Breathed. Her fingers gripped something, *hard*. She looked down. The cool polished wood of the armchair rests.

She was awake, the dim light of dawn greeting her, a stark contrast to the darkness of her slumber.

Sound pierced her ears—her phone alarm, she realized. Hand shaking, she snatched up the phone from the side table and punched Stop, then tossed it onto the still-made bed in front of her.

As soon as the room fell silent, a knock on the door made her shriek.

"Klara?"

It was Callum's voice outside the room. She collapsed back into the chair, relaxing for a split second before her chest tightened up again at the memory of last night. The date, the dance, Aion, the secrets storming across Callum's face. His *face*. The tightness burst as it all came rushing back, letting wave after wave of emotion out until she was a shivering mess.

"Klara?" he repeated. Did his voice sound strained, too, or was she imagining it? "If we dinnae leave soon, we'll miss the ship."

A grin pulled at the corners of her mouth. She couldn't help it. Though she had loved it since she was a little girl, Callum was definitely going to be disappointed by the dinghy-like ferry that would transport them to Orkney. She cleared her throat. "Don't get your hopes up. It's not exactly a ship."

Klara pushed away the urge to call him in, to melt into his arms like she had last night as the music swelled around them and shut out everything except his promises to protect

her. She wanted him to chase away the dream that clung to
her like a shadow.

But he was right. They had to get going. "Wait for me
downstairs," she said. "I'll be there in a minute."

As Callum's footsteps grew softer and finally disappeared
down the hallway, Klara looked around the room. She wanted
to savor the last bit of quiet before the trip ahead, whatever
it would bring. Sunlight filtered in through the window. It
struck the bed in golden rays that glittered with specks of dust.
It's just normal, everyday dust, she thought with relief.

Maeshowe. Their next mystic center. She'd never been herself, but she recalled her grandmother's description of the ancient tomb. How, underneath the most normal, boring hill
you could possibly imagine, a maze of dark passageways lay
waiting for thousands of years. She could picture the empty
alcoves that once likely held the remains of the long gone
dead as well as the angular runes inscribed upon the walls.
They were messages from people who built a civilization
stone by stone.

Maybe not so long gone. She thought of Llaw and Callum.
The invisible net tightened around her again. Like the past
was closing her in its fist.

Her phone dinged. She looked down. A message from her
dad blinked on the screen.

Hi honey. Are you OK?

Tears pricked her eyes and flowed down her cheeks. After
everything she'd gone through, five little words were all it
took to finally, really shatter her. She closed her eyes, letting

her nose fill with the imagined smell of mingling old wood, honeysuckle, and burnt toast that wafted through the halls of Kingshill Manor. But she was far away from everything she now called home, she remembered with a pang. Same country but it felt like another world.

She opened her eyes and stared at the message, wiping away tears. Her fingers twitched with the overwhelming urge to answer with the truth. *No. Nothing's okay.*

Instead, she said, Yep! Miss you! ☺

Klara scooted her back against the solid headboard and brought her knees to her chest, kicking her phone away as she did. Her whole body ached. She must have been clenching her muscles while she'd dreamed.

Nowhere was safe for her now—not even her dreams.

She had a feeling that where they were going would be no exception.

CHAPTER TWENTY-TWO

CALLUM

A boat larger than Callum had ever seen carried them to Stromness, a town carved into the rock-hewn shores of Orkney. Maeshowe was close. Callum could practically feel it sparking in the air around him. The cairn that hid ancient burial chambers under its gentle green slopes—and within it, he hoped, more information to help Klara battle Llaw.

He knew that with the help of the bean-nighe, he could help Klara more than with the strength he had now. Callum just didn't know what he would have to forfeit to obtain what he desired. He waited all night, in his room, for the bean-nighe to appear, but she never showed herself. He pushed the thought aside, knowing that for now, he had to work with what he already had. Though the temptation of gaining more, for her, was still ever-present.

Until now, he'd felt like a mule in the horse's paddock in Klara's century, but this far north, everything seemed unchanged by time. A sense of peace settled over him. At least until a carriage screeched to a halt an arm's length away from Callum, sending him stumbling backward.

"Watch it!" Klara shouted at the receding machine, even though Callum was entirely at fault. She turned back to him. She flashed a smile to a woman who passed by them on the road. A mangy mutt clipped along at her heels.

Neither had spoken of last night, only of the journey to Maeshowe that still lay ahead.

In the light of day, their encounter seemed like a sweet, impossible dream—Klara's body against his, his lips on her throat, like there was nothing in the world that could keep them apart. The sensation that it invoked in him now, however, walking side by side with her, was real beyond any doubt. Callum stared straight ahead, careful to avoid her eyes.

That was easy enough—Klara was focused entirely on her phone. She led them through the town, occasionally stopping to purchase food and drink that Callum ate eagerly. Brice fed Callum no more than he needed to; indulgence was saved for Christmas or if he won a large sum in a match and even then, it was not promised. After years of fighting for every morsel, the joy of having food for the taking—salty crisps in glimmering pouches, bread warm to the touch and filled with sweet, steaming fruit—still had not lost its shine. Eating so freely felt like letting infection drain from a wound. Klara watched him devour an apple. Heat flushed his cheeks as he wiped juice from his lips.

She stopped abruptly, a tendon of delicious bread dangling

from her free hand. "Can you grab the map from my bag? My GPS isn't working well up here."

Callum unfolded the map, revealing a tangle of intersecting lines. He marveled at the details and Klara's ability to decipher the tiny markings.

"A journey like this would've taken me days back home." He ran his fingers over the paper valleys and roads.

"I can only imagine," she replied. "The world is a much smaller place than it was in the sixteenth century. Have you ever even been on a boat before?" She glanced sidelong at him. The mischievous glint in her eye made the thought of her lips and tongue burn suddenly bright in his mind.

"There's a first time for everything," He blushed furiously.

She winked and turned her attention to the path ahead.

She had sensed his thoughts. Callum blushed harder and cleared his throat. "Brice couldn't be bothered with boats when there was a perfectly good stretch of land connecting us to London and Britain's other ports."

Klara traced a line on the map with her finger. "It looks like we can walk to Maeshowe. It's a little over four miles, so—an hour and a half on foot? But I bet we can do it in an hour. I can teach you to walk like a New Yorker.

"The only way of getting to Maeshowe is with an official tour. Like with a guide," she clarified for him. "I don't know of a way around that, so I'm thinking we should go there with the last tour, then find some way to stay behind."

Callum nodded. "If the guides, as ye call them, give us trouble, I can subdue them."

Klara raised an eyebrow at him, leaving him with the now-familiar feeling that he had said something foolish.

"Or we could barter with them for their discretion?" he offered. "People can be bought."

"Let's skip the subduing and bribing for now. You can't solve every problem with your fists, especially in this time," she admonished. "In this case, all we have to do is buy a bus ticket and hope the guide is too exhausted to count us properly on the way back."

Klara paused. "Do you think we can trust Arianrhod's warnings?" she asked, eyes fixed on the road.

Callum didn't respond right away. She was right but they didn't have many options. "We could run away to the coast?"

Klara glanced at him. "What good would that do?"

Callum shrugged. "I dinnae ken. I am trying to give ye an option, though not a viable one it seems. We only have one way out..."

"Yeah." Klara breathed. "I know."

They began their hour-long walk to Stennes, where the bus would take them to Maeshowe. The smooth road stretched before them, quiet save for the soft bleating of sheep that dotted the encircling farmland. A loch dipped into the land on their northern side. The water shone silver and blue under the morning sun, long-winged birds wheeling above. It reminded Callum of the sea they had crossed, which still lay salty on his tongue.

"Do you think Thomas spoke to the gods?" Klara asked.

Callum's jaw clenched. "He often acted like it, though he told me nothing specific. Nothing useful to ye now."

Darting a glance in his direction, Klara surveyed him. "You're sure? Nothing that could—"

"Nothing," Callum said. Guilt made his words taut. He

wished he knew something, anything, that could help Klara move forward safely.

Questions wrestled inside Callum. If Callum had questioned Thomas—if he could have put aside his fear and bothered to ask—could he have prevented his friend's death?

Could he prevent Klara's?

Klara seemed to notice his turn inward. She grabbed Callum's hand—a jolt shot straight to his heart at her touch—and looked into his eyes. "I'm sorry to bring up Thomas again, really. But he's our only key to this. Our only clue." She stepped away from him and bit her lip, looking away briefly and back again. Her green eyes were soft. "I wish he was here."

Her words—so easily offered, so sweetly spoken—disarmed him completely. A lump worked its way into his throat. The thoughts he'd been holding at bay, though they had been snapping like feral dogs in his chest, broke free. He gripped her hand tighter, and she rubbed her thumb gently along the base of his palm.

Thomas should have lived.

He'd have known what to do.

Seeing his grief, Klara stepped forward again and leaned into his chest. Callum's arms encircled her shoulders without his willing them to do so, his chin coming to rest lightly, perfectly, on the crown of her head. This was nothing like their last embrace—yet it still brimmed with a passion that penetrated all the way to his core. He gripped Klara tighter and closed his eyes, letting the tears spill hot down his cheeks. With a shuddering breath, he opened his eyes again—

And saw her.

A figure knelt on the shore of the loch. A woman, judging

by the long blond hair that trailed and whipped the ground at her feet. Callum relaxed slightly, though the hairs on the back of his neck did not. Bent low, she worked her arms over the water at a strange, unnatural clip. *A washerwoman*, Callum realized dimly. It felt wrong, out of place for Klara's time, even this far north. She raised a stone in her fist and brought it down suddenly, striking the clothes piled at her knees. Callum flinched.

With the stone still gripped in her hand, the woman straightened, lifting something from the water as she stood. A square of fabric. No, a shirt.

His shirt. The one he'd worn when he'd found Thomas.

His gut turned to ice. Hanging heavy between her hands, the cloth dripped with blood that dropped from its hem into the water below.

A tremor gripped Callum's body as he realized who she was. *What* she was.

Bean-nighe.

He had done it.

The bean-nighe—the omen of death—turned to him. Time seemed to slow. Her handsome face twisted and melted into a horrifying mask punctured by black, unblinking eyes and a mouth that opened to reveal a yawning maw of darkness.

Klara pulled away. "Callum? You're shaking."

He held her head fast in between his hands. She could not look; he would not let her. Anyone who looked upon the bean-nighe was destined to die. But when he looked at the shore again, the washerwoman was gone. Only a small stain of red in the water remained. It burned and flashed in the sun before it, too, vanished.

Though the thought of him needing her aid chilled him to the bone, he had succeeded.

He had called her to him.

CHAPTER TWENTY-THREE

KLARA

Silence fell between them until the paved road turned into cobblestone streets. Though he grasped her hand now, Callum had turned distant again, preferring to look at anything—the ground, the sky, at one point a passing mote of dust—rather than her.

Klara tried not to care. She had bigger things to worry about, and she tried to understand that he was in a strange land and time, had lost everything. He was allowed to process. But under the swath of pale blue sky in the world she was supposed to be saving, she did care. She wished they could just...be together. Without all of this hanging over them.

"Acting like everything is normal" had always been her superpower—aside from the *actual* superhuman abilities bestowed upon her by a goddess, the ones she couldn't fully reach. She'd been honing the ability to sweep things under the rug for her whole life. If she'd learned anything in the last six months, it was that it was important to lift up the rug and check on all those discarded things, to blow the dust off and make sure they didn't come back to haunt you. Failing that, to make it less frightening when they finally did.

Callum? Definitely haunted. Big, scary, haunted.

Klara flexed her fingers, wondering half-seriously if the god's power within would help her start over with Callum. Take back the desire she felt for him, the kind she thought could only exist in romance novels, take back the intoxicating kisses and his arms around her waist—

Her stomach hitched. He wasn't like any guy she'd known. His sense of honor would make him risk anything for her— and it was only more complicated now that kissing was involved. What the hell had she been thinking?

She cast a glance at Callum. His muscles pulled underneath his shirt. His face stormed under loose dark curls and the depths of it made her throat tight.

Okay, she knew what she'd been thinking. She was still thinking about it. And she knew that if it were up to her, she wouldn't take what had happened between them back.

Would Callum?

Sitting astride two deeply blue lochs, the town of Stennes was no more than a handful of white plaster houses with colorful wooden doors. Trying to quell the questions roiling inside her, Klara guided them to the Maeshowe bus, which rumbled and sputtered on a corner. They stood on the edge of a sea of boarding tourists. She kept her head low and pulled the jacket hood over her head as they slunk to the back and settled in empty seats.

The sword loudly clanked within its bag as Callum placed it on the ground, drawing the glance of an elderly couple in the row ahead of them. Klara's pulse quickened—but the woman only flashed a watery-eyed smile before turning around.

Of course they didn't know what was inside the hockey bag, but nevertheless, it still had her on edge.

At the front, a bubbly, freckled woman with mousy-brown hair beckoned a few more stragglers aboard before the doors wheezed shut. She adjusted the mic of her headset, tapping the foam gently until it let out a scratchy *puh*.

"Welcome to Mae*showe*," she said. Her accent deepened with affection.

The bus groaned into motion. Callum stiffened beside her. "You're about to visit what is Scotland's most famous burial site—perhaps the world's. The tomb dates back to Neolithic times—older than Stonehenge." She swept her gaze across the aisle. "Built only from rock and dirt, this incredible architectural feat was accomplished with no 'modern' tools to speak of." The tour guide leaned forward, lowering her voice to a raspy whisper as she continued, "And it was made to house the bodies of the dead."

A chill flew up Klara's spine. Did it house the secret to her powers, too?

"At least that's what scholars think." The guide cleared her throat and straightened up. "Interestingly, no bodies have been found in Maeshowe. But that is only the beginning of the cairn's mysteries. As you likely already know, the passageway was laid to align exactly with the path of the setting sun on the winter solstice."

Meán Geimhridh. The winter solstice. The shortest day. The longest night. Her scientist brain churned, considering it in astronomical terms: during the solstice, the earth's northern hemisphere was the farthest from the sun it could be. Farthest from the light. The cold expanse of space unfurled in her mind. She imagined its darkness spilling onto earth in the lengthening shadows of winter.

Then there was solstice on earth. Grams used to tell Klara about solstice traditions when she was a little girl, instructing her in the old ways. She concentrated, trying to conjure the feeling of the grip of Grams's hands as she lifted Klara to clip mistletoe from the towering oak tree in the yard—*Just like the ancient druids, my little druidess*, she said, *we'll hang the mistletoe to bring fortune*. Klara's eyes fluttered open. The solstice was a time for hope, life, and the renewal promised by the coming spring. So many pagan and druidic traditions were about hope and connection to a world we didn't understand, like Samhain and connecting to the Otherworld and the world of the dead.

For her, Samhain might mean coming death—the undoing of time itself. But she knew better, this season of time, autumn, meant so much more, especially to those who worshipped it.

Klara had come to know that with each season, Sabbat rituals for the Celtic druids and others who worship such things, the ever-evolving celebrations of darkness turning to light, then back again, was a sequence that ebbed and flowed like the tide. Giving the Celts these events to look forward to, to honor, and believe in, bonded them to the worlds beyond the Mundane Realm. Realms that lived in a parallel, but simultaneous existence. The Otherworld being one of them.

One that she now knew all too well.

Klara buried her hands in her sweater pockets, trying to ward off the stubborn shiver that climbed her neck. She thought of Thomas. Had he been searching for the light that came after darkness?

The tour guide's voice jostled Klara from her thoughts. "It is on that day that the inner walls of Maeshowe are illuminated with sunlight. They were designed for this purpose. Why? We're not certain…"

Klara wrapped her arms around herself, trying to absorb as much knowledge as she could, as if she could form a shield with facts and data even though facts and data had been failing her miserably.

The vehicle groaned to a halt and the chattering crowd disembarked, Klara and Callum clinging to the back. A pale green field lay before them. Maeshowe stood starkly in its center, jutting up from the earth.

At first glance, it was no more than a lone, grassy mound. It looked like any hill that Klara and her mom might have rolled down when she was just a kid, spinning until they were too dizzy to walk straight.

"Come on," Klara whispered. She took Callum's wrist and slunk around the back of the bus while the crowd of people surged in the opposite direction, toward the cairn.

At the front of the mound was a small, low entrance. Klara watched the tourists file inside, holding her breath until they disappeared into the hill.

Even as Klara took a step, she realized she was not walking of her own accord. She was being drawn forward again—right toward the hill. The more she resisted, the harder it pulled. Fear spiked through her.

"Callum—" she choked.

He placed one hand on her lower back and withdrew the sword with the other. "Ye're supposed to feel something, lass. That's good."

The warmth from his palm eased her tension. But then she thought of the woods. "The last time I felt something, I almost got my head bitten off by Llaw's beast."

"We've slain those beasts, twice," he said. "We can slay another one of them again."

She laughed weakly, trying to force a smile, though her stomach clenched. "Third time's the charm, right?"

The sky turned dark around them, and the sun dipped as night rolled through the landscape. She sent out a fervent hope into the universe that the tour guide didn't notice they were missing. After what seemed like an eternity, Klara heard the rumble of the bus kick up and grow fainter as it pulled away. She breathed a sigh of relief—and the space it carved out in her chest immediately filled back in with fear.

"Ready?" Callum asked.

He took the lead this time, sword ready. They hopped over the low-lying fence that surrounded the hill and hid on the other side, out of the sight line of the bus that brought them here.

They walked to the tomb entrance and stopped. Her gut tumbled and thrashed. On one hand, it helped lessen the pressure in her aching chest, but on the other, she felt an urge to stay away, this one from her head. She was trespassing, not only on the souls that may have once resided in the mound, but against the Fair Folk who were said to dwell within it. By all accounts, these fairies weren't the kind you'd find in Disney World. She thought of Oode and her coat made of human skin.

She shuddered. She highly doubted Tinkerbell would do that. Though… Tink did try to kill Wendy on a few occasions, so maybe she wasn't that far off.

Trying to push the image of a murderous Tink out of her head, Klara took another deep breath and ducked into the mound's narrow passage. She put on her phone's flashlight. The ceiling was so low, she had to stay hunched over to go deeper into the tomb. Its rough-hewn walls pressed in on all sides, squeezing her. Klara had never thought herself as claustrophobic but as another rush of panic flooded her limbs, she reconsidered.

She felt like a trapped animal.

But there was no room for doubt, or fear. Only forward.

Behind her, Callum's tall frame was doubled over even more severely than she was. Fortunately, it was only a short shuffle before the cramped passageway opened up into an arching cavern. Her stooped back unfurled. Callum emerged from the passageway just behind her. It was so tight in the tomb, she could feel his breath moving the hair on her temple, tickling her ear.

"This must be the central chamber," Klara said. She stepped back into him to take a better look, and stand a little closer to him. It was a small comfort to feel him next to her. Her voice filled the room, penetrating beyond her cell phone light. She aimed the light around the room, illuminating the walls that curved above their heads. Unlit torches were suspended from sconces on the walls. No flames burned, but an acrid stench still hung in the air.

"Look," Callum breathed, touching her shoulder and pointing at something ahead.

Klara moved her light, where a square of runes was carved into the ground. She gently hooked the tips of her fingers around the pads of his, and took a small step closer, trying to prolong the comfort his nearness brought for a moment more. Each rune was no larger than her hand. She felt drawn to them, just as she had felt drawn to Callum in the fairy circle, to Cernunnos in the Fairy Glen.

She turned to Callum, reluctantly dropping her hand and feeling the absence like a cold breeze. "Wait here," she said, gathering all her strength. "Just in case."

As she moved closer, the pull eased with each step, then all together disappeared when she stepped into the square of runes. She winced, expecting a burst of power, exploding inside her like a supernova—either that, or the appearance of the beast once more.

"Do ye feel anything?" Callum asked.

She waited a second longer, then shook her head.

"Maybe I'm not doing it ri—"

A pearl of light hung in the air in front of her, so small that she mistook it for something in her eye. Her feet rooted to the spot. The pearl grew—first slowly, then quickly, its whiteness expanding and spinning like a snowball rolling down a hill. The spin stopped abruptly, and it flattened in the air in front of her, casting her in a blazing white.

Klara cried out, at first in shock, then in agony. It felt as if she was being scorched alive.

It was the worst pain she had ever felt in her life, cutting to the very core of her. It was as if her skin were being peeled by a dull blade, and the muscle underneath doused in acid. The world seemed to be pulling her apart down to her atoms. Every fiber of her being screamed for relief.

"Callum!" She shouted, but her voice faded and spun into the bright windowed abyss opening up in front of her.

Then, just as soon as it had come, the pain stopped. The air in front of her crackled, then grew suddenly dense, as if a small storm was gathering. The whiteness before her shimmered and filled with color.

She saw the stone ceiling of the tomb once more.

Only this was not the abandoned chamber that she had been standing in, strung up with electric lights. It was lit with torch flame. With a lurch of her stomach, Klara realized she was seeing Maeshowe as it had once been. Another light came from the passage into the chamber, a wan glow that barely reached to the toe of her boot before it was swallowed by the dark liquid shadows of the interior.

The light was moving. Coming closer.

The walls—they were changing. The wood paneling fell away, revealing the alcoves behind them. These, too, disintegrated before her eyes, fading away with a *whoosh*. The dim light flashed, faster and faster, days and nights passing.

She was moving through time—or time was moving around her while she stood perfectly still, the eye in the center of a storm.

People came and went, bearded and robed. A group of men

set light to a fire beside them, axes and round shields in their hands. *Vikings*, Klara thought, carving runes upon the wall. Then they, too, were gone.

Rubble fell, crashing to the ground around them, revealing the sky above. Men emptied the fallen earth and stone.

Clouds tore across the heavens, the sun and moon cresting across an alternating gray-blue and starry-black skyscape. Then the view was blocked, the modern men closing the ceiling once more. Light, electric and artificial, flared into existence and expired. The scene turned back again, the sun and moon spinning like a top.

And then, just like that—the scene around her came to a standstill again. A bright-eyed boy dressed in a plain cloak stood in front of her, clutching a torch. His freckles spread like wildfire across his cheeks and a roguish grin. Recognition gripped her when her eyes landed on a small brown leather notebook tucked under his elbow.

Thomas.

His eyes blazed. His arm moved, reached out to her. The space bent and melted around his outstretched fingers—like there was not air but something else between them, something thicker than air, maybe time itself—leaving behind a faint trail of glowing dust in its wake.

"The Otherworld." His voice was low and deep, reverberating as if reaching her through water. "It's the only way."

His eyes met hers, and widened. "Are you like me?" He reached his empty hand toward hers. "What power you must hold..." Before a conscious thought formed in her head, Klara reached out, too, inhaling sharply when their hands connected. Power welled in her, rising like a tide in her limbs.

Then, with a feeling like someone hooked a blade into her, she was yanked forward, the power flowed out of her at the place their flesh touched. The fire rose in Thomas's eyes.

No.

Klara didn't say the word—didn't even open her lips to speak it—but it burst open in her mind with so much force that she thought she might shatter. She wrenched backward and clasped her hand to her chest.

The world lurched again, and Thomas was gone.

CHAPTER TWENTY-FOUR

KLARA

Klara came to slowly, half-expecting to see the face that had just been staring back at her. *Thomas.* But as her vision came into focus, all she saw was the low ceiling of Maeshowe hovering above her. The smell of peat and dirt filled her nose. Her bag lay sprawled on the ground next to her, along with something else that glowed faintly in the dark shadows. A torch.

"Callum?" she called. The name echoed and bounced off the walls. No answer came; only more silence. A chill wrapped itself around her but she tried to push away the fear.

Mustering what was left of her strength, she sat up and scooted over to the light, picking it up. It was almost out. The end of the wood glowed a deep red. The memory of one of her Grams's joints popped into her head with sudden force.

In spite of everything, in spite of the fact she was laid out in a thousands-year-old tomb, she smiled. Her Grams smoked a joint every Christmas.

Her stomach tugged and dropped as the homesick feeling swooped over her.

"Shake it off," she muttered to herself. Her words were immediately eaten up by the dark that surrounded her.

Gently, Klara blew on the embers until they sparked into fire again. A few seconds later, the flame grew to full height and dashed light across the walls. With a jolt, she realized it was the torch that Thomas had been holding.

Klara inhaled, gears working in her head. She'd brought it through time.

"No *way*," she said to the dark.

Klara brought it closer. She needed light. Warmth, too. The encounter with Thomas left her feeling like a layer of her had been pulled away, exposing rawness underneath, though she couldn't see any of it.

They had connected across centuries, actually *touched*. Of course, Klara had touched Callum, and he was a time traveler, but she wasn't responsible for bringing Callum here—she hadn't opened up a hole in time itself and reached across it like she had with Thomas. Or like they had, together. Bringing the torch closer to her, Klara inspected her hand in the dim, flickering light. The skin on her fingertips were kissed red where Thomas had grabbed her. Grabbed her? She struggled to remember—the only thing that was crystal clear was the memory of the feeling that had flooded her body when they'd made contact. Power, like thousands of volts of electricity, a bolt of lightning...

Klara shivered, then shook her hand like she could just brush the feeling off. Though it faded slightly, it also lingered and pulsed.

As sensation flowed back into her body, the red skin began to ache. She ran her thumb across her fingertips and drew it back immediately, wincing with fresh pain.

Easing herself to her knees, then to standing, she moved the torch across the circular room, looking for Callum. Maybe he'd passed out, too. Her stomach lurched again. Maybe he'd been seen home when she reached back through time, maybe—

Then she saw them. Drag marks scraped across the dirt floor. "Callum!"

Klara screamed, vaulting up against the weakness that spread throughout her body like poison. She stumbled. It kept trying to drag her back to the ground. Steadying herself against the walls, she gripped the torch with one hand and lurched forward, head reeling and stomach spinning as she tried to follow the drag marks across the dirt.

On the verge of throwing up, she finally burst outside. Breathing in the cool air and the bonfire-laced scent was like getting splashed in the face with water. "Callum!"

He called back. The sound was a strangled scream that sent Klara's heart racing in her chest. She whirled around. Callum crouched in front of the beast, sword raised. With a twist of her heart, she noticed the blood splashed across his leg. His limp.

"Klara, run!" He swung as the beast darted its open jaw forward. Even at this distance, she could see its fangs glisten and the shadow of its giant body shroud him in darkness. Its serpent head darted and wove, while its feline body rippled with muscles, tensing to attack Callum again.

Focus, Klara.

"Shit, *shit*," she breathed. Unlike the last time she'd faced the beast, there were no trees to hide behind, only fields upon fields of flat green. They would have to kill it, *again*, turn it into a pile of dust like Callum had in the tunnels.

"Run!" he shouted.

The beast roared and lunged at Callum, who dodged its gnashing teeth by only a few inches. Gathering all the courage she could, Klara sprinted toward the grappling pair.

"Klara! The other way!"

"Why! So it can eat me in a few minutes?" she shouted.

The beast turned to face her. Its tongue darted between its fangs. Sniffing.

Klara could have sworn it *smiled*.

Callum grunted, then lunged again, this time striking the beast's neck with the broad side of the sword. Rearing its head, the beast cried out. Then, it swung down in a flash—missing Callum by several feet—until it twisted sideways, sinking its teeth into Callum's side.

Callum's eyes flew wide, white with pain and fear, and blood poured from his wounds. She heard the *snaps* of several ribs breaking.

Despair gripped Klara. *"NO!"* she shouted.

As soon as the sound left her mouth, the beast and Callum froze.

Before she could breathe again, before she understood what was happening, she watched as their bodies began to twist violently. Hers, too. The moon above flickered. Burning nausea rose in her throat but her body went completely cold. She couldn't move but she felt the charge gathered inside her. It was the same one that had gripped her when she and Thomas had touched, only slightly fainter. Then, the feeling hooked her torso and *twisted*.

Someone gasped. *She* gasped. The world shifted suddenly beneath her feet and she only barely caught herself from stumbling over.

When she looked up again, the beast and Callum stood in front of her, both paused in confusion in positions they'd been moments before: Callum, *standing*. His side whole. Not bleeding. Just staring at the sword in his hand, face blank with confusion. The beast, standing just feet in front of him.

"We traveled back in time," Klara breathed. She laughed. "Holy shit. I did that."

The beast got its bearings first.

"Callum, duck!" she shouted.

Callum snapped into action just as the beast swung its head—*Again*, Klara thought dizzily—only this time, Callum flattened himself against the ground, raising the sword to instead clash with the monster's head. At the impact, the sword flew end over end toward Klara, stabbing into the ground within reach.

Klara didn't have time to think. She grabbed the hilt and ran headlong toward the creature. Its eyes darting between them, the beast shrank back, screeching.

Leaping as high as she could, Klara bore down and drove the blade into the monster's open mouth.

The weapon tore out of her hands and the force sent her sprawling backward. Her body hit the ground with a thud.

She blinked stars out of her eyes and scrambled up. The beast staggered toward her, dislodging the sword with an angry toss of its head.

Not dead.

Yet.

An odd sense of calm overcame her as she stared into the beast's snake eyes. What surprised her most of all was the soothing voice that suddenly filled her head. Cernunnos's voice.

It comes from the breach between worlds.

Limping, the beast closed in on her. It faltered, stumbling on its left front leg, though its hungry eyes remained fixed on her. Klara stayed perfectly still, feeling her feet root into the ground, willing every ounce of her energy at the beast, willing herself to focus—on every scale and hair that composed the creature's hide, on every bloodred speck that swirled in its eyes, on the exact curve of its hooves and the way they shone in the moonlight. She held the entire being within her mind, imagining down to the smallest atom where it had come from.

And where it must return.

The powers of a god, she thought. *I'll have to be good enough.*

She brought her hands downward in one swift motion. A cry ripped out of her from somewhere deep in her chest. With it, the beast came toppling down, and down, though its body never hit the ground. It had dissolved by then, until nothing more than a shimmering curtain of gold dust remained.

CHAPTER TWENTY-FIVE

CALLUM

Callum and Klara had found refuge at another small inn, near Stromness by the Ring of Brodgar, called Hag's Head, where he leaned into the warmth of the hearthstones behind him and took stock of his injuries. The electric light of Klara's world was dazzling, but false—it made him feel a stranger in his own skin. For a moment, he felt close to home. But the din of this pub was nothing like The Black Hart on fight night. No matter how the heady smell of spilled ale tried to trick him into thinking they were one and the same.

Klara returned from the front desk—he knew what to call it now—holding a small white case with a red cross emblazoned on one side. Leaning over him, she peeled back his torn pant leg to reveal a blazing scarlet gash. The edges of his torn skin were blackened and singed. The beast's fangs had grazed him.

"*Ow,*" she hissed under her breath.

Callum gently grabbed her wrist. "I thought ye said ye weren't hurt."

A smile flickered across her face, then fell just as soon as she turned her attention back to the gaping wound in his leg. "I'm not. This just looks like it hurts."

He dropped her wrist. "'Tis nothing," he said.

But it *did* hurt. Not just the wound—Callum ached all over. The emotions that had flowed through his body and animated him after his fight with the beast had dulled over the course of their brief walk to the inn. Now that they were resting, his whole body trembled.

He craved the amber-colored liquid stacked over the bar in glowing bottles. He craved the deep dreamless sleep that might have followed any other fight at Rosemere, interrupted only by Thomas's thunderous snoring. Anything to ease the pain. But he was determined that Klara would not see him hurt.

The beast had come again, but the bean-nighe had not returned. Had he missed his chance forever after losing it at the shores of the loch? Had he not called the spirit correctly? Without her, he would never have the strength to protect Klara, not truly. He would have to find another way.

Klara retrieved a small package from the healer's kit and tore it open with her teeth. Inside was a napkin that she unfolded and pressed against his wound. The wretched thing burned even worse than the beast's venom. He bit the inside of his cheek to stifle the cry that leaped from his chest.

"I don't know if rubbing alcohol does anything against magical wounds, but it's all we've got." Her nose twitched as she lifted the cloth. "That venom is nasty. I think your pants caught most of it…"

The smell of alcohol filled his nose. He breathed in through clenched teeth. "I prefer the venom," he grunted.

No one had ever tended to him in this way, other than Thomas. But Klara was tender and gentle. He didn't mind her ministrations at all. He languished in relief and warmed at her touch, wanting nothing more than to close his eyes and kiss her again.

"Ye saved my life, Klara," he said, reaching up his good hand to cup her cheek.

"No biggie. You saved mine, didn't you?" She smiled at him and leaned into his touch. "The beast came for you when I was…"

Klara trailed off. Eager, Callum waited for her to continue. She had not yet told him what had happened in Maeshowe. He did not want to push her, but the troubled look that splashed across her face now made a knot form in his stomach.

"'Tis not the same," he insisted. "My life isn't worth as much as yours."

Klara scoffed. "That's ridiculous, Callum."

She turned away, but he caught her hand and squeezed, willing her to look at him. "I died, didn't I? But you sent us back in time."

Klara stared at his hand on hers, then moved her gaze up to his face. Her eyes melted with firelight. He expected her to smile and quip, to correct him that she'd saved him

again, to veil her feelings in wit. But instead, she only nodded slowly.

"I saw you dying. It was..." she said, voice breaking. "It
was awful."

Callum nodded in return. He knew what it felt like to see
someone die. Only Thomas hadn't come back. The last of
his warmth drained away in the alley. By now, his body had
been dust for hundreds of years. With a wrench of his gut,
Callum wondered who had buried him, if they had done it
properly, though he knew in his heart the answer was *no*.
Guilt wrapped around him, stealing his breath.

But Callum *had* come back. Which meant he had a purpose, and that purpose was standing in front of him. Now he
only needed to find a way not to fail her.

Klara stared at him. All the color had fled from her face.
He pulled her closer, savoring the sting that came with the
pull of his muscles, and pressed his lips against her knuckles
in a quick motion.

"I'm here. Not dead yet."

"Right," she said softly, pulling her hand away. "Not yet."

Her eyes full, she turned but he was faster. He reached out
and grabbed her hand once again. She turned to him, a loose
tear slipping free from her emerald eyes, down her cheek.

She didn't brush it away, so Callum did for her. His thumb
swept over the apple of her cheek, her eyes fluttered shut at
the action.

He hated seeing her cry.

"Believe in me, as I do you," he said.

Eyes still closed, she leaned into his hand.

A moment passed.

"Kiss me," she murmured.

A pleased shock rolled through him as his lips descended on hers, slow and meaningful. A calm spread through him and he could feel as she melted against him. He slid the palm of his hand down to the back of her neck, she shuddered.

They kissed like this for what could've been minutes or hours. Callum didn't want it to end, damn any pain.

"Okay," she murmured against his lips. "Shall we patch you up?"

He chuckled. "Sounds like a good plan to me."

She gave him another quick kiss, then turned to get the kit.

Klara fumbled with the box, then withdrew a thumb of cloth. Gently, she wound a soft strip of it around his leg. The threads immediately soaked through with mottled red. If Callum's ears did not deceive him, he heard a faint *hiss*, too, when the cloth touched his skin, followed by a puff of faint smoke.

"Damn it," she said. "It looks *bad*, Callum. It looks like…"

He grinned, clenching his teeth harder as he did. "Like a monster took a wee bite out of me?"

"Oi, do you two need a room?" a voice called out from across the room.

Klara flushed red. They turned. The bushy-browed owner of the Hag's Head Inn stared back at them, a wry smile on his face. He'd given Klara the healer's kit she was using to tend to his wounds.

"Like we need any more attention," Klara whispered at Callum. "Come on."

She urged Callum up and over to where the man stood, then slammed the kit down in front of him. "Thank you."

Thick eyebrows lifted. "Will that be all?"

"We will take a room, actually," she said sweetly. She pulled the thin black card from her bag and slid it over the counter toward him. "Do you have one available?"

The man nodded and handed her a key.

One key, Callum thought.

Upstairs, Klara set her bag down at the clawed foot of an armchair. The room was plain and clean, a four-poster bed tucked at the far end. Callum resisted the urge to collapse onto it. Small paintings were strung along the wall. Shadowy hills were visible outside a long row of windows. Above and below were the blanket of stars in the dark sky and a shining loch. Klara stared out the window, her eyes unfocused.

Callum stepped closer to her. "What's wrong, Klara?" They were alone now—no need for secrecy any longer.

She looked at him, mouth taut. "I saw Thomas."

Callum stilled. At first, he did not understand her meaning, but the realization crept over him like cold water. "He's alive?"

Klara shook her head. "I'm not entirely sure," she said quickly. "What I do know is, I saw him in the past."

He tried to mask his disappointment, but judging by the concern in Klara's eyes, he did a shite job of it.

"It's like I opened a window in time," she continued. "First, I saw all these glimpses of history, like I was flipping through pages in a book. But then the page stopped on Thomas, and there he was. He was standing in front of me just like you are now."

"How did you know it was him?" His voice was thick with hope.

"Callum, he had his notebook." She dug through her bag for the leather-bound pages. "This very one."

"Your powers must be getting stronger." Pride swelled in Callum's chest and he reached for her. Klara did not seem to hear him. She stared somewhere out the window, face fixed in thought. "The portrait—he must have seen me by the time he died. He must have drawn me right after."

Callum stepped closer to her. "Did he say anything?"

Klara snapped her head to him then. She bit her lip. "He said, 'The Otherworld. It's the only way.' There was something about him, though, Callum." She paused. "It's like he was looking for me."

"Perhaps he was," Callum said excitedly. "Perhaps he knew to search for ye, perhaps he discovered something about how to defeat Llaw and strengthened his powers more than we imagined."

"Maybe," Klara said. "He definitely seemed...confident." She shifted from foot to foot. "But, Callum, something about him was wrong."

"Wrong?" Her words sparked in him. Too many people in Rosemere had judged Thomas and Callum—for being poor, for being rough.

But Klara only grew more confident, and stepped out of his embrace. "There was something off, Callum. Some kind of energy—"

"Thomas is the most trustworthy man I ken," Callum insisted. He heard the tinge of desperation in his voice.

"To *you,* of course. You were best friends." Klara paused. She then softened her gaze. "I know what I felt, Callum. I just don't know what it means yet."

"Well what does it matter now? He's *dead*."

Callum turned from her and strode over to the window. The sounds of his heavy footfalls faded, leaving a heavy silence between them in its place. Klara came up behind him and laid her head on his shoulder. "I'm so sorry, Callum."

Callum reminded himself that Klara did not know Thomas, and this was as new to her as it was to him. But he knew Thomas well enough for the both of them. He turned back to her. "His words, they must mean something…significant. Could it have been an offer of help?"

"Well I've been thinking about that, too. It reminded me of something Arianrhod said." Klara stared at her hands. "You're right, my powers are growing stronger. They must be the key."

"What do ye mean?" he asked.

"You're not going to like it," she answered.

Klara stretched her arms out in front of her, a kind of wonder and fear dancing in her eyes and the way she flexed her fingers. "I think the Otherworld may be the only place Llaw couldn't reach me. And with my powers…"

Callum waited for her to finish. When she didn't, his mind filled in her meaning. "Ye think that with your powers, ye could escape into the Otherworld?"

Klara nodded. "If I can figure out how. I'm still catching up to the whole 'gods are real' thing but based on what we know, it seems like I could stay there forever, if necessary."

Callum's heart twisted. The most selfish part of him rebelled, urging him to say there must be another way. He could no longer imagine a world without her.

"We must find a way, then."

Klara nodded, then spoke again. "I think I can send you back, too. I'm not sure how, but—"

He cut her off. "I will not go back until ye're safe."

She joined him at the window. "Callum, Samhain is nearly here. We're out of time." A bitter laugh escaped her. "I don't know how I can possibly win against Llaw, but if I'm going to send you back, it has to be before I try to make it to the Otherworld. I can't send you back after I'm gone. And you have to go back. You can live a whole life in your time, you can—"

He gripped her shoulders and in doing so, cut off her speech. "No."

She glared at him, her mouth set in frustration. "Callum, you can't die for me."

"I'll not die for ye, I'll die for time itself—for our world to go on—" he said, even though it was a raging, blinding lie and he longed to take it back. Of course it would be for her. But he didn't take it back. "I'll be with ye until the end. Until ye're safe."

Klara's brow flinched. She placed her hand on his chest. "I don't want you to die at all. I can send you back," she said. Her voice was ragged and desperate and it tore at him.

"I dinnae want to go," he said quietly. The words were simple and plain and true. He stared at her and did not blink. "Do ye want me to go?"

The light in Klara's gaze shifted. Her eyes shone. "Callum..."

Callum moved closer and wrapped his arms around her, lifting his chin to pull her as close to him as possible. Her body tensed. But instead of pulling away, she leaned into him, tilting her head so that her cheek pressed against his chest.

"I dinnae want to go," he repeated, breathing the words into her hair.

His lips found her hairline and lingered there. He felt her arms encircle his waist. He closed his eyes as she slid her palms up his back, felt his muscles tighten in response to her touch. The pressure of her hands, the gentle insistence of her fingertips, was an answer to his question.

Klara wanted him here, too.

Sensing his thoughts, she leaned away from him slightly and looked up into his eyes. In the span of a shared breath, they were kissing.

Everything that was fierce and gentle in Callum flowed out of his touch and into her, then back again, until there was no end or beginning to their embrace. He held on to her and she him, as if this was the only thing holding the entire world in place. Perhaps it was, he thought dizzily.

A knock sounded on the door.

Callum froze in place. The tension in Klara's body shifted all at once, like the wind changing direction. Blood thrummed in his ears.

Without moving, hardly breathing, he took stock of their surroundings. The door was two paces away, the sword only one. If he moved quickly enough—

"Klara?" came a deep voice from the other side of the door. Not one that Callum had ever heard before. Klara's eyes went wide with fear unlike he'd ever seen before. Before he could leap for the sword, she answered.

"Dad?"

CHAPTER TWENTY-SIX

KLARA

Klara didn't embarrass easily, but at the thought of her dad catching her in a hotel room kissing a banged-up, yet very handsome Callum, she burned. This was *not* part of her plan. Then again, none of this was.

She opened the door a crack and slipped out, closing it quickly behind her. "Uh, hi, Dad. Long time, no see, huh?"

Shit. She forgot her phone tracking was on.

"Let's take a walk."

Klara had killed a mythical beast, but all the courage zapped out of her as she trailed behind her dad. Outside, they walked to the low farmer's wall that separated the road from the property. Her dad finally turned to her, crossing his arms way more theatrically than he needed to, and stared at her, as if he couldn't look away.

"You…okay?" she tried.

He shrugged. "Just waiting for you to tell me what on earth is going on."

Klara laughed. *If it were only just earth.* "I wish it was that easy."

He groaned, leaving no doubt as to where Klara got it from. "Come on, kiddo. Really?" Klara winced and glanced down, unable to meet his eyes. Guilt knotted her stomach. She had the powers of a goddess inside her—somewhere, at least—but the way she felt his gaze on her left her feeling like a little kid.

After a few more seconds, her dad sighed. He sat on the stone wall, patting a spot next to him. She sat. The slabs of rock were cool against her legs.

"I take it you found out about college?" she said.

He tilted his head at her. "You think?"

She closed her eyes. Her decision not to go to school, and to keep it from her dad, had seemed so far away since Callum had appeared. Like it was from a past life that no longer belonged to her. But her dad sitting next to her now was a reminder of all the things she hadn't shared with him—and still couldn't.

The word *sorry* made its way up her throat, but she held it in. She had to. It was tangled with a million other things she couldn't say. If she spoke the word—if she told any slice of the truth—she wasn't sure if she would be able to stop.

Instead, she asked, "How did you find out?"

"The school called to return a deposit. Some housing deposit thing we paid months and months ago."

Looking at her, his stern expression broke. A small, sad

smile formed in its place, which was a thousand times worse. "You've always been honest with me."

She pressed her lips together and said nothing. His eyes widened.

"At least for the most part?" he asked.

"I know, Dad. You're right," Klara said, only slightly relieved that it was true. She knew their bond wasn't the typical father-daughter relationship. If she wanted to, she could tell him anything, and he trusted her completely. The fact that she had shared so much with him only made her recent evasion sting more.

"I changed my mind about college. I thought I might get it back, or at least I was hoping to, but it just never happened. I wanted to tell you, but—" She paused. "It was Mom's dream. I felt like I was crushing it by not wanting to go."

Her dad's brow furrowed in concern and in the next second, his arm wrapped tightly around Klara. "Her dream was for you to be happy, honey."

Klara breathed out. Even though this wasn't exactly her top concern right now, finally telling the truth felt like coming up for air. "And that's not the only thing going on right now," she added.

He was still nodding, still squeezing her with reassuring pressure. "Yeah, I kind of guessed that. Why couldn't you tell me what was going on in your head? Did I do something? If I did—"

"No," she said firmly, heart breaking that he could even think it was his fault. "I just—" She breathed, bracing herself. "Right now, I'm dealing with something else kind of...big."

"You can always talk to me, kiddo. I know I'm an old fogey,

but I have grown up before, you know." He smiled down. "Or did you think I was born perfect?"

Klara snorted. "This is different, Dad."

She stopped. She wasn't sure if she was afraid he'd believe her if she told him the truth, or not believe her. But either way, she was sure he wouldn't just let it go. And if he knew…

She thought of Llaw. His blade. Tonight was Samhain, and he was coming. She couldn't risk putting her dad in danger.

Klara sat up straighter, trying to muster a confidence she didn't feel. "I need to figure it out by myself."

Her voice cracked on the last word. Saying it out loud, she realized how true it was—both here and with Callum—and how badly she wanted it not to be true. But if the Ring of Brodgar didn't activate her full powers, tonight she could die. It was the final mystic center, and although the others went more or less to plan, she was hesitant to believe she was in the clear. Especially because now, she'd be doing it alone.

Her dad shifted, resting one hand on his hip. "Because a boy's involved? Listen, I know I'm not your mom, but I—"

Her cheeks burst into flames. "Dad, *please*—"

"Let me *finish*, Klara," he said, his voice as stern as it ever got, which was not very, but still enough to make Klara realize he was serious. "I hope I've created some kind of trust between us. I might not agree with everything you do and I am not going to try to manage your life, but I did chat with your Grams and she mentioned that you showed up with a young man at her doorstep."

Oh, Grams… "That would be Callum. And it's not quite what it looks like, but maybe a little bit what it looks like.

There's a bigger picture, I swear." Klara sighed. She let her head fall onto his shoulder. "Really, it's not about Callum."

He nodded, taking this in, then leaned back to look pointedly at the window of the inn, where Callum stood brooding in a window. "Has someone told Callum that?"

She sat up straight and elbowed him. *"Dad."*

She glanced at the inn, laughing to see Callum look so moody. "God, he is intense, isn't he?"

He leveled his gaze at her, not budging.

She groaned. "Okay, it's complicated."

"Ah," he said, craning his head back to look at the stars. His face screwed up with an exaggerated thoughtful look. "It was complicated between me and your mom once."

Normally, she would have groaned and told him to stop. But right now, hearing about the past felt like water in the desert. "It was?"

His eyebrows flew up. "Really? You're not going to invoke the Geneva Accords and tell me that talking about me and your mom's love life is a human rights violation?"

"I'm not that dramatic," she said.

"That was an exact quote," he said.

Her dad leaned back, earnestly thoughtful this time. "Well, I wanted to map our whole life out down to the minute. I had our house picked out, our kids' names decided, the date on which we'd be able to retire and how much we would have in our retirement fund down to the cent. She hated it—she wanted to live day to day, take life in the moment. And of course, she was right." He laughed softly. "I even bought the champagne for that day before I even asked her to marry me. I spent an entire paycheck on it, actually."

"Really?"

"Yep." He laughed. "We drank it the night before our wedding. Word of advice? Don't get married while you're hungover."

"Noted," she said.

"Another word of advice? Eight-hundred-dollar champagne goes down the same as fifty-dollar champagne."

"Just think of all the pitfalls I'll avoid with that indispensable advice."

Side by side, they craned their necks to look at the stars. After a moment, he scooted back to better look at her and took something out of the inside pocket of his coat.

"I didn't only come here to scold you. Open your hand."

Klara did. He placed a gold chain in her palm, its stone cool against her skin. The gem glimmered red in the moonlight. Her breath caught.

"Mom's necklace."

"It's yours now."

Klara lifted the necklace higher, letting it twist in the moonlight. She hadn't worn it before, not really. To her little kid eyes, it had seemed like the most expensive and precious thing on earth. Looking at it now, she felt a similar sense of awe—not at how much the necklace cost, but at its history. It had been passed down through her family through generations. Now it belonged to her. After her mother died, every time she tried to put it on felt like saying goodbye.

Hands shaking slightly, she clasped it around her throat with her dad's help. The pendant fell just underneath her collarbone. It sat heavy on her chest, like it belonged there.

"Mission accomplished," her dad said wistfully.

Klara laughed. "You drove five hours to give me this?"

He shrugged. "Actually, my main goal was to make sure you hadn't run off with a mystery man." His smile fell and his expression turned serious again. "I wanted to make sure you were okay. And this is the first time you've really left the manor since—"

He stopped. Klara saw his Adam's apple move as he swallowed. She grabbed his hand and squeezed.

"I hated the thought of you being out there somewhere without a piece of your mom to carry with you," he said. "And it was worth it. Your mother would've loved seeing you in that."

A tear escaped her father's eye. She had never seen her father cry until her mother died. Since then, it happened often, and it always made her uncomfortable. But this moment was different. Now it made her feel less alone.

Now that she was about to go on a quest that could lead to her not coming back at all.

He sighed. "Okay, Klara. I won't push any more. You don't have to tell me anything you don't want to, but can you promise me one thing?"

She bit her lip, ran her fingers over the necklace's cool stone. "What?"

"Not to lie to me anymore?"

Heart reeling, Klara wrapped him in a hug, half nodding, half holding in a sob. She squeezed him hard, like squeezing him would make time reverse. He sputtered, pretending to suffocate in her grip.

After a few seconds, her dad cleared his throat and pulled away. "Well, have the best time at this very real spiritual retreat that you're sneaking off to in the middle of the night, like a perfectly normal person who doesn't lie to her dad at all. And make sure Grandma Laura makes some of those shortbread cookies for me. I've been craving them since the last batch."

She wrapped him in a hug again, so he wouldn't see the tears that spilled down her cheeks.

"I'm sorry for not telling you, Dad. I really I am," she said, meaning it with her whole being. Just like she'd feared, the whole truth rattled in her chest, desperate to get out. It took every fiber of strength to keep it inside. "I just—I need to do something, and I can't tell you what. I'll be back as soon as I can."

Klara hooked her elbow in his and squeezed. Now that he was here, she didn't want him to go. Not when she didn't know what lay ahead. Not when him leaving might mean forever.

Her father took a deep breath. "Everything within me is telling me to take you home with me but I know you. I trust you." Klara could tell how hard this was for her dad, as it was for her. "Well it's probably best for Finley and the manor guests that I get going."

Tears pricked her eyes. Finley. "You're worried he's not getting enough treats, aren't you?"

"What can I say? The dog has preferences."

Standing just outside the doorway, she watched him walk toward his car. Every instinct screamed at her to chase after him, hop in the passenger's seat, and blast Metallica until her eardrums bled while she drove straight back to Kingshill Manor.

"Oh, and, Klara?" he called back.

Klara sniffed back the sob building in her chest and hoped he couldn't see her tears shining in the moonlight. "Yeah?"

"I booked an extra room for Callum." The car beeped. "Don't want you to be too crowded."

"Thanks, Dad. I love you."

"Love you, too, kiddo." He raised an eyebrow. "When this is all over, though, you can bet I'm going to want to get to know this mystery man of yours."

He stopped and looked at her—really looked at her—before opening the car door. "Just promise me—you'll be safe?"

"That's the plan," she said, voice cracking on the lie. The lie she'd promised not to tell.

She waved as she watched him drive away. She stayed out there long after his headlights faded into the darkness, arms folded and tears flowing freely. Under the starred sky, she thought of what she'd read about the mortal men who'd been invited into the Otherworld—how they were scrutinized on their honor by the *aes sídhe* of the mound. With those parameters, Klara thought, she didn't stand a chance.

CHAPTER TWENTY-SEVEN

CALLUM

As Callum and Klara walked outside, firelight illuminated the air around them, emanating from crackling torches that lined the pathways spidering out from the inn. People of all ages, all dressed in vibrant colors, had gathered for a celebration. Dusk had fallen. The horizon was barely visible. Samhain had nearly arrived. Llaw was coming tonight.

Klara stopped. "Happy Samhain," she said darkly, shifting the weight of the sword higher on her shoulder.

Callum looked at her, examining her face. Her lips glowed in the firelight, and in profile she looked like a Celtic warrior queen of Thomas's tales. He tried to memorize every line of her lovely face—the strong line of her nose, the swoop of her jawline, the eyes which so often danced but now looked steady and serious. He wished Samhain had never come. He wished they had more time.

Tonight Llaw would come for her. But not if Callum could get strength from the bean-nighe first, at least he hoped. He knew she had the power within her but that it still felt farther away than her home in America. But that the Ring of Brodgar could help her and that was what centered him in the midst of all this hardship.

A few paces away from them, an elderly man knelt at the skirt of an unlit bonfire. Flame leaped from the tip of his offered torch. Within seconds, fire consumed the tower of branches. Heat kissed Callum's face. He breathed deep, inhaling the scent of scorched wood and smoke. So much had changed in five hundred years—but not the smell of a bonfire.

It felt like home.

Bonfires would burn all over Scotland tonight in honor of Samhain. Gathering his courage, Callum took Klara's hand, telling himself it was only to give her strength. Her fingers wove into his with such ease that his heart nearly stopped. Then she took her hand away again, as if only now just realizing what she had done.

Callum's heart quickened. How could he lose her, after all they had been through together? Though he had known her merely days, he felt close to her. Closer to her than he had to anyone before.

The words pressed at Callum's lips. If he didn't tell her now, would he have another chance?

"Klara..." he started.

"Yeah?" Klara tilted her head, narrowed her eyes when he said nothing. "What is it? What's wrong?"

He didn't have the strength to say what lingered in his heart. Instead, he looked at the celebration. "The fire is meant to protect us from whatever may pass through into our world. That is why 'tis lit on Samhain," Callum said quickly. "Dinnae be afraid."

She turned away. "Do you really believe it could stop Llaw?"

Callum did not want to lie to her anymore, so he said nothing. The flames looked suddenly pale.

"Do you think anything can stop him?" she said.

"*Ye* can, Klara," he said forcefully. It was the only thing he felt certain of. He put his palm over his chest and knelt to show fealty to her. "I swear it, with all my heart."

"Oh my god, *Callum*." Blushing, she grabbed the front of his shirt and pulled him up to his feet. They stood chest to chest, just barely a hand's length between them. "But—how do you know?"

"Because I believe 'tis your destiny," he said softly. "My purpose is here, my heart is here."

"I don't want to be your purpose, Callum. At least not like this." She looked up, into his eyes. "I don't want to be the reason you get hurt, or worse." Her eyes welled with water, glowed fervently like a candle burning low. "I want to be the reason you want to live."

A group of girls ran past them, so close that Klara eased into his chest. Their long, white dresses trailed behind them like horse tails. But it was their pointed ears that caught Callum's attention. He stiffened, wrapping a protective arm around Klara's waist.

"Fair Folk," he breathed.

"Wait." Klara put a warning hand on his arm. She followed the girls with her eyes. "I think they're just cosplayers, but—" she laughed, shaking her head and in doing so, stepped out of his grasp. "I really have no idea anymore. Demigods? Beasts? Time travelers? Why not fairies?"

A troop of young men stumbled after the girls. Their ears looked far less convincing. "Costumes," he said.

Music struck up: flutes, a fiddle, a bagpipe. The cheerful tune contrasted too sharply with his mood, making him flinch. A gray-haired man swung a young child in a lively jig, twirling past them in a flurry of moving limbs. But as the crowd began to dance around them, forming and reforming in time with the instruments, he felt himself lighten. For a moment, Callum forgot the man made of shadows that may already be stalking the hills around them. The wild beauty of this place—and its people, so like his own, with Klara among them—stole his breath.

He took her hand again, clasping it against his chest. "Listen to me, lass. I dinnae ken what has happened between your time and mine, but I ken that humans have faced greater hardship."

Klara balked. "Greater hardship than defeating a superstrong demigod and saving time itself?"

"Maybe not but I was taught as a child about the Battle of Flodden, which had stained the battlefield red with the blood of many thousands of men." Smiling, he gripped her hand tighter. "Great kingdoms have risen and fallen. Great heroes have fought impossible battles—and *won*. I suspect that has not changed in your time?"

"Not exactly," she said.

"Then ye have to draw strength from that. People survive. They go on to wage another battle, or fall in love—"

Her mouth twitched into a smile that snagged his heart. "Not both?"

"If they're lucky." He flicked his eyes to the sky, not wanting her to see what was in them.

"I want to dance." Klara pivoted suddenly, causing her dress to fan out around her. "If I might be walking to my death and setting off a series of events that will make time itself cease to exist—I might as well enjoy myself for a moment."

"Ye're *not* going to die—"

She pulled Callum's hand with surprising, insistent strength. They fell into step with the other whirling bodies.

When he and Klara touched, Callum shivered with heat that felt like cold. He remembered what she had told him about electricity,

"What?" she shouted.

"Electricity!" He raised his voice to be heard over the music. "Can it exist in a man?"

Klara tipped her head back and laughed, hair falling behind her in red waves. "It does, actually, but the charge is so small that you don't even notice it."

"I feel it when we touch."

Together, they spun and spun until the world blurred around them, colors melting like candle wax.

Callum had faced the threat of death and even death itself, but here, in this moment, his heart filled with joy at the sight of her bright face. He hadn't thought it possible.

Happiness was a separate world, as distant and foreign to him as a lone star in the sky.

But with Klara, perhaps it was possible.

They stumbled to a stop. The heat from the fire and dancing bodies shimmered in the air around him. His vision teetered and tripped. He pulled Klara to him for balance and caught her by the waist, gazing deep into her eyes.

Samhain was an unspoken promise—a wish—that another year was coming, another spring, another festival, another, another...

Her plump lips parted as if she were to speak but instead, she loosened a breath, then slid her hands across his chest. They slipped up his body and around his neck, leaving shivers in their wake. He sucked in a breath.

Callum wanted to kiss her. He pulled her even closer, lifting her so she was on her toes.

She made the next move, as she pushed her fingers into his hair. He moaned, feeling euphoric. His lips descended to hers. When they met, passion instantly hummed through his veins as their lips gently glided together.

The space around them evaporated like mist, leaving just them. Only them.

The way she made him feel...it was unlike anything he had felt before. Comparable to the likes of a raging sea but equally as calm as a breeze drifting across a meadow. He wanted to get lost in her and never be found.

This feeling, he knew, was love.

He didn't know how long they kissed for, nor would he be the one to break away first. He would happily kiss her forever.

"Callum," Klara whispered breathlessly against his lips. He eased her back down, but still held her close. "I need to tell you something. I—"

In a moment of feeling bold, he put a finger to her lips. "Ye dinnae need to say it, Klara, I love ye, too." He pressed his lips to hers and felt her melt into him.

A voice boomed, breaking them apart. A stout man clambered onto a slightly raised platform and peered over the heads of the crowd. "Our pilgrimage begins!"

The man picked up a horn at his feet and blew into it. The crowd shifted suddenly. A laughing woman and her husband jostled between Klara and Callum, knocking him backward and onto the ground.

"Sorry, laddie!"

Callum looked for Klara, but saw no sign of her flashing red hair. But something else caught his attention—from his vantage point, he glimpsed greasy wet hair at the edge of the crowd, walking slowly in the opposite direction of the revelers. The feet were bare. Then, a soft dirge reached his ears, as if floating on the wind. A chill raked his skin. At first, the sound was so quiet that he was not sure he heard anything at all—but it continued, low and lamenting.

Bean-nighe.

Panic forced him to his feet. At his full height, he could see the shape of a figure in the distance, kneeling at the shore of the loch.

The bean-nighe was not searching for Klara; it was not Klara she'd appeared to, nor Klara's clothes that she had washed in the loch waters, frigid as death itself. She was there for him. He was sure of it.

I have seen the bean-nighe, my friend. Thomas had said these words to Callum. Then, days later, he had died. The knowledge should have terrified Callum. Instead, it offered a strange sense of comfort, a feeling like looking at your reflection in still waters—like recognition.

If Callum was fated to die—well, he would face his fate.

But first, he would have something from its messenger.

Pushing his fear aside, Callum shouldered his way through the dregs of the crowd in pursuit of the bean-nighe. He reached for the dirk tucked into his waist, resting his fingers gently on the leather-wrapped hilt, not sure if he would need it. Following the bean-nighe's song, he crept forward cautiously, knowing that unless he caught her by surprise she would owe him nothing.

A short distance away, he found her: she crouched at the shore of the loch with her back to him. The knobs of her spine stuck out through a thin, dirty shift, and the smell of rotting flowers hit his nose. The strands of her matted hair trailed in the stream. He stilled. She made no indication that she was aware of his presence, and it made him bold. Her long curtain of hair flowed past her waist and over the ground.

Gathering his breath, he plunged forward and grabbed her by the arm, bony and emaciated, her skin like vellum beneath his fingers. The water lapping at her feet was obsidian dark—just like the swell of her eyes as she wrenched around to face him.

Callum's blood turned to ice, but he maintained his grip. The bean-nighe only smiled serenely as she looked up at him, eyes dark marbles in a sunken face, lips taut over a hint of sharp teeth.

"Do you know what happens to men who find me?" she said. To Callum's shock, the bean-nighe's voice was much like a human's: soft and lightly accented, with only a hint of music.

"Aye. Death," Callum growled, attempting to sound courageous. "But I also ken that a man who takes the bean-nighe by surprise will be given one of his most ardent desires—and she will have no choice but to give them."

"By surprise." The spirit spoke slowly, like the words were a delicious fruit. A light danced in her eyes, though she and Callum were far from the dying bonfire. "Who is to say I did not let you catch me? I *am* lonely, as you rightly know. That's what all the stories say." She pouted. Then, as if she could not stand it, she flashed another wolfish grin. "But I am not as lonely as they say."

"Is that why ye have been following me?" he said.

"Brave boy," she whispered. Her dark eyes bore into him. "Though you are not brave enough, I sense." She looked at her arm where he grabbed her. "That is why you followed me."

Callum blanched. Was he so obvious? So desperate? His grip on her loosened.

The bean-nighe took advantage of his reaction. She wrenched her arm back with sudden force, dragging Callum into the water until he was submerged up to his knees, then swung her free arm toward him. He grabbed her by the wrist and tightened his hold once more, steadying himself against the violent shaking that seized his limbs. "How do ye ken that?"

"I owe you no answers, and it is not time yet for you to understand, though such things are beyond your understanding," she hissed. "But consider this: You are only a mortal. What is life to you? What is death? It may not be what you think, foolish boy."

Anger flared in Callum. "I am a man," he snapped. "A

man with someone to live for, and that's more than a lonely wretch such as ye can ken."

The bean-nighe cackled, a terrible sound that rasped along his spine. "You will know when death has truly found you. But if you wish, I grant you the strength of ten."

Callum paused. "Could the strength of ten men beat a questing beast? A demigod?"

She smiled, her teeth rotten, "That is up to you, laddie."

It was vague, but he had to take the chance. For Klara, for Thomas, for himself.

"I wish for the strength of ten men."

With the words came fire, ice, pain.

Callum released the bean-nighe's arm, fingers pulsing and stinging. Strength burst from his heart and poured outward, burning like molten lead through him. His head arched back with the flow of it through his body, mouth tipping open and reaching for the night sky as if it wanted to swallow the moon whole.

The strength released him just as suddenly, and Callum collapsed into the water below. The bean-nighe was gone, the only evidence of her was a ripple in the water. What she left behind in him—strength, like he'd never felt before—curled like smoke in his veins. He clenched his fist, felt his heart drum in his chest. A war cry. He could help Klara now, protect her—

Klara.

Callum charged out of the loch, flinging water off his skin with his great, pounding leaps. He reached the inn grounds swiftly—to find them completely abandoned. The bonfire raged, sending sparks toward the sky. Garish red cups stuck up from grass like discarded fruit. Klara was nowhere.

She had left without him.

"Shite," he hissed, running his fingers through his hair. *"Shite."*

Callum was alone.

Or so he thought, until an unearthly howl shattered the quiet.

Callum ran. There was no thought, only speed. The bean-nighe had promised him the strength of ten, but as he charged toward the Ring of Brodgar, desperate to close the distance between him and Klara, Callum felt the strength of an entire army working through his body, through his pounding heart.

He reached the ring of stones, chest heaving and burning. The massive slabs rose to the stars and shining moon, casting great shadows that spilled over the earth. Among those shadows, a flash of red hair—

"Klara," he breathed.

Then, Callum watched as she disappeared, red hair turning into mist.

CHAPTER TWENTY-EIGHT

KLARA

Klara hated this feeling.

It reminded her of visiting the pool with her family when she was young. She insisted on jumping off the tallest diving board with the big kids. With each step she took, the more frantic her heart beat, the rougher the board scraped the bottoms of her feet. At the top, the sun bore down on her from above. She wanted it to melt her on the spot.

All she had to do was get to the edge of the board and do it. *Just do it.*

"Can't she just jump already?"

"Hurry up."

"Loser."

Klara gripped the massive slabs of rock that jutted up from the earth, trying to steady herself, trying to wipe the silly memory from her mind. She was not a kid anymore. She was standing on the edge of the Ring of Brodgar, not a public pool in central New York in a frilly bathing suit. She was in the middle of Scotland, caught in a war between gods and their offspring, with a power trapped inside her she didn't fully understand and one she *definitely* hadn't asked for. But she couldn't get the scent of chlorine out of her nose.

The wind whipped her hair.

No one was there to taunt her now. It was Samhain and she couldn't bear to say goodbye. Callum was a dark smudge in the distance. She had been forced to leave everyone she loved behind: her dad, Grams, Finley.

Breathe, she thought to herself.

She was doing this for everyone she loved. Klara was alone—though she wouldn't be for long.

Llaw would find her soon. He would kill her soon. If she didn't escape first.

Callum. Her mind strayed to him. She hadn't realized how much she wanted Callum by her side until he wasn't. Until she'd left him without saying goodbye, not knowing what the outcome of tonight would be.

Klara felt deeply for Callum. So much so, that it scared her. They had done more over the last five days than most do in a lifetime. But there was still so much that they hadn't done. Go to a movie. Callum hadn't ever tried popcorn, for god's sake.

She clamped her eyes shut, trying to suppress the panic that tightened her throat. Her mother had taught her to block out the bad. So, she took a deep breath, tucking away the idea of Callum in a corner of her mind. She ignored the whispers of doubt circling in her head like vultures, the fear gnawing away at her stomach.

Be brave.

She stepped forward. The Ring of Brodgar was massive—much larger than what she'd expected. A shallow ditch encircled the outer edge, followed by another circle made out of tall standing stones, at least four dozen of them in total. The stones reminded her of an assembly of ancient warriors, stern and still. She crossed the ditch, lifting the plastic chain that met her on the other side. It was a pitiful attempt at security to block her path to the stones.

When she was a kid, everything was all right after she took a step forward into the known, even into the unknown.

So she leaped.

The falling was over in a flash.

The cool water would wash over her, fanning out her hair like a mermaid, slowing her movements and silencing everything on the land above. Then, she would always burst easily through the water's surface again and take a deep gulp of a breath.

That's all you had to do, her mother had said. *The hard part is being brave enough to jump.*

Entering the Ring of Brodgar was nothing like that. It was only the beginning.

Klara inched into the circle, moving toward its center. Nothing pulled on her to guide her steps because *everything* pulled. Her insides lashed and stormed.

Nothing happened.

Tears stung her eyes. She had traveled across Scotland fighting monsters, and had nothing to show for it except a lot of cuts and bruises and even more questions. Her shoulders sagged, causing the hockey bag to slip down her shoulder. The sword shifted within, reminding her of its presence— its weight.

Klara took the bag off and eased the weapon out. She felt lighter without the heft of it on her back, but the lightness didn't stop the fear that the sight of the blade brewed within her.

The sword suddenly felt right in her hands. Still, Llaw'd had a lifetime of training, she'd only had a few hours.

If she was going to win this fight, she would have to use her power, her wits. Her heart. There was no technical training for that. She closed her eyes, and focused on her heart—the string that had pulled her in the right direction every time before. Her gut, her intuition, her destiny, whatever it was, it would take her to what she needed to do. She waited, and then, like a twinge, she felt it—the yank around her rib cage. She looked at the ground and felt electricity zing between the sword and the center of the circle.

Klara marched to the center, gripped the hilt, and lifted the weapon as high as she could, angling the tip downward. Then, with all the strength she could summon, she drove it into the earth at her feet.

She screamed. Her heart drummed in her neck, sending waves of adrenaline into her limbs. Trembling, she pushed it down harder, until all that was left above ground was the hilt, gritting her teeth until her jaw felt like cement.

Her nerves crackled with electricity, and even though she should be thinking of anything, *everything* else, she thought of Callum's face—the wind lifting locks of hair off his forehead, the impossibility of him crash-landing into her life. She thought of her mom again, wishing she were here to tell Klara that everything was all right, that she was brave just for trying...

Then: mist.

Slowly, it seeped into the edges of her vision—too slow for her to startle, yet too fast for her to do anything but react.

Klara stood, looking at her hands through the curling tendrils. She turned them over and felt the cool brush of mist against the skin of her palms. She shot one last look behind her and watched as the sky, ring of prehistoric stones, and field around her melted into swirling silver and white.

"Shit," she whispered to herself.

The mist closed in on her and gathered around her feet. She took a step. The mist clung to her like a shadow, as if she were in a Stephen King novel.

Well, she didn't like *that*. If you ended up in his books, you'd probably end up dead. Or worse, wishing you were.

"Hello?" Klara called into the blankness. Her voice, small and weak, was immediately swallowed by the whiteness around her.

She took a few steps forward—not that it mattered. She could not see the ground beneath her feet, nor tell whether she was moving forward or backward, or any direction at all. Everything looked the same. Her mind was warped with disorientation. The fog continued to intensify, and as it did, her heart pounded.

A shape drifted in the veil of fog. A figure.

Her pulse sped up. "Hello?" she repeated.

There was a reason Klara hated horror movies. It was the

suspense, the lead-up to a jump scare that always nearly killed her. She didn't need to fear being murdered, because she would die of fright waiting for the killer to pop out from a closet or under the bed. Right now, she felt fear churning in the marrow of her bones.

The silhouette continued to approach, dispelling the mist as it did. Klara froze, biting back the instinct to run by clenching her teeth. She wished suddenly that she had kept the sword. She dropped to her knees and felt for the handle, but found nothing but air as it dropped behind her.

Then, the mist fell away like a dropped curtain. The Ring of Brodgar still surrounded her, but it was changed. The sun shone down in glittering, golden rays. There was no sword stuck in the earth at her fingertips. In its place stood two slippered feet. A woman's feet.

Klara snapped her head up—and all the air rushed from her lungs.

"Mom?"

CHAPTER TWENTY-NINE

CALLUM

The moon hung low in the sky, now just a sliver of pale yellow over the horizon. With each passing minute, Callum's strength churned under his skin.

He paced, scouring the rolling hills that skirted his vision. Nothing. No sign of Llaw. No howl. The bonfire burned low, a faint orange spot in the distance.

Then—

The howl came again, though Callum could not tell from where. It seemed to be carried on the breeze. A shiver raked down his spine. Klara had told him that wolves no longer roamed the wilds of Scotland. Even if she was wrong, such animals would be unlikely to be in a place so bare of woods to hunt in.

Likely not a wolf, then.

Callum closed his eyes and let his senses focus. He had always been a decent tracker and patient hunter, perfecting his stillness while Thomas lazed about and sang songs, sometimes scaring a hare from its den with sheer luck. Now that *he* was the hunted, Callum had even more need of his senses. Fortunately, they had grown sharper with his newfound strength—almost painful. The soft sound of the breeze turned into a roar in his ears. The scent of the wet earth below his feet flooded his nose, mixing with something else now: wet fur, animal breath.

He concentrated, reaching further still, trying to catch the direction of the scent on the breeze. A droplet of rain fell onto his cheek, merging with the sweat that had broken on his brow.

Then: another howl pierced the sky, this one was far closer than the last. The eerie animal wail set his teeth on edge. It came from the north. He was sure of it. He turned in that direction and watched.

Shadowy forms converged on a distant hill.

Llaw was coming.

Callum stirred. Gripped and re-gripped his dirk. He had come to collect on his promise.

Fear pierced Callum's chest, along with a fierce hope that Llaw couldn't reach Klara, wherever she was. That Klara would not return.

Another sound reached his ears. At first it was no more than a patter, easily mistaken for the rain that now came down in sheets. As it grew louder with the shadows' approach, Callum discerned it: paws hitting wet ground, too heavy and wild to be dogs. Suddenly, he thought of Klara's dog, Finley.

His heart twisted, longing to be in Kingshill Manor with no concern other than giving table scraps to the slobbering mutt.

He squinted, trying to discern what shapes shifted in the shadows. They were near enough now that Callum could count four of them. Closer still. They had the appearance of wolves, all thick fur and snapping jaws.

The pack loped over the low hills with their noses held low to the ground. As they got closer, the creatures took shape in Callum's eyes.

Not wolves.

These beasts looked as if they were plucked straight from the pits of Hell. They were twice as large as any wolf Callum had seen, with fur so dark and oily as if made from shadow itself—the same as Llaw. Two sets of ruby red eyes burned on either side of their large heads.

Callum crouched. There were no teachings on using a dirk against a four-legged beast from Hell. But the bean-nighe had not lied. Strength poured through his veins. These creatures were not friends. He was at The Black Hart again, Thomas on the sidelines, and all he could do was wait for his opponent to strike.

The lead beast gathered speed. One, two, three more footfalls and it was soaring through air, flashing claws outstretched toward Callum.

He dropped, flattening his body against the ground to avoid the snarling beast. It arced over him, leaving behind the scent of sulphur. He sprang up and turned, already crouched when the animal pivoted and lunged at him again—slower now without its charge.

Instinct guided Callum's limbs. One hand grasped the

beast's muzzle, the other the meat of its neck. Callum felt the crunch of its crooked and uneven teeth under his fingers as he tightened his grip, then used the beast's own weight to swing it away—and let go.

The creature sailed through the air. With a sting of fear, Callum thought for a fleeting moment that it flew. But it was him who made it fly. The creature yelped in pain when it landed and skittered across the hard ground. Callum's muscles sang with strength.

"Hellhounds," said a familiar voice.

Callum whirled. Llaw. Smiling.

The memory of Kelpie's Close reared in Callum's head— the raining of Llaw's fists, the searing slash of his blade. The ocean of blood that pooled in the alley, the smell of death. His friend. Dead.

The hound recovered quickly and leaped again.

With a cry, Callum fell to his knee and thrust the dirk upward, catching the creature's soft belly with his blade. How easily Callum pushed the blade through. The terrible sound of ripping flesh filled his ears. Hot blood splattered in his hair and face. He tasted iron.

The hound shrieked, writhing above him, then fell to the ground beside Callum. The hound's exposed, tangled intestines shone in the moonlight. Bile stung Callum's throat at the sight.

"Very good!" Llaw jeered.

There was no time for a retort. The other beasts were already bearing down on Callum, harder than the first. The three formed a wall of fur and fangs, snarling.

"Come on, ye scabby dogs," Callum snarled back.

He stood, fists drawn.

The one on the right attacked first, launching into the air with jaws aimed for Callum's throat. He slammed his fists into the beast's chest. Bone bent and split under the force of his knuckles, the sharp *crack* louder than the pounding of his heart in his ears. Another hellhound's teeth snapped closed over his shoulder, just barely missing his neck. Callum pulled the hound close then thrust him away, into the other leaping hound. The two collided and collapsed in a tangled heap of claw and fur.

"Fight me yourself, coward," Callum shouted. Blood darkened his shirt.

In response, the whimpering hound—the one Callum had thrown—clawed to its feet and made to crouch again. But Llaw whispered something Callum could not hear and obediently, the beast-dog sat at the hem of his cloak.

The other two hounds untangled themselves and sprang up. Callum met the mass of coiled animal muscle with a swift kick of his boot, but the other sunk its claws into the front of Callum's chest. The bite of fang and flesh tore a scream from his lungs. Callum plunged his fingers into the hound's matted, oily fur and pulled him off. He faced Llaw and lifted the twisting, yelping creature over his head.

Llaw's gaze trailed from the suspended hound to the flow of blood down Callum's arm and chest. His head tilted slightly in interest. "What have you done?"

"Let me show ye," Callum growled.

He threw the beast through the air. Before it landed, the other scrambled up on three good legs and leaped again, this time grazing the meat of his thigh before Callum dug a hard knee to the side.

He had been in fights like this before. When the opponent just kept coming, and he weakened in each exchange. Though strength thrummed in him, it would still deplete— Llaw would watch as his hounds drained Callum, then step in to pick him off like a wounded animal.

Experience told him to stop defending. Go on the attack.

He picked up his dirk and charged, closing in on the beast to the left, and swung down. The blade sunk deep, then slipped out of his hand as the beast wrenched itself away. The other black blur hurtled toward him. Callum had just had enough time to pull his dirk free from the lifeless body as the last advancing hellhound slammed into him and the hound's flesh collided with his blade.

Its movements grew weaker and finally stopped. Callum kicked it away just as it turned to dust, disgusted and alive with fire inside, feeling every inch of his own rain-numbed skin. Red rivulets ran down his wrists, both the beasts' and his own.

"You look tired," Llaw said.

"I do beg to differ."

Callum charged him. Llaw crouched low with a sneer on his face but Callum slid at the last second, hooking his feet between the crook of the man's legs. With all the strength he could summon, he heaved himself around. With a cry that made Callum's blood surge with triumph, Llaw tumbled along with him.

Not thinking, not feeling anything but the scrambling of the devil's limbs against his grasp, Callum recovered and descended again, this time with his knees on Llaw's chest. Llaw pushed away with brutal force, but Callum landed neatly on his feet. When Llaw shot up, Callum gripped the demigod and lifted him into the air, finding him surprisingly, thrillingly light.

"You were right," Callum said. "This is amusing."

His muscles screamed as he plowed Llaw into the ground again. Llaw groaned, a muted, gurgling sound that was so human it made Callum hesitate as he lifted his dirk—

Llaw kicked his feet and stood again, narrowly missing the swing of Callum's blade. The demigod ducked, but using his momentum Callum ran his knee into Llaw's gut.

Llaw stumbled, but did not fall. He struck back, driving a hard fist into Callum's throat. Callum staggered. A second blow knocked the dirk from Callum's hand, sending it tipping end over end into the darkness.

Llaw was strong. He stole the remaining breath from Callum's belly with a sharp kick, sending his body reeling like he had run full force into one of the standing stones. Pain flared in his injured shoulder. Callum fell to his knees. Llaw drove a fist into his chest.

Now on his back, Callum stared up at the dark sky, his breath rattling in him like dice in a wooden cup. His ribs were jagged, shattered inside the bruised and bitten shell of his body.

It wasnae enough, he thought.

Dizzily, he looked for his weapon, though his sight was scored with blood and sweat and rain. He reached blindly for it. Llaw caught him by the arm. The steel manacle of his fingers closed around Callum's wrist.

"True strength is earned," he said, then dragged Callum up and—

Callum tumbled, unseeing, through the air and landed with a sickening thud. Broken bones shrieked with pain. He could not stand. He could not move.

His vision faded, along with the beat of his heart.

He thought not only of dying, but of living.

He thought of Klara.

All the hours they had spent together, trying to save time, and now they were still left short of it. Not for the sake of the world, but for themselves. With Klara, he had lived a lifetime in the last few days—more time than he thought he would ever have, yet not enough.

Then another thought slammed into him, breaking him more completely than Llaw ever could.

There had been four hounds, but he had only killed three. He had not defeated Llaw. Callum had failed for the last time.

CHAPTER THIRTY

KLARA

"My sweet girl," the woman breathed.

She bent down, outstretching her arms as if to pull Klara up. Klara lurched backward, shooting a protective hand out. "Wait," she said, choking the word out.

Her mom, Loreena—or whatever likeness stood in front of Klara—stopped, her arms raised in an attempted embrace.

Klara blinked once, twice. The sound of her heartbeat thudded in her ears. "I don't understand," she said finally.

"That's okay," her mother said gently. "But weren't you expecting to see me, Klara? I felt you reaching for me."

"I—I—" Klara sputtered.

Her mind was in full revolt. It didn't feel real, it couldn't *be* real. She squeezed her fists until her knuckles turned white.

A panic attack was pulling at all her edges. She froze, powerless to stop it.

The last time she'd had an attack was the day her mother died. She had doubled over on the tile hospital floor, only a few paces away from her mother's lifeless body. The shape of her mother's feet—tucked neatly under the faded blue hospital sheets, perfectly still—was burned into her memory forever.

But Klara hadn't been there when her mother took her final breaths. She was downstairs getting coffee. Just before she left the room, her mother had been talking like everything was normal—about a recent soccer match, of all things—if a little weakly. But when she returned, her mother was gone. Klara's life was forever changed in less than ten minutes, turned upside down and left to hang.

Of course, Klara had imagined what seeing her mom again would be like—practically every time the door opened, she pictured her walking through like nothing had happened. But that was a dream: a wish that would never be fulfilled.

Now her mom was here. That, or Klara was dreaming. Maybe she had died, too.

The woman—her mom—stepped a little closer, lowering her arms slightly. "Klara?"

Panic gripped Klara now. The week's events finally caught up, enveloping her completely before breaking her hardened exterior into a thousand tiny pieces. Klara choked back bitter tears. "This is a trick," she said. "It has to be."

Her mother smiled. "It's not a trick, Beara."

Beara. Her old nickname. Tears stung Klara's eyes. "Is it really you? Mom?"

Pulling her long hair over one shoulder, her mother sat

down beside her. "Do you remember the trip we took to Twin Lakes?"

Klara stared into her eyes, which grew distant, as if being swept away into the memory. "How could I forget?"

Loreena grabbed her hand. Klara didn't pull away. "We were on that dinky paddleboat," she said. "Our plan B after the horse-riding disaster."

Klara let out a half sob, half laugh. But her mom hadn't finished.

"We got to the center of the lake when we thought we saw a huge cruise ship in the distance, which made no sense. Why in the world would there be a giant ship in the middle of a lake?"

"Then what happened?" Klara asked, half wanting her mom to prove herself, half wanting her just to keep talking.

"We got close enough to see that it was not in fact a giant ship, but instead a marina."

"Mom." Klara's voice cracked with emotion. "I missed you so much."

But that voice. It was her mother's voice. Slowly, she encircled Klara in a side hug. At first, she was gentle, hardly touching her; then, she brought Klara closer, squeezing her tighter than Klara thought possible.

The scent of vanilla filled Klara's nose. Her mom's perfume. The image of her sitting at her vanity, taking out a small vial of amber liquid from the drawer burst into Klara's head. She dabbed her wrists with it every morning.

"Mom," she said into her shoulder.

Her mom wrapped her tighter. "A time-travelling Scots-

man practically shows up at your door and you're questioning your dear old mother?"

The tears burst forth, hot and fast, as if Klara's lids were a
dam that had broken. Her arms lifted and squeezed back au-
tomatically, hugging her mother close by their own volition.

Her mother.

Klara didn't care if it was real. It *felt* real. Time melted
around them as they held each other. After some time passed—
a minute or an hour, Klara had no idea and didn't care—her
mother released her. She stood and pulled Klara up with her,
holding her at arm's length, taking her in with shining eyes.

Klara did the same. Her mother looked just as she had before the chemo. Full cheeks, red hair, a barely noticeable scar
under her left eye from a childhood sledding accident. Crow's-
feet crinkled the corners of her eyes as she smiled.

"You're too thin," she said.

Klara gave a snotty laugh. Loreena rubbed her upper arm
and gave her a warm smile, then hugged her again.

"How's your father?"

"He's doing all right. But he misses you. We both do."

The half lie tripped easily from her tongue, guilty though
it made her. How could she tell Mom that she heard him crying every night? How she had to swallow her own grief to
help keep his cheeks dry? That Klara had just left him, alone,
at Kingshill?

Klara looked around them. "Did *I* do this? Are we in the
Otherworld?"

Loreena pushed a lock of hair behind Klara's ear. She
cupped Klara's cheek, and her hand was soft and warm. Although she smiled at Klara, a sadness lingered behind her eyes.

"Yes," said a voice behind her.

Klara whirled. Arianrhod stood before her, resplendent in flowing white robes cinched at the waist with a golden belt.

"Very few mortals have been allowed to enter here. Mortals must have been invited, or earned their way in—" She paused, gaze lingering on Klara. "And even then, it was a rare occurrence," the goddess said.

"Then how did I get here?"

The crescent moon of a smile appeared on Arianrhod's otherwise stone-still face. If Klara wasn't mistaken, a hint of approval flitted across her brow, then vanished.

"You possess a part of me, Klara. More importantly, you found a connection to this place. One that bridges realms. In other words, a very strong one." Arianrhod turned her attention to the sun, then back again. "One that Llaw cannot find."

"Does that mean—" she paused, glanced at her mom, then back at Arianrhod "—that Llaw can't enter here?"

The goddess nodded.

The tension seeped out of her body. For the first time since Callum had shown up, a sense of calm flickered inside her chest. Klara wouldn't be hunted, or constantly on the run for her life, or subject to a madman's mad whims. How much longer could she last on earth, if she was forced to share it with Llaw?

"You're sure?" she asked Arianrhod.

"He may know where you are, but he will not be able to reach you," her mother said.

"But he'll know where I am?" she repeated.

Klara recalled Llaw's promise to her—that he would find her, wherever she was. He had traveled impossible distances to find the Pillars of Time and he killed them, one by one. He had found a way to warp Arianrhod's powers to travel through time itself. He had bent *physics* to his will. The thoughts made her gut turn, curdling the sense of calm that had only just settled there. But it made her certain of one thing: there was no guarantee that Llaw wasn't going to bend heaven, earth, and the Otherworld to find her here.

He was part human, after all. A human that craved power. That made him more dangerous than any god.

"He'll find a way to get here," Klara said.

"He has not succeeded in centuries of trying."

Klara remembered Llaw's speech. He talked about ushering a new age of gods and men, which she had scoffed at and dismissed. He yearned for a world that gave him power, though he didn't deserve it. Not anymore, at least.

But the power *had* existed, Klara realized—it existed here, where she stood, in the Otherworld.

"That's what he wants." Klara shifted on her feet, growing eager as understanding dawned on her. She felt her mother's protective presence next to her. It kept her bold. Safe. "He wants to walk among the gods as an equal—"

"He will never be welcome among them," Arianrhod said, cutting her off. "Like other mortals, he cheats, steals, and kills."

"I know," Klara said. In another life, she might have felt sorry for Llaw. But the things Arianrhod said about him were true.

The goddess leveled her gaze at Klara. Her expression was unreadable. "But if you stay, Klara, you will be safe, but stagnant. Time moves differently in this realm. Remain for a year and everyone you love will pass away, even if they live until their bones grow brittle."

"And what of you?" Klara asked, knowing the goddess wanted more than to protect her.

"I will slowly regain what I have lost. When your life reaches its mortal end, Llaw will spill the power he has stolen through the years, and I will recapture it."

Arianrhod paused. "He is powerful—but he will wither, and he will die. He may have my blood running through his veins giving him a longer life, but he isn't forever. Even for a demigod."

Klara let herself envision it for a moment: a life here, in a realm without pain, suffering, need. The man who sought to kill her would rot on earth. The idea pulled at her chest, tempting her. But just as quickly, she shook her head.

"But if he cannot be one of you, and he cannot come here because he doesn't have a connection to it—" she glanced at her mother "—then he'll murder to get here, to get your powers. He isn't all-powerful but he can become so…and he will ruin the Mundane Realm to do so."

The image of her Grams and dad floated into Klara's mind. Here, standing in the presence of a goddess in the cradle of another realm, she knew what to do.

"I came here to access my powers," she said. "To defeat Llaw, not hide from him."

Klara swallowed, avoiding her mother's gaze for fear it might make her burst into tears, which didn't seem very godlike now that she was in Arianrhod's presence. "Can you help me?"

"I am the Silver Wheel. The goddess of life, death, rebirth, with a throne in the stars." Arianrhod stared at Klara. "It seems like there is something in you that needs to be born."

Relief, along with fear, washed over Klara. She was pretty sure that was goddess for *yes*. The goddess nodded to her mother.

Her mom embraced her. "Sometimes I get really annoyed with myself for doing such a good job raising you," she whispered, then pulled away. The sad smile on her face nearly tore Klara's heart in half. "It seems like we don't have much time."

The words hurt more than everything Klara had felt at Maeshowe. A different kind of pain, sharp and sweet, plunged into her.

Six months had passed since her mother's death, and she longed for closure. It was at least within her reach, even if her arm was outstretched, her fingertips fumbling against it in the dark. But being here, with her, and thinking about saying goodbye, Klara realized she might never come to terms with the idea she'd never see her mother again.

A sob forced itself out of her chest. "I don't know what to do, Mom."

"Yes you do, honey," her mom said.

More sobs followed. They were sharp-edged heaves that ripped her up from the inside, but Klara let them flow. Her mother brought Klara's hands to her heart until her sobbing quieted.

"I need to go back," she said, addressing Arianrhod but refusing to look away from her mother. The feeling was urgent now. "Now, before too much time passes."

Her mother squeezed her hand. The gesture sent a wave of warmth and love rushing through her. She stooped slightly to press her forehead against her mother's. "I wish I could stay, more than anything," Klara said.

"I know you think I'm a cheeseball for saying this," Loreena said, smiling through tears. "But I will always be with you."

"Not a cheeseball," Klara whispered.

"Listen to your Grams. Take care of your dad." Loreena planted a kiss on her cheek. "I love you, *Beara*. Now close your eyes."

"To the moon and back," Klara replied.

Klara closed her eyes. Tears streamed down her cheeks.

Her mother's hands gripped her. They radiated warmth; the warmth spread through her veins, then grew hot—but this was not pain. Not at all. It was renewal.

The fire spread through her, washing her body clean of what was, replacing it with what is. And yet somehow, at the same time, it was only revealing what had always been.

For her whole life, she had been one of billions. But her true self—her secret—was hidden within. In that moment, Klara could see herself suspended in the space between worlds, hair blazing around her like a halo of fire. The dormant power fully awake, no longer buried and forgotten.

When Klara opened her eyes again, she was still inside the Ring of Brodgar—but Arianrhod and her mother were gone. Instead of sun, the skies were smeared with gray clouds and sideways rain pounded against her face.

Exhausted, Klara collapsed on her knees and bent her body over the ground, allowing her tears to mix with the green and mud and rain.

A howl pierced through the storm. A human cry.

Klara bolted upright. There was no point in wiping the

tears from her face. Everything was rain. She could hardly see two inches in front of her. She could barely see the ridged hills in the distance, nor the rocks that rose to the sky around her.

She stood and turned in a circle, trying to locate the source—to find Callum. Another howl tore through air... followed by a sharp yelp.

"Callum!" she shouted.

Before she could wrench the sword out of the ground, Callum's limp body landed at her feet.

CHAPTER THIRTY-ONE

KLARA

"Callum!" Klara screamed, shock heaving through her body like a sickly current. The pain of saying goodbye to her mother was replaced by another type of agony.

It tore through her like a blade.

Klara collapsed over him, as if her body could shield him from the injuries that had already riddled his body. She placed a hand along his damp cheek, she could see the clammy beads of blood masking his face.

"I didnae imagine death would have such a sweet embrace." He murmured from his bloodstained lips.

The face she had kissed—the one that had kissed her back. She watched as his beautiful eyes fluttered shut.

An ugly sound escaped her lips.

"Callum," she croaked. "Wake up…please wake up."

She choked on her words.

"Come back to me." She smoothed a hand across his brow, around the sharp corners of his jaw and down into the damp crease of his neck. His limp, heavy head was cradled in her palms.

Nothing in the slightest stirred him, not even a shiver or a flicker of his eye under his closed lids.

The moonlight darkened around them like a slow-moving shadow.

The lunar eclipse. She craned her neck to the night sky. The eclipse had started to take its hold across the land.

She took him by the shoulders, carefully, as she didn't want to disturb his wounds.

Callum wasn't moving. His chest was motionless but covered in gruesome wounds and dark bruises.

A sob escaped her lips, just as bile rose in her throat. She took a heaving breath. It was sour and revolting.

"Come back to me," she pleaded through the putrid taste that encased her mouth. Her pleas were of no use. So, she held him.

Her hands were tainted red with his blood and her vision became blurred.

It was then, at the final moments, that she realized, he was it for her. He was the man she loved.

And now he was gone.

The realization hit Klara and she slid back, horror plain across her face just as death was upon his.

An ashen white slowly replaced his usual bronzed glow.

This cannot be how it ends. This wasn't supposed to happen.

She wanted to pinch herself and wake up from this nightmare, but she knew that this—this devastating, irreparable moment—was her reality. Nothing she could do would change it. It didn't matter if she had a goddess's blood running through her veins. She was alone, with a power she didn't understand and the boy she...loved...dead.

The startling realization made her ache even more debilitating.

How could she love a man she had only just met? She didn't have the answer...but it didn't matter now, she was alone.

Hot anger rushed through her body and she slammed her fists against the ground, sending mud splattering. The damp earth, like ichor between her fingers.

Wait.

She *wasn't* alone.

Cernunnos.

You do not need my help, Klara. But know that I am always here. That's what he had said to her.

He had said that she had summoned him.

Could she do it now? She had to try, for Callum.

"Cernunnos!" she yelled into the rain as the earth warmed beneath her as if he were responding to her plea. *"Help him!"*

At first, nothing happened.

Then, as if responding to his name, the rain pounded harder, coming in sheets, but it was anything but cold. The air around her grew warm as if she was before a fire. Hope flickered through her—but it was cut short.

Llaw's boot slammed against her chest, pinning her to the ground. The hound by his side—another beast plucked from the Otherworld—crouched. With its sickeningly sharp claws carving up the earth as it moved, the creature inched toward her until its snapping, snarling jaw was nearly pressed against her throat.

She turned her face away from the hound's acrid breath. Her body was angled alongside Callum's, which lay prone. His blood slicked the grass.

"Callum?"

He wasn't moving. His chest was motionless. Her chest heaved, even under the weight of Llaw's boot, which felt immense—but not heavier than the fear that pressed down on her.

Callum is dead. It's too late. Llaw's blade was meant for me.
He died for me.

Her own body shook. Klara could feel it now. Her power, electric in her veins. It moved within her, a tectonic plate breaking in half in her core. Fury filled in the cracks left behind.

The shadow of the waning eclipse acted like an extension of his darkness. He tipped his head down to look at her. To her surprise, he did not look angry, nor did he glare at her with hatred. Instead, he smiled, as if bemused by the very sight of her. A slick of white hair fanned down to his shoulders. Behind him, the shadows seemed to darken, as if a mass of monstrous beasts waited just out of sight. The hem of his cloak swirled around her in waves.

Days ago, she might have said he looked godlike—but she would have been wrong.

He looked tired. His eyes were ringed with darkness, as if he had not slept in days. A shudder passed through her. How long had he walked the earth? Hundreds of years? Thousands?

His unkempt appearance gave her a sliver of hope. But below the casual facade, she could see a crack.

Leaning forward, he pressed his foot down on her chest until a rib snapped.

Pain ricocheted. She cried out which only made the pain worse.

The hound barked sharply in her ear, its rancid breath hot against her face.

"Of all the words I could use to describe tonight," he said, "I never would have thought that *surprised* would be one of them—"

Klara grasped Llaw's boot. Through the pain, another feeling grew. Power—it surged inside her, surpassing her ache. It collected inside her. She had once thought she wasn't capable of defending herself against this monstrous man. But now, she could, and she sure as hell would.

For Callum. And for herself.

In a swift movement, Klara expelled the power through her hands, pushing it upward with all of her strength.

Llaw flew backward with the force of it, eyes flung open with alarm. He landed on the other side of Callum's body.

"Don't *touch* me," she shouted, her voice booming out of her chest like it never had before.

The hound leaped next, barely grazing the flesh of Klara's arm as she sprang up just in time to shove it away. It yelped and collapsed with a thud.

The eclipse was almost total, as if a symbolic reference to Callum's life. She wished it were not; the thought ruptured her soul.

The darkness that was once Llaw's ally was now hers.

Cursing, Llaw scrambled up and drew his sword.

"You shouldna be able to do that," he said, laughing.

Klara glanced quickly at her own sword. The thistle handle jutted out of the ground, only a few strides away. "You find this funny?" she spit.

"*Yes,*" he hissed. He smoothed down his mussed white hair with a gloved hand. "A little girl, thinking she knows how to wield the strength of a god? If not comical, then it's just pitiful."

But the smile had been wiped from his face. Instead, there was a flash of fear there, and Klara relished it.

Llaw moved one foot forward but shifted his weight back. A fighting stance. She mirrored him, while a small voice inside her thought, *Callum taught me that.*

"You are *pathetic,*" she said. "Honestly, I almost feel sorry for you."

"And why is that?" he said.

She tried to stand tall, but her side burned where Llaw had cracked her rib. "Because I know what you want, Llaw, and you'll never get it," she taunted. "All of the lives you stole will have meant nothing. They'll have died for nothing."

"You *know* nothing, child," he said. "Enough games."

Klara scoffed. "That's rich, coming from *you.*"

"Your blood belongs to me," Llaw said.

He threw himself toward her, sword outstretched, aimed right at her belly.

"You can't have it!" she cried.

Klara charged forward, diving aside just before she and Llaw collided. Her feet left the ground. She willed time to slow and it did—the space around her seemed to melt with the billowing black of Llaw's cloak, which was suspended in the air. His blade whistled as it arced toward her, the sound of its scream stretching and deepening in the hollows of her ear. She turned her chin, ensuring the sharp silver passed only a few inches from her cheek.

Then everything sped up. The ground came up fast, then faster as she lost her grip on time. Her side struck the hard earth, and the impact made her rib sing with pain—but her fingers found the handle of her own sword and grasped it, tearing it out of the earth as she rolled into a kneeling position.

She steadied herself just in time to see Llaw pivot. "You want to be a god. You want to walk among them in their realm, the Otherworld. You want to be *welcomed*, celebrated, blessed, but you never will be," she said. "But I've been there, Llaw. I was *welcomed* there. Invited to stay. And I came back."

A confused look crossed his face. "Impossible," he growled. But he soon bore down on her again, eyes blazing.

"I was able to enter because my mother wanted me there. Unlike yours. You have no connection—your presence holds no weight in the hearts of the dead or the eternal."

He stood up straight. "You speak the truth. I've been around long enough to know it when I hear it." The corner of his mouth quirked up in a smile. A true one this time. "Perhaps then I should just destroy it all."

Klara thought of her mom. She thought of Callum. Power burst within her, a supernova of energy at the very core of her existence.

She swung.

The hilt shuddered in her fingers as the blade met resistance—as it cut through the flesh and bone of Llaw's arm. Then the sword was free again, a swath of blood on silver the only evidence that she hadn't missed.

Llaw fell to his knees. He stared at the space where his hand had been, confused, then grasped the nub of his wrist.

Klara rushed forward, then held him in place with the tip of her weapon. He lurched forward, but she pushed him back again, trying to force down the nausea working its way up her throat, trying and failing to ignore the blood from his wound. Llaw did not—he stared at the blood, which poured out of him red and shining silver, mingling with the rain.

He coughed, a burbling sound that made her own blood run cold. "All that work," he said. "All that blood."

"I didn't want to do this," she choked out.

"It's only a wound." His strange eyes snapped up to hers. "You haven't won."

"But I will," she said. *Because I have to,* she thought.

Her chest ached. *Because you killed the person I was falling in love with.*

More blood seeped from his wound, soaking the wool of his cloak. The light in his eyes dulled.

"But, Klara," he warned, "this is not your last reckoning. Death is still coming for you."

"Death is the only way you'll get to the Otherworld, Llaw," she said. "It's your only hope." The air flashed suddenly cold. Mist gathered around them. It was different this time—the fog came in thick gray fingers, rolling in like clouds before a storm.

Longing flitted across his face. "Then we shall see."

He reached up and wrapped his hand around the hilt of her sword—and pulled the blade into his chest.

He shuddered violently, like he'd been pushed onto her blade. Klara grasped Llaw's cloak, determined not to let him escape. The fingers of mist thickened around her, seeping into her hair and clothes.

She felt his body go limp.

Deafening silence descended upon the land, replaced only by a haunting hoot from an unseen owl.

Then, as if she were within a supernova, light burst across her vision.

Shock rushed through her as she felt the sword yanked into the air, and she came with it, stomach tumbling and tossing like she'd been thrown into the sea.

And then, as suddenly as it had begun—it stopped.

EPILOGUE

KLARA

Klara opened her eyes.

Stars greeted her. Millions of them, crisp and twinkling in the sky that no longer poured rain. Head reeling and chest aching, she slowly sat up. Droplets of water dripped from the ends of her hair and onto the hard, cold ground below.

She blinked, willing her eyes to adjust to the darkness around her. A crescent moon hung in the sky above.

Hadn't it been full just moments before? she thought to herself.

She slowly eased her body back and met a hard, sturdy object... She turned her head and squinted into the darkness. As her eyes adjusted she could make out shapes...unfamiliar ones.

She was boxed in by squat buildings. Dust caked her lips. The sword lay by her side. The blade was stained with blood.

Llaw's blood.

Her heart shuttered.

Callum...

Where was he? She thought frantically. He needed her, and she needed him. But he was gone.

Panic rose within her, heavy and stifling.

Her fingers sunk into cracks in the road. No, not cracks, grooves. There were cobbles beneath her hands. They were wet with something. Sticky. She raised her hand close to her face, to inspect it—

Her skin was sticky with blood.

"Ye're not supposed to be here." A voice said in a low, slow whisper.

Her heart leaped and she grappled for her sword. "Who's there!"

Despite the pain, she stood. The sword held out before her, as Callum had taught her.

Klara backed up, scanning the darkest shadows in the alleyway, heart thundering in her ears.

"I said, who's th—" Klara's words were cut short as she sharply backed up into something.

No, she thought in horror. Not *something.*

Someone.

Klara turned swiftly, too quickly. She stumbled back.

A man stood before her.

Even in the dim light, she could see the mop of bright red hair and intense blue eyes.

Shock slammed into her.

She knew that face but the knowledge did anything but ease her fear.

He was a ghost. Or at least he should've been.

"Thomas?" she breathed.

He appeared before her just as he did in the mystic center.

But how? Was she in the Otherworld, seeing the dead like she had seen her mother?

"You're dead." The words tumbled from her mouth before she could stop them. She stood, the sword forgotten on the ground.

"Do I look dead to ye?" said Thomas.

"Callum saw you die," she exclaimed.

He lifted up the edge of his shirt. "Nearly." His torso was wrapped tightly in a bandage but Klara could tell a wound lay underneath, as blood seeped through the fabric.

If he was alive, then...

No.

Realization hit her like a rogue wave. "Where am I?"

She looked around again: the tiny houses, the cobblestone street, the crescent moon, the clearest skies she had ever seen...

Instead of *where* she was, Klara should have asked *when*.

"Rosemere," Thomas said easily, as if it didn't just shake her whole world.

Impossible.

Klara collapsed to the ground.

She knew only a few things to be true in this moment, in her current reality.

Thomas was alive.

Callum was dead.

And somehow she had ended up five hundred years in the past without any clue how to get back home.

★ ★ ★ ★ ★

ACKNOWLEDGMENTS

This book is the novel of my heart and soul. It marries my passions of Scotland, romance, and mythology together in a way I hope you love. After working on it for over six years, I have so many wonderful people to thank for inspiring, helping, and motivating me throughout this process. So here we go!

First and foremost, I want to thank my incredible agent, Joanna Volpe. It is wild to think you have other clients when I feel like the only one. Without you, I don't know where I'd be, and your attentive care, friendship, and all-around beautiful nature have fueled me throughout our years together. I adore you!

Alongside Joanna, I have to thank her immaculate team at New Leaf Literary and Media: Jordan Hill, Hilary Pecheone, Kathleen Ortiz, Abigail Donoghue, Jenniea Carter, Devin Ross, and Veronica Grijalva. Then, of course, I have to send a massive thank-you to my absolutely brilliant editor, Kate Sullivan. Thank you for believing in me and spearheading the process of making my words into a readable novel #YouRock.

I want to thank my publisher, Bess Braswell, for seeing this book's potential. You are a massive reason why it is in the hands of readers today, and for that, I am immensely grateful. I adore Inkyard Press, and being a part of the Harper-Collins family for five years now has been an absolute honor and privilege.

To my parents, Joan Zielinski Alsberg and Peter Alsberg. Throughout my life, I have struggled with seeing my potential since struggling with ADD and dyslexia, but your unwavering support and love have led me to where I am today. Even though you both aren't here physically to see it, I will forever feel your presence in each word I write and every book I publish. I love you both so much.

To my godmother, Marcia Longman (aka Mama Marcia). In a world of uncertainty, I know I can always rely on you to be a beacon of light that helps guide my way through the darkness. I love you. To Nancy MacNeil, for always supporting me and only ever being a phone call away.

To my friends and family:

To my twin, Marisa Alsberg Hanebrink. I know you don't read much, especially after you got my book wet at the pool that one time, but your support of my writing career means the world to me, and I am so proud to call you my support system and my sister. To my other sisters, Anna Camilla Rosenfeld, Stephanie Alsberg Stafford, Jennifer Alsberg, and Nikki Alsberg, and to the family I have now come to know, Cooper MC Schirf and Ginna Goodenow-Schirf. To Kolin Pound, Adrienne Dagg Pound, Marina Andreeva, and my twin flame, Sarah Alsberg.

To JD Netto and Laura Sebastian, you are such rocks in my life, and I'm forever grateful our paths crossed. To Lilly Santiago, Gabby Gendek, Natasha Polis, Kaitrin Kelorra,

Carmen Seda, Ambar Driscoll, Francesca Mateo, Ben Alderson, Casey Ann, Jessica Scoffin, Ryan La Sala, Joanna Hazel, Lucy Richardson, Tina Morris, Alexa Wejko, Elizabeth Sagan, James Trevino, Kasia Lasinska, Destiny Murtaugh, Alexandra Christo, Caitrin O'Neill, Tobie Easton, Lindsay Cummings, Christine Riccio, Ariel Bissett, Roshani Chokshi, Margot Wood, Laura Stevens, Alwyn Hamilton, Samantha Shannon, Katie Webber, Elizabeth May, Amber Skye Noyes, Jackie Sawicz, Annmarie Morrison, Christina Marie, Anna James, Jenna Clarke, Emma Giordano, Regan Perusse, Sarah Grunnah, Tashya Marcelle, Julie Dao, Tom Rainford, Jessica Taft, Alison Jensen, Taran Matharu, Tristin Antonelli, Catherine Chan, Pegah Adaskar, Andrei Frimu, and Esme White. If I forgot anyone, you know who you are and know that I am so grateful for the support around me!

To my fur babies, Fraser and Fiona. No matter where I go in this world, you are both always by my side, which is not technically your choice, but I'm happy to choose that for you. I love your floofy booties and infectious smiles!

To my amazing online family. I am so grateful to have had us all grow up together, and I wish I could give each one of you a hug for all you've done. I adore you and appreciate you all more than you know. ♥

And last but not least, to Sam Heughan. Thanks for inspiring me to write about another sexy Scot—but know you'll always be my first.